WAR

(The True Reign Series, Book 3)

BY

JENNIFER ANNE DAVIS

WAR

Cover Design by: Marya Heiman
Typography by: Courtney Nuckels
Editing by: Cynthia Shepp

ISBN: 978-1-940534-60-2

Content Disclosure

For more information about our content disclosure, please utilize the QR code above with your smart phone or visit us at www.cleanteenpublishing.com.

To Addison
The third in my own personal trilogy
You are my inspiration for Rema
May your spunkiness and love for life never cease

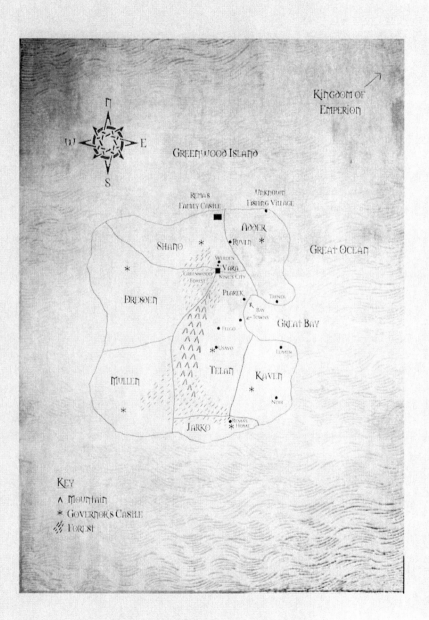

KINGDOM OF
EMPERION

GREENWOOD ISLAND

REMA'S
FAMILY CASTLE

UNKNOWN
FISHING VILLAGE

ADDER

RAVEN

SHAND

GREAT OCEAN

WERDEN
VARA
KING'S CITY

GREENWOOD
FOREST

DRUSDEN

PLAREK

TRENDE

R. BAY
TOWNS

GREAT BAY

HUGO

USAVO

LUMEN

TELAN

KAVEN

MULLEN

NORE

JARKO
REMA'S
HOME

KEY
∧ MOUNTAIN
✳ GOVERNOR'S CASTLE
/// FOREST

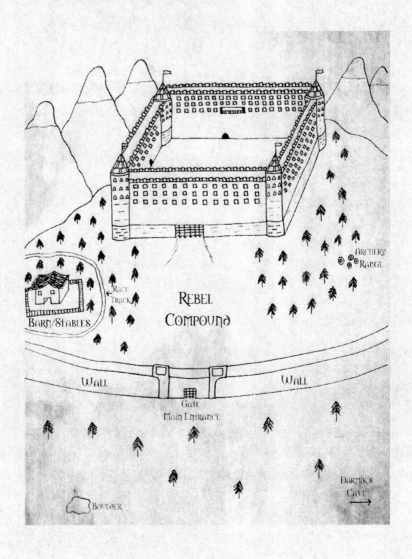

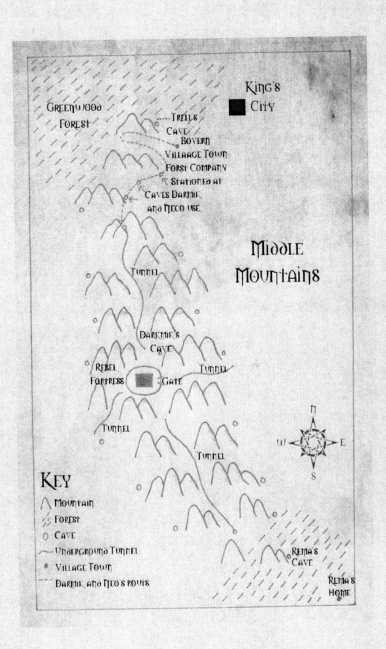

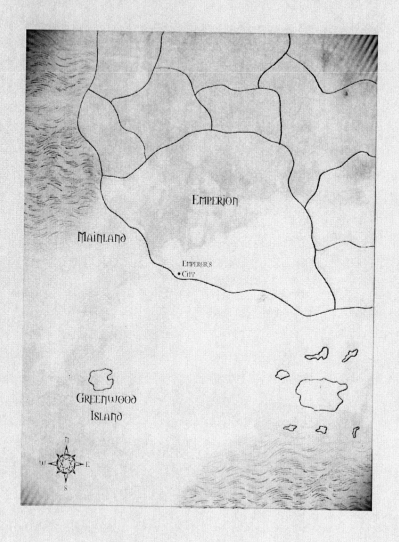

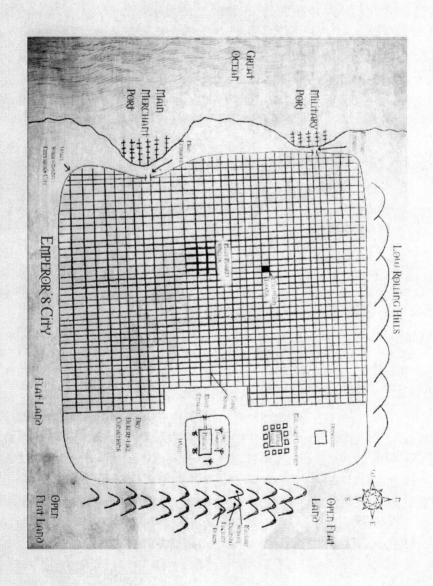

Prologue

Mako

Mako knelt next to the rickety, wooden shack, observing the Emperion ship. It was difficult to see the details of the vessel since it was the dead of night and a thick, heavy fog concealed the moon and stars.

"No one's about," he mumbled to Darmik and Savenek. Even though a few men roamed the pier, Mako didn't see a single person aboard the large boat.

"Maybe we beat Captain here?" Savenek suggested.

It was possible. Mako had led them down the east tunnel of the Middle Mountains. They traveled for three days straight to get there to the town of Plarek, located on the Great Bay. If Captain had gone a different way, it could easily take him another two days to arrive.

Darmik shook his head. "Something's wrong. I can feel it."

"There's only one way to find out," Mako said. Logistically, he couldn't send his men to attack the ship. Besides himself, there were only six people. The probability of Emperion soldiers lying in wait, unseen, was too great for such a small band of rebels.

"I'll go," Darmik offered.

Mako hesitated. He couldn't afford to lose Darmik—he was their best bet at rescuing Rema. However, if soldiers were indeed waiting, they most likely would not harm Darmik since he was a prince. Mako nodded. "If it's safe for the rest of us, signal with your left hand." Wasting no time, Darmik slid into the shadows, making his way toward the ship.

Mako whispered to Savenek, "Go and tell the others to hold their positions back by the storefronts, but to be prepared." The boy crept away.

Mako watched Darmik approach the bottom of the ramp. Crouching low, he ascended with his sword drawn. When he reached the top, he ran and jumped over the railing, landing on the deck, disappearing from sight. No shouts rang out, no warning cries arose, and no sounds of fighting were heard.

A few moments later, Savenek rejoined Mako. "Audek, Neco, Ellie, and Vesha are ready when you are."

Mako nodded, watching the ship for any movement.

"Is something the matter?" Savenek asked.

"No."

"You seem…tense," Savenek commented.

"Because I am. Now be quiet and keep your eyes open."

Savenek sighed. They sat side by side in silence, waiting.

Darmik finally appeared at the bow of the ship, giving the all-clear signal.

"Let's go," Savenek said. The two of them joined Darmik aboard the vessel.

"They're not here!" Darmik said, punching the mast.

"Savenek," Mako ordered, "go and check the marina's log. See if another ship has recently left." The boy hurried away.

On the pier, there was hardly any activity since the majority of business was conducted during the daylight hours. A few sailors tended to a boat, while others slept just off the wharf.

"There are two Emperion soldiers below deck. I knocked them out and tied them up," Darmik said, pacing.

"We can question them when they wake," Mako said. Darmik's eyes sliced over to him, seemingly aware of the mistake he'd made in rendering the men unconscious. "In the meantime, I'm going to ask the people on the pier if they've seen anything. Let's go." They descended the ramp. Mako was glad to be back on solid ground.

Savenek ran up to them. "They left! The ledger states that a merchant vessel set sail an hour ago for Emperion."

Darmik suddenly shouted, "Get on the Emperion ship, now! We're leaving!"

"Calm down and think like a commander," Mako scolded. "We need to talk about this."

"There's nothing to discuss." Darmik leaned in toward him. "Every minute we stand here arguing, adds to the distance growing between Rema and us. If we want to save her, we have to leave immediately." His eyes shone with fury.

Mako understood Darmik's fear and frustration. Yet, in order to have a solid plan in place, they had to think and act rationally. "Why did Captain take a merchant boat instead of his own military vessel?"

"The merchant ship was slated to leave in the morning," Savenek said. "It was fully stocked and the crew nearby."

"What about the Emperion crew?" Mako asked. "Where are they if they're not on board?"

"The crew and soldiers are inland," Darmik muttered. "They infiltrated the army at King's City, a two-day's ride from here."

Since Captain's military ship wasn't ready to sail, he chartered a regular merchant boat. Mako glanced at the Emperion ship docked nearby. "So we need supplies and a crew to sail that thing?"

Darmik nodded.

"Savenek—go find a crew for hire. Check the local taverns. Darmik—tell Neco and Ellie to acquire food and water. Have Audek and Vesha obtain any other provisions you deem necessary. Then I want you back here, out of sight. As soon as we have everything, you can set sail."

"What about you?" Darmik asked. "Aren't you coming with us?"

"No," Mako said. "I can't leave the rebel army. We need to go forward with our plans and prepare for battle. We'll be ready when you get back from Emperion."

The boys took off running.

Mako handed the sailor a large burlap bag of coins.

"This will only be enough to get them there," the man said.

Glancing at the ship, Mako watched Savenek sprint up the ramp, carrying a crate of food.

"I understand," Mako mumbled. He pulled out another bag of coins, handing it to the sailor.

The man took the money and slipped it under his weathered jacket. "Once the food and water are loaded, we'll set sail." He turned and boarded the ship with his crew.

These sailors came highly recommended by the local tavern owner—a man who worked with Mako's men on more than one occasion. He promised that they were good, hardworking, and loyal sailors.

Savenek ran down the ramp, stopping before Mako. "Everything's on board."

"What about the items Darmik requested?"

Savenek rolled his eyes. "It's all there—the weapons, uniforms, everything."

"Good." Mako didn't know what else to say to Savenek. The boy was like a son to him and was the only family he had. This could very well be the last time he saw him.

"Stop," Savenek said, putting his hands on Mako's shoulders. "I'll be fine. You trained me to be a competent soldier."

Mako nodded. "Be careful. Emperion people are very different from us."

"Let's go!" Darmik shouted over the ship's railing.

"We'll be back with Rema, I promise."

"Don't make promises you can't keep."

Savenek smiled. "I'll return with Queen Amer. Then we'll invade King's City and retake the throne. I promise." Excitement shone on the boy's face. He spun around and sprinted up the ramp, joining the others. Mako hated having to place his trust in someone he once considered his enemy; nevertheless, Darmik had been to Emperion before. If anyone could sneak into the kingdom and rescue Rema, it was Darmik.

The sails went up into the dark night, the fog slithering around them. Water slapped against the boat as it slowly moved away from the dock, disappearing into the thick, ocean mist.

ONE

Rema

Rema peeled her heavy eyelids open, and everything swayed before her. Rolling onto her side, she vomited. When she moved to wipe her mouth, she discovered her wrists were tied together with thick rope.

Where am I? What is going on? The last thing she remembered was standing in her bedchamber, an arm snaking around her chest, while a cloth was placed over her mouth and nose. Then, everything went black.

She pushed herself up, her arms shaking and head pounding. Sitting on the hard, wooden floor, it felt as if everything around her was moving. Vomit rose in the back of her throat. She took deep breaths, trying to calm her queasy stomach. Glancing around, it appeared she was in some sort of dark storage room. A few beams of light filtered in between the wood plank walls. Several crates of food, boxes, and barrels of water lined the walls. Rema tried to stand, but her ankles were also bound together, so she crawled to the corner farthest from where she had thrown up.

Leaning against a barrel, she closed her eyes, waiting for the nausea to pass. Was she somewhere in the fortress? Who would have done this to her and why? Trying to focus on her surroundings, Rema felt as if she was moving up and down. Maybe it was a side effect from the toxin she had ingested.

She heard voices shout above her. Several feet pounded on the wooden floor. All the floors in the castle were stone. The only wooden one was in the barn, and that was only one level. Cold fear prickled through her. Where was she?

More yelling and feet stomping above, and then a loud groan as the floor shifted. Rema was thrown sideways, and a couple of the wooden boxes toppled down beside her. Pushing herself up, she crawled over to one of the crates and used it to pull herself into a standing position.

It definitely felt as if the floor moved. Since her ankles were bound, she hopped toward the door. The wood groaned, and the floor shifted again. Rema lost her balance, falling to the ground. The door flew open, and light burst into the small room. A figure dressed in black walked toward her.

"You're finally awake," said a male voice she didn't recognize. The man towered above her. There was something about the way he spoke—it was foreign and unlike anything she'd ever heard before.

"You're the Emperion assassin," she whispered, her heart pounding in her chest. The emperor probably knew she was the true heir to the Emperion throne and would stop at nothing to see her killed.

He crouched down, leaning toward her. "I am," he said, his voice soft and low. "Welcome aboard The Scorpion."

Everything made sense—the vomiting, the feeling that the floor was moving, the food in the storeroom. Rema was on a ship.

"I'm taking you to Emperion. The emperor wants to *see* you beheaded." He grabbed her arm, yanking Rema to her feet. "I can't have you die before we get there." He tossed her over his shoulder and exited the room.

Rema squinted against the bright sun as the assassin plopped her back onto her feet. Her fear vanished as she beheld the magnificent sight before her. Enormous, ivory sails vigorously flapped against the wind. The vessel cut through the ocean, which surrounded her in every direction. She hopped to the railing, looking over the side in amazement.

Rema wanted to scream with joy and hug someone—she was on a boat, sailing across the ocean! Granted, she was going to be executed, but she'd faced that situation before and lived. It would do no good to dwell on the negative. Rema always wanted to see the world, and this might be her only chance to do so. Besides, an opportunity to escape could present itself.

"Why are you smiling?" the assassin asked in his

odd accent.

Now that she was outside, she could see her kidnapper. He appeared to be in his early thirties and had a tall, stocky build, blond hair cut close to his head, and freckles covering his face. She'd never met anyone else who had blond hair like hers before.

His eyes narrowed, studying her. Rema glanced away, not answering him. She took a deep breath, smelling the cool, salty air. The sun warmed her skin.

The assassin grabbed her hands. Rema tried jerking them away, but his grip was too strong. His deft fingers untied the knot, and her bindings fell to the ground. He knelt and fumbled at the rope around her ankles.

The man stood before her. "You do understand you're going to be executed?"

"Yes," Rema said, gazing back out at the ocean. The water went on as far as she could see, in every direction.

"Then why aren't you crying?" he asked, puzzlement clear on his face.

She laughed, and then looked at her captor. "I'm on a ship, sailing across the ocean." *The ocean!* "I haven't been on a boat before, nor have I ever left Greenwood Island." She never imagined being on a ship could feel so liberating. The man shook his head. "Let me ask you a question," Rema said. "Why did you undo my bindings?"

He smirked, leaning against the railing next to her. "Something tells me you aren't going anywhere."

Which was true—she couldn't swim her way to

land. She'd have to wait until she was off the ship to get away.

"If you make one move, I'll gut you and take the pieces to the emperor." Something sharp dug into her side. Glancing down, she saw the assassin holding a small knife to her stomach. She hadn't even seen him move. If he wanted her dead, he could kill her before she realized what happened. The knife disappeared and he stood there with his arms crossed, studying her. "You seem all-too content to be aboard this ship."

Rema closed her eyes and tipped her head back. The wind whipped around her, tossing her hair every which direction. The ship had a steady rhythm now that she had gotten used to it. Opening her eyes, Rema laughed. "This is magnificent!" Never in her wildest dreams did she envision being aboard a boat.

The assassin shook his head at her again. "Well, since you seem to embrace your situation, I'm going to put you to work instead of keeping you in the storage room."

Rema's shoulders relaxed with the prospect of not being locked up.

He furrowed his eyebrows and thought for a moment. "Follow me." He turned and headed toward a narrow set of stairs.

"What's your name?" she asked, hurrying after him.

"Captain," he answered, climbing the steps two at a time. "However, the man in charge of this ship is also bestowed the same title, so you may call me by my real name—Nathenek," he spoke over his shoulder.

"Where are we going?" She wanted the opportunity to explore the boat.

Nathenek abruptly spun around to face her. "Aren't you the queen of Greenwood Island's rebel forces?"

Rema wasn't sure why he was asking. *He* kidnapped *her*. He should very well know who he captured. "Yes." She placed her hands on her hips.

Nathenek took a step closer to her. Rema refused to back away and show fear, even though she desperately wanted to put space between them.

"You don't cry when I inform you of your pending execution. You haven't barked orders or made any demands. You are unlike any noble woman I have ever met."

Rema laughed. She wasn't raised as a noble woman, but as a simple merchant girl. "Do you usually converse with the people you kill? Does it make it more fun to get to know them before murdering them?"

"No," he said, his eyes darkening. "I'm given a target and I hunt them down, killing them quickly. This is the first time I've…traveled with my assignment."

"Well, you're not what I imagined an assassin would be like."

Nathenek remained in her personal space. His hair was so short that it didn't move in the wind. He wore a uniform similar to Darmik's—dark black pants and a simple tunic bearing the emperor's crest. Instead of blue accents, they were emerald green.

"Have you met many assassins?" he asked. "Do you employ them in your rebel army?" Nathenek cocked his head to the side, awaiting her response.

Rema squinted against the bright sun. "As far as I know, you're the first one I've met."

"You can be sure I'll be the last."

A rope came loose, and a sailor scrambled to catch it. Nathenek whipped out a dagger, throwing it. Rema turned to see the knife pierce the rope to the mast. At least if he decided to kill her, he'd be quick. Rema swallowed the lump in her throat.

During her brief stay with the rebels, she'd undergone enough training to have some ideas on how to escape. Once they arrived at Emperion, Rema would make every attempt to do so. For now, she would try and get to know this strange man as best she could. Perhaps he had a weakness or soft spot she could uncover and use to her advantage. Nathenek spun on his heels and headed inside. Rema followed him through a doorway. It took a moment for her eyes to adjust to the dark room.

"This is the galley," Nathenek said. "You can help the cook." He pointed to the young man next to him who stood with a large knife in one hand and several potatoes piled before him on the counter.

"The kitchen?" Rema asked in disbelief. "Because I'm a girl, you assume I want to work in the kitchen? Cooking?" Without meaning to, she pointed her finger at Nathenek's chest. "You may not be like other assassins, but you *are* a typical man."

The cook stopped chopping the potatoes and stared at Rema. "Ain't no girlie working in here with me."

"I need to do something with her," Nathenek mumbled. "There has to be a job for her here."

"Can I please work outside instead of in the galley?" Rema asked. She wanted the sun and the ability to see the ocean, not to be cooped up inside a windowless room.

"You need to talk to the ship's captain about the girlie," the cook said. "He won't want her messin' up stuff or gittin' in trouble. Ships ain't meant to have girlies on board."

"Fine." Nathenek grabbed her arm, pulling her back out onto the upper deck.

Rema had to walk with a wide gait in order to maintain her balance as Nathenek dragged her along to the other side where a man, dressed in a crisp, blue uniform, stood, looking into a long tube of some sort. Rema guessed he was the captain, and therefore in charge of The Scorpion.

The man put the tube down and turned to glare at her. "What's she doing above deck?" he barked.

"I plan to put her to work," Nathenek said. "What job can she do?" He still had a tight grip on her arm. Rema wanted to pull free, but something about the ship's captain made her stand still.

"She can't be up here."

"I don't want her down in the storage room during our voyage. Emperor Hamen expects her delivered alive."

"She's not going to die from being tied up down there. On the other hand, she will have…problems if she remains up here. I won't vouch for her safety. Some of my men haven't been with a woman in a long time."

It felt as if she'd jumped into the icy water of the Sumer River. The thought never even crossed her mind that the sailors on board would violate her.

What if Nathenek didn't care what these men did to her? What if he allowed them to abuse her, so long as they didn't kill her? She glanced over the railing. The drop was high, but nothing she couldn't handle. Yet, once she was in the water, how far could she swim? How long would she last? Was death by drowning better? Probably.

Nathenek's hands squeezed her arm, and she let out a small cry. His eyes assessed her before focusing back on the captain.

"Very well," he snapped. "I will keep her with me." He dragged her back down the steps and through another doorway.

"Please not the storage room," Rema begged. Not only had she vomited in there, but there weren't any windows. "If I'm going to die soon, can't you grant me this one small mercy?"

Inside, the rise and fall of the ship felt worse. Her stomach rolled. The assassin hauled her down a short, narrow hallway lined with several doors. He pulled out a key, about to unlock one of them, when a man stepped into the corridor behind Rema. She spun around and came face to face with Trell.

"What are you doing here?" she asked. Did Nathenek kidnap him, too? He didn't answer. Instead, he stood there, staring at her. "Trell?"

The old man glanced at Nathenek. "What are you doing with her?"

Nathenek unlocked the door and shoved Rema inside, slamming it closed behind her. She heard the two men speaking in hushed whispers, too quiet for her to discern any of the words. What was Trell doing here? If Nathenek didn't kidnap the old man, then was he helping the assassin? After all, Trell was from Emperion.

Groaning in frustration, Rema examined the room. It was small, about seven-feet-by-seven-feet. A bed stood against one wall, with a footlocker at the end of it. A small, wooden desk sat under a round window.

Nathenek came in, locking the door behind him. He grabbed the chair from the desk and shoved it under the handle. Rema froze. She had no idea what to do. This strange man before her could violate her, and no one would stop him. She quickly ran through everything Savenek had taught her. But then what? Even if she managed to get free from the assassin, where would she go? Should she—could she—jump to her death? Most likely, if she tried anything, she'd end up with a knife in her side.

"Why do you suddenly look so frightened?" he asked.

Biting her lip, Rema glanced at the door.

"Oh," he said, "that's to keep you safe. So no one

can get in. I always secure my bedchamber. It's habit." He walked over and plopped down on the bed. "This is my berth. You can stay here until we arrive at Emperion. It's not much, but at least you have a window."

"Why is Trell here?" she demanded. "Did you kidnap him, too?"

"I'm not going to discuss the old man with you."

Rema let the issue drop, for now. She was afraid if she pushed too hard, he'd throw her in the storage room.

She still found standing difficult, so she slid down to the ground and leaned against the footlocker. "How long?" she asked, holding her head against her hands. She would not vomit in this room.

"Excuse me?" Nathenek kicked off his boots and lay down on his back.

"Until we get there," Rema clarified.

"Two weeks." He crossed his ankles and slid his hands under his head, appearing relaxed.

Rema noticed all the furniture was nailed to the ground. The boat lurched to the side, and then resumed its up and down motion.

"Since I can't work, what are we going to do all day?" she asked.

Nathenek sighed. "Unfortunately, there's not much to do. This is my first assignment off the mainland. On the journey to Greenwood Island, I studied maps, terrain, and city placement. I reviewed Darmik's history at Emperion's military school. I thought he'd be assisting me. Things obviously didn't turn out the way I expected."

He let out a deep breath. "I also exercised daily. That's it."

Rema knew she needed to do some form of training or exercise to maintain her strength; otherwise, she'd have no chance of escaping.

"For the next two weeks, am I just going to sit here?" she asked.

Nathenek didn't respond.

If she couldn't be up on the top deck, this journey would be miserable. Her stomach felt queasy again.

"What did you think of Greenwood Island?" she asked, trying to focus on something other than feeling so awful.

"It was cold, wet, and green."

"Is it very different from Emperion?"

"Does it matter?" His head tilted to the side so he could see her.

"I guess not. I'm just trying to pass the time."

Nathenek sighed. "I didn't particularly care for it," he admitted.

"Because it's so different from what you're used to?"

"Yes and no." He focused on the low ceiling above him. "I grew up in the military. My family sent me into service when I was eight years old."

Rema gasped. "So young?"

"It is typical. Families are required to send a certain number of children to the emperor's service."

She tried to recall what Maya had taught her about Emperion. It wasn't much, but Rema wished she'd paid more attention. She never thought there would be a reason to know the details of the empire.

"I excelled in stealth warfare. I was put on track to be part of an elite team. When I was fifteen, I saw my first battle." Nathenek remained quiet for several minutes. Rema wondered if he was done talking, or simply mulling over thoughts from his past.

"I won't go into details," he suddenly continued. "But when the battle was over, I was a changed man." Rema thought she heard a hint of sadness and regret in his voice.

"I was then recruited to the emperor's personal guard. One day during duty, the emperor approached me and asked if I would serve as one of his assassins. To be chosen is a great honor, and I accepted. I am one of only three dozen that do his bidding."

"How many people have you killed?" Rema asked, not really wanting to know the answer, but thankful he was talking to her.

Nathenek shook his head. "Up until this trip, I killed eighty-two."

There was something odd and strange about the way he phrased his answer. Rema pondered what he'd said.

Realization dawned on her, and it was as if a cold bucket of water was tossed on her head. How had she forgotten about the massacre in Jarko? Her arms shook, and it was hard to breathe. This *man* was responsible for the deaths of hundreds.

Rema sprang to her feet and rushed to the bed. She jumped on top of Nathenek—her hands wrapping around his neck. There was an intense desire to watch the life drain from him. She squeezed harder.

Tears streamed down her face. "How could you kill all those innocent people?" she screamed.

His blue eyes locked on hers.

He wasn't fighting back.

What was she doing? Rema let go, staring at her hands. Had she really just tried to kill a man?

Nathenek reached up and took hold of her shoulders. In one swift, fluid motion, he flipped her over and onto the bed. He now straddled her.

"How could you?" Rema choked out. "All those innocent people in Jarko. You just killed them." She couldn't stop crying.

"I told you, I'm a soldier. I grew up in the military. It's ingrained in us to follow every command." His voice was soft, yet there was a dangerous edge to it.

"Let me go," Rema demanded.

Nathenek released her and stood next to the bed. "Don't ever touch me again," he said. "Otherwise, I'll kill you."

"Why didn't you fight back?" Rema asked. "Why did you let me strangle you?" She sat up on his bed.

"Why did you try to hurt me?" he countered.

"I don't know," Rema whispered. "I wasn't thinking."

"Exactly." His face scrunched in some emotion

she didn't understand. "It was done from passion—hate. It wasn't consciously or purposely done."

Rema slid her feet to the floor, but she didn't stand. She just sat there, thinking about what this assassin said.

"In Jarko," he continued, his voice gravelly, "it's not what you think."

Why was he explaining anything to her? He was a killer—it was what he did for a living. She didn't need to know the details.

"I'm not sure how to say this so I make sense and you understand."

"You don't owe me an explanation," she mumbled.

"I know." Nathenek sat on the ground before her, looking into her eyes. "I'm a soldier," he said. "I'm given an order, and I always carry it out. In Jarko, no one would speak about you. I was convinced you were hiding somewhere in the region. Normally, I am hidden in the shadows when I kill with my dagger. But in Jarko, everyone saw me. When we couldn't discover your location, Prince Lennek gave the order to burn everyone's homes. When people ran out screaming, he ordered them to be shot with arrows."

Nathenek bowed his head. "It reminded me of battle. Something I loathe."

"Lennek gave the order? Not you?" Lennek had always appeared disinterested when it came to the army.

"Yes," Nathenek said. "I was sent for you, and only you. I had no business killing anyone else. Especially women and children. Prince Lennek gave the command,

and we all carried it out. That's when I left him and started hunting you on my own."

"Why are you confiding in me?" Rema asked. Did it make him feel better to confess his crimes? Especially to someone who was sentenced to die? "You're an assassin. You should be used to it."

Nathenek knelt before Rema. "You asked why I *allowed* you to strangle me. I was simply trying to explain myself. My *crimes* are orders I'm following. Not an act of passion." He stood and glanced out the window. It was too high for Rema to see anything but blue sky. "I want to remind you to *never* touch me again." His voice was hard, cold, and lifeless. He gestured toward the bed, indicating it was time for Rema to move. She slid back to the floor, leaning against the wall.

"You are my eighty-third assignment. I have been given eighty-two assignments, and all were completed on time and without a single issue. You are the first to present a complication. Luckily, Darmik led me to right to you. He was so injured that he never noticed me following him." The corners of his mouth rose in a faint smile.

Nathenek lay back down on his bed. "I will hand you over to the emperor, and my eighty-third assignment will be complete."

She was trying with all her might not to think about Darmik, but now, she couldn't keep the images and worry away. What did he think happened to her? Did he know the assassin had her? Or did he assume she ran away? Or was she presumed dead?

Closing her eyes, she felt Darmik's soft lips against hers. His strong hands caressing her back.

Oh Darmik, she thought, *I'm so sorry for being captured. I love you.*

Two

Darmik

armik clutched the railing, digging his nails into the wood. *This could not be happening,* he thought. His worst nightmare had come true—Rema was taken from him, and by an assassin, no less. Darmik would kill anyone and everyone who harmed her in any way. His stomach rolled just thinking about her alone with Captain. He punched the railing with his fist while letting out a ragged scream. The thought of her stepping foot on Emperion soil was almost too much for him. If there was any chance of saving her, it was up to him, and he was running out of time.

Glancing up at the stars, he tried not to let his imagination get the better of him. It would do no good to envision what was happening to Rema at this very moment. Was she scared and alone? Injured or hurt? He, after all, knew exactly what Emperion did to their prisoners.

The sails of the ship were fully extended, the boat

traveling at a fast speed.

"Standing at the bow of the ship in the dead of night won't get us there any faster," Savenek said as he came to stand next to Darmik.

"What are you doing out here?" This man had no right to worry about Rema—that was Darmik's job.

"I couldn't sleep," Savenek admitted. "Between vomiting and my pounding head, this journey isn't off to a very good start."

"It'll pass," Darmik said, smiling. He crossed his arms and leaned against the railing, staring at the man before him. "Why do you think Captain took her alive? Why not kill her and take evidence to Emperor Hamen?"

Savenek bent over the railing and vomited. Darmik had to admit the motion of the boat wasn't pleasant, yet he felt no compulsion to throw up. He hoped Savenek was tougher than that in battle—otherwise, they'd never make it out of Emperion alive.

Savenek wiped his mouth with the back of his hand. "I've been wondering about that," he said. "It's almost as if he wants you to follow him."

"Why? For what purpose?" Darmik asked. The chilly wind whipped around his body.

Savenek slid to the floor, leaning against the side of the boat, next to Darmik. "I don't know," he said. "I can't even think when I feel this awful." His face was unusually white.

Darmik paced on the deck, trying to figure out Captain's plan.

"How can you even walk?" Savenek moaned. "My legs can barely hold me up."

Neco came out from below deck, carrying a bucket. He dumped it over the side of the ship.

"Not you, too!" Darmik said, exasperated.

Neco glared at him. "Everyone below deck is vomiting." He turned and went back inside.

Darmik resumed pacing. "Captain left me a calling card. It said, *Thank you for the hunt. Although it was a little tedious, you led me right to her. —C—*." He clasped his hands behind his back. There had to be a reason for Captain's actions. This was a highly skilled, professional assassin. "Maybe it's a clue and not a calling card?"

"You're overthinking it," Savenek said. "He is probably taunting you in order to make you feel guilty. After all, it's your fault Captain found her in the first place."

Darmik stood before Savenek, glaring down at him. "But I want to know if your theory is correct. If Captain wants us to follow, then are we walking into a trap?"

Savenek rubbed his face. "Why would he care about us?"

Darmik squatted eye level with him. "That is precisely what I'm trying to figure out."

Savenek jumped to his feet, vomiting over the side of the ship again.

Darmik shook his head. There was a lot to do before they arrived on the mainland and, right now, no one was capable of focusing.

"I'm going to go to bed," Darmik announced. "When you feel better and are able to strategize and plan with me, let me know."

Savenek, still bent over the side, raised his hand in acknowledgment. Darmik rolled his eyes and went below deck.

After tossing and turning for several hours, worrying about Rema, Darmik finally gave up on sleeping. He stretched and put on his boots, curious to see if anything happened during the night. When he stepped into the hallway, a foul stench assaulted him. He covered his nose and ran to the ladder, quickly climbing. As he stepped onto the deck, the fresh sea air cleared his nostrils. However, he was not prepared for the sight before him. "You have to be kidding me," he said.

Neco scowled at Darmik while rubbing Ellie's back as she vomited over the side of the boat. Savenek was sprawled on the ground, a green-faced Vesha knelt next to him, and Audek hung over the railing.

"Is every single one of you sick? How are we going to plan a rescue attempt when none of you can even walk? I planned to go alone, but all of you insisted on coming. I told you this wasn't going to be easy." Darmik looked to the sky, trying to gain as much patience as he could muster. "You have until the end of today, and then

I expect everyone to start strategizing with me. Is that clear?"

Several people moaned, but everyone nodded in understanding.

Darmik turned and went to speak with the helmsman.

The elderly gentleman smiled as he approached. "I take it it's their first time at sea?" He laughed.

"Yes, the whole lot of them." Darmik folded his arms. "Any news?"

"No." The helmsman shook his head. "I have a man posted on the main mast whose sole purpose is to search for the merchant vessel."

"It had several hours of a head start," Darmik stated. "If we can't catch it, I want to arrive before it does."

"If your map is accurate, and Captain is headed to the main merchant port like you suspect, then I believe we will be able to dock well before them."

"Excellent."

"There is one additional matter that needs to be addressed," the helmsman said, ducking his head as if embarrassed. "I need someone to clean the sleeping quarters. And I don't have any men to spare."

Darmik sighed. "Fine, I'll do it. Just get us there as fast as you can."

Darmik was sick to his stomach—not from

cleaning below deck or from the motion of the boat—but because of what he'd seen. He knew this was a military ship, built for speed. Apparently, it was also designed to transport prisoners. The first level consisted of the sleeping quarters and kitchen. Under that level were the weapons room, storage facility, and human cages. Inside each cage was a trough for a small amount of food and water, chains for the prisoner's wrists and ankles, and a bucket for bodily functions. Near the cages was a table lined with several instruments used for torturing someone. More terrifying than that sight, was seeing evidence that all the cages had been used, including the torture table.

After making the gruesome discovery, Darmik went to get some fresh air. What if he was too late and couldn't save Rema? Or his uncle refused to release her? He could be torturing her right now.

He rubbed his hands over his face. He knew, better than anyone, that he couldn't allow himself to think about it. Emperion used psychological intimidation as an effective way to torture not only prisoners, but also their enemy. Darmik couldn't let them succeed. He had to focus on the task at hand—saving Rema. He would be no good to her if he started thinking about the *what-ifs*. He swore to devise a plan to save her, no matter the cost.

"Don't tell me you're getting sick now," Savenek said, coming to join Darmik at the bow of the ship. "Serves you right."

Darmik shook his head. It was hard to convey the ruthlessness of Emperion to someone who had never been there—someone as egotistical and arrogant as Savenek.

Savenek leaned on the rail next to him. "I assume you have a plan."

"No, I don't," Darmik admitted. "There are too many variables. I have a couple of ideas, but nothing set in stone."

He smiled. "Then I'll just have to come up with something myself."

Savenek certainly seemed like he was in a good mood. He'd obviously found his balance aboard the ship.

"If you're ready to start strategizing," Darmik said, "then go inside and get everyone. We'll meet in the room at the end of the hallway. There's a table with several chairs in there."

Savenek didn't move. "I know this is a near impossible mission; that it's unlikely we'll survive. But I feel like there's something I'm missing. Something you're not telling me." He bent forward over the railing, focused on the rough ocean below.

Darmik propped his elbows next to him. "What you're missing," he said, "is an understanding of your enemy."

Trell's words came back to him. When he showed Darmik the archives room, he'd said, Most battles are won by those who understand their enemy. I've always found one only has to look to the arts. Sculptures, books, paintings. They reveal the true identity of a culture. If you understand that, then you know your enemy. You can find their weakness and attack.

"Emperor Hamen is nothing like my father. I fear we are a step behind Captain—that he is playing some sort of game we don't even understand yet." If Darmik failed to save Rema, he would be dooming his companions to death. He wished they had stayed behind.

"Tell me about the emperor, so I have an idea of what we'll face."

"There are no words to describe him." Darmik closed his eyes, trying to banish the memories. "I will say this—he always knows his enemy. He figures out what they want most, love most, and uses it against them."

"But he's your uncle, right? That has to help."

Unfortunately, that strained relationship was their only hope of saving Rema right now.

"Go below deck. See what's on the bottom level. That will give you a small glimpse of what we're about to walk into."

Savenek's eyebrows bent inward. "Below deck?" Darmik nodded. Savenek shrugged his shoulders and left.

Darmik stared out at the great ocean before him. He never thought he'd return to Emperion—the war-driven, land-hungry, empire.

Unwanted images flashed through his mind—standing before his entire military class, naked, being whipped—being submerged underwater, held down, unable to breathe—having to take the new cadets, only ten years old, and beat them with a stick for crying out in the middle of the night because they missed their parents—and a completely lethal, obedient army that carried out any and all orders the emperor gave, without question.

What was this savage empire going to do to Rema? Simply execute her? Or would the emperor destroy her? Darmik's uncle held little regard for family. He never showed any kindness toward him when he was there for his training.

"I figured you were up here making yourself go mad," Neco said, patting Darmik on his back.

Darmik rubbed his face. This was probably what Captain wanted—to torture him.

"You need to get inside," Neco said. "Let's focus on a plan." Darmik nodded, unable to speak. "Savenek's in there making a fuss," he continued. "Let's go put that pup in his place, yeah?"

Darmik looked at his friend.

"Don't even say it," Neco said. "We all *chose* to be here. You're not responsible for us. All we ask is that you lead us."

Darmik would never make an effective leader if he didn't pull himself together. Rema needed him. He had to be strong for her. "All right. Let's go devise a plan to get Rema back."

The two friends ducked and stepped through the archway. As Darmik descended the ladder, he heard Savenek yelling. Maybe it hadn't been the best idea to send him down to see the area where prisoners were kept, but Darmik wanted him to have a clear picture of what they were going to face.

He followed Neco into the room at the end of the hallway. Audek, Vesha, and Ellie all sat at the table while Savenek walked around, waving his arms, ranting on about something regarding Rema.

The room fell silent, and all eyes went to Darmik.

"Your uncle is one sick and twisted person," Savenek sneered. "I hope you don't take after him."

Darmik stood there, staring at him.

"Well?" Savenek said. "Tell us your plan."

Darmik was fed up with him. He wanted Savenek on his side, and he needed his trust and loyalty. Right now, he had neither. He clenched his hands into fists.

Neco shook his head. "Not in here, Darmik," he said. "Please go to the top deck were there's more room."

"I'm afraid I'll throw him overboard," Darmik said, seething with irritation.

"So?" Neco chuckled.

"What's going on?" Vesha asked.

Darmik pointed at Savenek. "You, top deck. Now."

Savenek jerked back. "Why?"

This was exactly why Darmik needed to do this. He turned and left the room, knowing Neco would tell Savenek he was being challenged. It was something Darmik did with the men from his army—if they wanted to move up in rank, they had to fight Darmik to prove their skills. The exercise established understanding and respect among his men.

Out in the open air, Darmik swung his arms,

stretching. Several of his wounds were still healing, but they wouldn't impede him. Hearing voices approach, he went to the middle of the deck and stood with his feet shoulder-width apart, waiting.

His mind drifted back to his first challenge. He'd only been at Emperion's military school for three days. The officer leading his squad was showing them how to do a flying sidekick while unsheathing a longsword at the same time. Darmik asked a simple question—why not use a dagger instead? Since he questioned authority and showed insubordination, the officer assigned five cadets to attack Darmik.

Granted, at the time, he had been seventeen and was serving in the King's Army back home, so he wasn't a novice. When the five cadets came at him, Darmik was shocked by the determination and brutality they exhibited. Since they weren't allowed to use any weapons, one cadet went to punch him in the stomach. Darmik blocked the blow, but another cadet kicked from behind, sending him to his knees. Before he could recover, another cadet grabbed his hair, yanking his head up. One punched his jaw, while another kicked his side.

As he sprawled on the ground, the cadets repeatedly kicked him until he passed out. When he woke up, he was still on the ground, covered in blood. Since there wasn't a medical ward at the campus, and no one would help him, Darmik was forced to crawl to the room he shared with the cadets who had done this to him.

His torso was purple, his face black and blue, one eye swollen shut, and he could barely move his jaw. From that point on, Darmik never questioned his commanding officers out loud—ever.

Savenek stood before Darmik. "You want to fight me?" He smiled, confident he'd win.

"No," Darmik said, "I want to challenge you. No weapons. Hand to hand only. First one to pin the other down, unharmed, wins. Understand?"

Savenek nodded. "What's the point?"

"To show you that you have a lot to learn. I am in charge of this mission, and you will give me the respect I deserve—no more snide comments."

Savenek stood, staring at him.

"Do you want to rescue Rema?" Darmik asked.

"Of course I do."

"Then I need your loyalty."

Neco folded his arms, standing next to Ellie, watching. It looked like he was trying not to laugh.

"I don't need to fight you to prove anything," Savenek said.

Darmik reached out and grabbed Savenek's shoulder, digging his fingers in.

"You're arrogant, and you don't understand how to follow authority. I am challenging you. Once I win, you will swear allegiance to me."

Savenek whacked Darmik's arm away. "My loyalty is to Rema, not you."

"If you want to save her, you need me. And I want

you focused and doing exactly what I say. Otherwise, I'll throw you overboard."

Savenek snickered. "What happens when I win?" His fist flew toward Darmik's face.

Darmik ducked and grabbed Savenek's right leg, throwing him off balance. Springing up, he kicked Savenek down. Savenek rolled to the side, getting back up. Bouncing on the balls of his feet, Savenek hunched over and came at Darmik, trying to tackle him to the ground. Darmik twisted and broke free, shoving him back. It was time to end this. Darmik ran and jumped on him, wrapping his legs around his neck, knocking him to the ground. He sat on top, victorious. Savenek tried to squirm free, but Darmik had him pinned down.

"Swear loyalty to me, or I'll throw you overboard right now."

Savenek growled, still trying to break free. Darmik leaned his elbows down harder on Savenek's neck.

Savenek banged his hand against the ground. "Fine," he said, seething with rage. "I concede."

Darmik loosened his hold ever so slightly. "And?" he prompted.

"I swear loyalty to you."

"No more disrespect. No more inappropriate comments. I want you on your best behavior. Understand?"

"Yes," Savenek agreed, his face red.

Darmik released him, jumping to his feet. He reached down to help him up. Savenek clasped his forearm, springing to his feet.

"I've never been beaten before," he said, wiggling his jaw and placing his palm to his face.

"I know," Darmik said. "Emperion is going to change all that."

Savenek smiled grimly. "I'm starting to get that impression."

"You two done?" Neco asked.

Darmik looked at Savenek, who nodded. *Excellent*, Darmik thought, *he is already keeping his mouth shut.*

Vesha ran over to Savenek, but he waved her away. Audek pouted, handing Neco a few coins.

Neco smiled. "Never bet against Darmik. He wins every time."

Darmik surveyed all five faces. They had a lot of work to do before they set foot on the mainland.

The hot sun beat overhead.

"Everyone below deck," Darmik ordered. "It's time to formalize the plan and prepare. You're all are going to play a vital role in recovering Rema."

THREE

Rema

Rema's head smacked the corner of the footlocker, awakening her. She sat up, her back stiff and hip throbbing with pain from sleeping on the hard floor. She spent most of the night thinking about Darmik. Her heart ached. They had finally figured things out, and a relationship was forming between them. He even revealed that he loved her—and she loved him. Now, she'd never see him again, nor would she ever see Aunt Maya and Uncle Kar. Even if she managed to escape the assassin, how would she get back to Greenwood Island?

There had to be a way out of this mess. Could she feasibly fake her own death? Make everyone think she jumped overboard, while secretly hiding on the ship somewhere?

"I'll tie you up," Nathenek said, making Rema jump.

She glanced over at him lying in bed, and noticed his cold, blue eyes staring at her. A chill ran through her body.

Pushing back the covers, his legs slid to the ground. He sat there, watching her. "If you give me any trouble at all, I'll put you back in the storage room."

"I understand," she said, trying to placate him.

"I don't think you do." He stood, wearing only his cotton sleep pants and undershirt. "I'm very good at reading people and understanding their intentions. If I see you plotting or thinking about escaping, that's it. There won't be a second chance."

Rema nodded, mentally kicking herself for being so transparent.

He pulled on his tunic, making himself presentable.

"Excuse me," he said, coming to stand before her. She slid out of the way, and Nathenek opened the footlocker, removing some clothes. "Here." He handed them to her. "They'll be big on you, but better than that thin nightdress you're wearing."

After spending time in the frigid Middle Mountains, Rema was actually warm. Still, she took the items, grateful for the more practical clothing.

"I'll be back in a few moments." He left, closing and locking the door behind him.

Rema hurried and yanked on the rough, wool pants. She slipped off her nightdress, putting on the undershirt and tunic. The clothes were huge, so she rolled up the sleeves and pants. She suddenly realized she no longer felt nauseous or queasy.

Stretching, she wondered what she would do all day. Hopefully, Nathenek would return with food because her stomach kept growling from hunger. He claimed he needed her alive and well for the execution, so he should feed her. However, if she was indeed stuck in this small berth all day, then she needed to find a way to maintain her strength. When the opportunity presented itself, and Rema was certain it would, she wanted to be fully prepared and able to escape.

Standing in the center of the tiny room, Rema started doing jumping jacks. After one hundred, she stretched her legs and arms. It felt great to move her body around.

The door latch rattled, and Nathenek entered. Rema quickly sat on the ground, hoping he wouldn't question what she'd been doing while he was gone.

Nathenek squatted, handing Rema a loaf of bread and a small water pouch. "That's all you get until tonight," he said, his eyes roving over her body, assessing her.

Rema tore the bread in two, saving half for later in the day. "Thank you."

Nathenek stood. "I'll be back."

"Where are you going?" Rema shoved a piece of bread in her mouth, wondering how long it had been since the last time she ate.

"Out on the top deck." He smiled, mocking her. "I don't want to be cooped up in this room all day."

"Good," Rema said, feigning pleasure. "I'd rather be alone. I'm much more interesting and make a far better conversationalist than you do."

Shaking his head ever so slightly, he turned and left, locking her inside.

Sighing, Rema finished eating and then took a few small sips of water, saving the rest for later. She stood, ready to get back to work. Closing her eyes, she envisioned Savenek and everything he taught her. She started running through the various drills she knew.

After several hours, exhausted and out of breath, Rema sat and devoured the last of the bread. She took a gulp of water and lay on her back, staring up at the ceiling. Thoughts of Darmik invaded her mind again, and tears filled her eyes, blurring her vision. After her almost execution, she thought she had been handed a second chance at life. When Darmik arrived in the Middle Mountains, *for her*, she was elated. It was as if all her dreams had come true. He gave up everything for her—his father, brother, crown, and army. Even the hideous "L" Lennek had carved on Darmik's chest was proof of everything he suffered for her.

When she kissed him, she felt truly loved and complete.

Now, here she was, stuck on a ship headed to Emperion. She reached for her key necklace and noticed it was gone. Panicking, she sat up and shoved the collar of her shirt aside, frantically searching for it. Either Nathenek had taken it, or the necklace had fallen off when he carried her down the mountain.

Glancing at the footlocker, Rema wondered if

her necklace was hidden inside. Standing before it, she tried lifting the lid, but it was locked and wouldn't budge. Frustrated, she kicked it.

Placing her hands on her hips, she paced around the room, searching for something she could use to break open the lock. She didn't see anything of use.

What would Darmik do if he were in her position? He certainly wouldn't give up. Closing her eyes, she pictured him before her. *Stay focused. You can do this. Maintain your strength, and when the opportunity to escape presents itself, take it.* Rema opened her eyes, a fierce determination taking over. She would not sit around wallowing in her situation. Squaring her shoulders, she prepared to run through her form again.

She vowed to get away from Nathenek.

She would not be executed.

And she most definitely would find her way back to Darmik.

Voices came from the other side of the door. Rema hurried and sat on the ground, trying to calm her heavy breathing. She wiped her forehead, removing the dripping sweat. The door opened and Nathenek stepped inside, his eyes sweeping the room and settling on her. Without saying a word, he handed a loaf of bread and a cup of water to her. After removing his tunic, he climbed into bed, facing the wall.

She was starving from exercising all day and quickly inhaled the food. "Is bread the only thing I'm going to eat for the duration of our voyage?"

"I haven't decided," Nathenek mumbled.

"Do you plan to keep me in this tiny room the entire time?"

Nathenek grunted. "It's the safest place. Now be quiet and go to sleep."

"You're an assassin. Wouldn't I be safe with you?" He didn't respond. "All I'm saying is that it's cruel to keep me holed up in here." Rema glanced around the room, not really wanting to sleep on the hard, wooden floor.

Nathenek rolled onto his back, looking up at the ceiling. "Why?"

Rema sighed. She needed to convince him to let her out of this room. "You're taking me to my death. Don't you think I want to feel the sun on my face and smell the ocean air before I die?"

"What difference does it make? You're going to die, regardless of being stuck in here or not. Wouldn't it be easier to not experience those things?"

The room turned dark as night descended. Rema could only see an outline of Nathenek's body.

"All my life I've been sheltered, people claiming it was for my own good. In some sick twist of fate, it seems I'm destined to go to my death that way." Rema lay down on the hard floor. "Can I at least have a blanket? Or would it be better for me to be miserable and cold, since I'm going to die anyway?"

"Has anyone ever told you how infuriating you are?" Nathenek snatched his top blanket, throwing it at her.

Rema grabbed it, wrapping the blanket around her body and shoving part of it under her head as a pillow. "Thank you."

"I didn't do it to be nice. I just want you to shut up and go to sleep." Nathenek rolled over, facing the wall again.

Rema smiled.

When she woke the next morning, Nathenek was gone. She folded the blanket, placing it on his bed. Rema stretched her arms and legs, preparing to exercise.

The door slammed shut, causing Rema to jump at the sound. She spun around and came face to face with Nathenek.

"What are you doing?" he demanded, his voice barely above a whisper.

"Does it matter?"

Nathenek sat on the edge of the bed. He pulled out a loaf of bread from the pocket in his tunic, handing it to Rema. "I suppose it doesn't," he finally answered.

She tore into the bread, devouring it all.

"Do you plan to exercise during our entire journey?" He folded his hands on his lap.

"As opposed to sitting here, crying?" she asked

around a mouthful of bread.

"Yes, actually."

"I'm sorry to disappoint you," Rema said, swallowing her food. "I have no intention of sitting here, wasting away. It's not in my nature."

Nathenek glanced up the ceiling, appearing lost in thought.

"Let me ask you a question," Rema said. "Would you sit here all day if you were in my position?"

"I suppose not." He stood and went to the window, gazing outside while she finished eating her food.

"Fine," Nathenek said after several minutes. "I'll take you to the top deck."

Rema's eyes widened in shock. Was he serious? Or simply playing with her?

"There is one condition, though." He faced Rema, waiting for her response.

"What is it?" she asked, dread replacing the excitement she felt a moment before.

"You have to dress like a boy."

She jumped to her feet. "That's it?" He nodded. "Deal."

Nathenek went over to the footlocker and opened it up. He handed her a cap. "Pull your hair up, so no one sees it."

Rema did as he asked, shoving her hair under the hat. He also gave her a belt, which she used to cinch her pants up higher, so she wasn't tripping on the material. "What about shoes?"

"I have an extra pair of boots."

They were huge on her, but after being barefoot for so long, it felt like a soft blanket surrounded her feet.

"How do I look?"

Nathenek stood before her. "Good." He adjusted the cap lower on Rema's forehead. "You remind me of my sister. She's stubborn like you." He patted the top of her head. "Let's go."

Nathenek led her through the dark, dank hallway to a ladder bathed in sunlight. "Stay by my side," he ordered as he ascended. Rema climbed right on his heels, eager to see the ocean again.

Nathenek stood on the deck and turned around, reaching down to help Rema up. He led her to the side of the ship, near the railing. She couldn't get over the sight of the ocean and just how much water there was in every direction. The sails billowed against the wind. One man hung on the tall center mast, while several others on the deck tended to the sails, mopped the floor, or assisted the captain with various tasks.

"What are your duties while on board?" she asked Nathenek.

"You," he said bluntly. "The emperor assigned me the task of hunting you down and bringing you before him to be executed. He gave me endless resources to do so."

A thought occurred to her—did Nathenek know why Emperor Hamen wanted her dead? Perhaps he was unaware of who she really was—the one person Emperor

Hamen feared—the legitimate heir to the Emperion throne.

She needed to tread carefully. "You mentioned I'm the first prisoner you've ever dealt with?" Rema casually asked while leaning against the railing and gazing out at the ocean.

"Yes. Usually I assassinate the target immediately. You're the first one that I've had to bring to the emperor for termination."

Even though the warm sun beat down on her, she shivered from hearing Nathenek's cold words. "Can I ask you a question?"

"You can ask," he said, leaning on the railing next to her. "It doesn't mean I'll answer."

She played with the end of her rolled sleeve, trying to decide how to phrase what she wanted to say. "Why does the emperor want to see me executed? Why can't you kill me like all the others?"

Nathenek's eyes sliced over to Rema, analyzing her. For a brief second, she thought he knew the real reason.

He looked back out at the ocean and answered, "I'm sure you know King Barjon is the empress's brother."

"I do."

"And you plan to kill him in order to take the throne."

"That is correct. But do you know why I want to take the throne?" She turned to face him.

"The rebels claim you are the true heir." He peered

down at her.

"I am," she said. "King Barjon slaughtered my family in order to gain control of Greenwood Island."

"Yes, I know all this." Nathenek crossed his arms. "What are you getting at?"

"I'm just wondering how well you know your history."

"My knowledge of Emperion is impeccable."

They stood facing one another. Rema wondered how receptive he would be to learn of her true lineage. Would he embrace it? Or kill her on the spot?

He leaned toward her. "How well do you know your history?" She was about to answer when he continued. "Because I doubt you know anything about Emperion, our customs, or how intimately your suitor, Darmik, is connected to the ruling family."

"I know the emperor is Darmik's uncle," she admitted.

Nathenek smiled. He didn't understand that Darmik had denounced his family and was no longer loyal to them. He looked at something behind her. She glanced back and saw a hooded figure go below deck.

"Why is Trell here?" she asked.

"Why do you care about the old man?"

"Because he's an elderly gentleman and his health is failing. I can't imagine what the emperor wants with him."

He rubbed his face. "You weren't supposed to know he was here," he mumbled.

"Why? Are you going to kill him? Or is he giving information to the emperor?"

Nathenek rested against the railing. "There's a group of dolphins." He nodded toward the water.

Rema saw the beautiful, dark gray creatures zipping along the surface of the ocean. "They're magnificent!" One jumped out of the water and dove back in. "I'm glad I got to see this. I never knew such creatures existed." She'd been sheltered far too long. There was so much of the world she wanted to see and experience.

He smiled.

"Are we here for any particular purpose? Or are we just enjoying the sun and view?" she asked, changing the subject.

"Nothing with me is ever for pleasure," he replied. "We're here to practice."

He moved away from the railing to the center of the deck, motioning for her to join him. "Since you've been exercising in the room, I assume you did some training while at the rebel camp?"

"A little," Rema replied, standing before him.

"Get me to the ground," Nathenek ordered.

Rema came at him, trying to knock him off balance. She shoved him, tried bumping him, and even attempted to trip him.

"I'm glad you're not afraid to get your hands dirty." He chuckled.

Rema growled in frustration. She had no idea how to beat an opponent down who was not only taller than she was, but weighed considerably more.

"Stand up tall," he ordered, placing her at an arm's length away. "You want to walk toward me. While my eyes are focused on your face, quickly move your right leg out and around my left leg." He demonstrated the technique for her. "Place your hands on my shoulders, jerk my body toward you, and then shove me back while using your legs to hook mine in."

Rema did as instructed, and Nathenek went down. "Good, now punch me." Rema lightly hit him. "Then run away." He hopped back onto his feet. "Let's run through the drill a few more times."

"Why?" Rema asked, adjusting her cap.

"What do you mean?"

"I want to know why you're bothering to train me when you're taking me to be executed."

"Since you insist on exercising in the berth, I figure you might as well do it out here where you can at least help me. I prefer to train on a daily basis with an opponent. It keeps my skills honed." Nathenek gestured to the ocean surrounding them. "And I prefer to practice outside."

His reason seemed weak, but she didn't care. Rema was ecstatic to be outside in the fresh air with the sun shining down on her, and learning skills used by an assassin.

They ran through the drill several more times until Rema had it down. By the time they finished, she was exhausted and covered with sweat. The ocean water looked cool and inviting.

"I wish I could take a swim," she mumbled.

"You could," Nathenek answered, "if we weren't out in open water."

"Oh," Rema said, dumbfounded. She'd only said that in jest. She didn't realize people actually swam in the ocean. The only other time she saw the sea was with Lennek, and that had been from the top of a very steep, rocky cliff.

"You didn't know that?" he asked.

Rema shook her head.

"I forgot King Barjon doesn't allow travel between regions." He reached for her hand, examining the tattoo on her wrist. "I have one, too." He tugged up his sleeve, revealing a crude, black tattoo of an "X."

"We get them when we enter the military. It denotes a person's rank." He pulled the fabric down, covering his mark. "Let's get you inside. I'm starved."

Nathenek led her back to his room, where he once again locked her inside while he went to eat dinner with the crew.

She was so exhausted that she grabbed the blanket from his bed, laid down on the ground, and fell asleep.

❧❧❧

The next morning, when Rema woke, Nathenek was gone. It was frightening how he could come and go without making a sound and waking her up. She supposed it was a necessary skill all assassins possessed.

A plate of boiled potatoes lay next to her. The food was cold, but she quickly devoured it. After eating and putting the blanket back on his bed, she began stretching. Her muscles ached from the drills she did yesterday.

"Good, you're awake," Nathenek said from the doorway, startling her. "Here's your breakfast." He tossed her a loaf of bread. "Let's go."

Rema caught it and hurried after him, eating along the way. "Do you have any water?"

He pulled out a small waterskin and handed it to her. She took a few gulps and then attached it to her belt for later. They were about to step onto the top deck when Nathenek said, "Fix your hat."

Reaching out, Rema felt the cap had slipped back, exposing some of her hair. She quickly adjusted it, making sure all signs of her womanhood were hidden. It was silly—certainly, the crew knew her identity. After all, she came on top deck the first day wearing her nightdress. Perhaps dressing like a man was simply to limit curiosity and attention? Whatever the reason, Rema trusted Nathenek had her best interests at heart—he would ensure her safety in order to deliver her to his emperor.

Out in the fresh air, she took a deep breath and smiled, enjoying the sun's warmth on her body.

"Today we're working with daggers." Nathenek pulled out two small knives. "Have you ever thrown one before?"

"No." Savenek had taught her some basic sword work, and she knew how to shoot a bow. But those were the only weapons she was familiar with.

"Why are you smiling?" he asked.

She didn't realize she was. "This sounds like fun." And it was something that could come in handy.

Nathenek shook his head. "You should have been born in Emperion. You would've made an excellent soldier." He stood with his feet shoulder-width apart, a knife in each hand.

"Emperion blood runs through my veins," Rema whispered.

"I figured it did. Your blonde hair and blue eyes give you away. Everyone from the lower class has your coloring." Bending his arms, he quickly threw one dagger, and then the other, embedding each in the wooden door fifteen feet away.

"Your turn." He motioned for Rema to join him. "Stand like me," he instructed. She stood two feet from him and imitated his stance. "Good, now stand like that, facing the door over there." He pointed to where his daggers were embedded.

Rema did as he said while Nathenek retrieved his weapons, yanking them from the door.

He stood next to her. "When you go to throw, there are a couple things to keep in mind." Rema nodded, trying to commit all he said to memory. "You need to relax, clear your head, and put heat behind it."

She raised an eyebrow. "That seems contradictory."

"It's not, trust me."

Yeah, right, Rema thought. She couldn't trust the man taking her to her death.

"Shake your arms, loosening them." Rema did as he said. "Excellent. Now, when you hold the knife, you need to keep it secure in your hand, but you don't want a death grip." He flipped a dagger in the air, catching it, and handing it hilt first to Rema. She hesitated, and then took the weapon. Nathenek dangled her water sack from his hand.

"How did you do that?"

"Just remember what I do for a living," he said, handing it back to her. "And don't try anything." She nodded. "Now lift your throwing arm back," he instructed. "Reach forward, lightly flick your wrist, and release." He threw his dagger, landing it in the door. "Your turn."

Rema did as instructed—arm back, forward, flick, and release. Only her dagger didn't strike the wood—it bounced off.

"Again," he said, retrieving the weapons.

Rema spent the remainder of the day and into the early evening practicing until she could somewhat accurately throw the dagger. She could hit the door, her weapon sticking almost every time, but she wasn't able to strike the target yet. Her hands ached—blisters formed and popped on her fingers, bleeding in a few places.

Nathenek finally made her quit for the night. When he locked her in the berth, she grabbed the blanket and collapsed onto the ground, exhausted. Her eyelids were heavy, but she forced herself to stay awake in order to eat. Luckily, he returned a short time later, carrying two bowls of soup. He'd never eaten in the room with her before. They sat cross-legged on the ground, across from one another. Rema wondered what had changed that he decided to join her tonight.

She stared at the wooden spoon. The thought of holding it in her hand was too much. Gingerly picking up the bowl, she brought it to her lips, drinking the warm broth.

Nathenek sat, staring at her. "I can put something on your hands to help with the pain."

Rema nodded and he went to the footlocker, pulling out a small jar and a strip of fabric.

"Do you want me to do it for you?" he asked. Rema didn't know how she'd put the medicine on her own hands, so she nodded. He opened the jar and used two fingers to scoop out some of the pungent-smelling goo. He rubbed it onto her raw skin and popped blisters. Then he wrapped the fabric around her hands. "They'll be healed by tomorrow."

"Thank you." Her hands felt tingly, the pain already going away. She picked up her bowl and sipped some more soup. "You could've let me suffer. You know, since I'm going to die anyway."

Nathenek chuckled. "I could have." He ate a couple of spoonfuls of soup. "I didn't do it to be nice. I simply didn't want you to drop the bowl and make a mess." He took another bite.

Rema suspected he was lying. As much as he tried to hide it, Nathenek was a good man. "Do you have a family?" Rema asked, wanting to understand him better.

"My parents and sister live in Emperor's City. My brothers, all seven of them, are serving the emperor, like me."

"You're not married?"

"No." Nathenek shook his head. "When I took the oath to serve Emperor Hamen, I vowed not to marry. Only the assassins in his elite guard are required to make this promise."

That was a harsh requirement when he was already devoting his life to the emperor's service.

"Seven brothers and one sister. You must've had an interesting childhood."

"All my brothers are older than I am, and they enlisted in the military at age twelve. I grew up playing with my sister."

Rema recalled him saying that he went into the army at eight. "Why did you enlist younger than most?"

Nathenek sighed, putting down his bowl. "It's obvious you know nothing of Emperion and our ways." He leaned back against the wall, stretching his legs out before him. "I don't want to go into details, but know that Emperor Hamen rules over the largest empire. The entire place is centered on conquering other kingdoms and maintaining its current holdings. In other words, it is solely focused on war. If the emperor wants more soldiers, he gets them, no matter their age."

Eight children from one family—all forced into the army. Rema feared asking if they were all still alive. "Your sister managed to avoid enlisting?"

"Technically."

"I don't understand." Rema finished the soup and set the bowl down beside her.

"I went in her place," he revealed. "And while she may not be serving in the military, her life is defined by it."

"Did she marry a man in the army?"

Nathenek chuckled. "No, most certainly not. She married a baker. But her oldest child is ten. In two years, he'll be required to enlist." He stood and removed his tunic.

"I'm sorry."

Nathenek turned off the oil lamp, sending the room into darkness. "Good night." He climbed into bed.

"King Barjon is an oppressive ruler. Not in the same way as Emperor Hamen, but ruthless nonetheless. I'm tired of one person controlling the lives of everyone— especially when the good of ordinary citizens is overlooked. A ruler should listen to and lead his subjects."

Nathenek didn't respond.

Not wanting to bother him, Rema pulled off her tunic, using it as a pillow. She lay down on the hard ground, wrapping the blanket around her body. She was so exhausted that she quickly fell into a deep sleep.

FOUR

Darmik

The only one without any training was Ellie. Neco offered to teach her some basics, but Darmik was concerned. He needed Neco focused on their task of rescuing Rema, not protecting Ellie.

Sitting around the table, Darmik outlined his plan. Their ship was headed to Emperion's military port, located north of the main merchant port, where he believed Captain was headed. Since the military ship was smaller and faster, Darmik estimated they would dock a few hours before he did. Once in port, Darmik would announce that he was there on a diplomatic mission. He intended to be escorted to the palace where he would speak with the emperor before Rema arrived.

"What do you plan to tell your uncle?" Ellie asked.

"This is where it gets tricky," Darmik said. "Emperor Hamen will perceive Rema as a threat. The only way he'll let her live is if she's not the true heir."

"What are you saying?" Ellie asked.

"I want to convince him he has the wrong person, and Rema is simply a commoner whom I'm betrothed to."

"How do you plan to do that?" Neco asked, raising his eyebrows with a skeptical look.

Darmik was surprised no one questioned him using the term *betrothed*. He stood and began pacing around the small room. "As you know, Rema bears the royal mark on her shoulder."

"You want to remove it?" Savenek asked.

"Or I could cover it with makeup," Ellie suggested.

Darmik nodded. "What do you think?"

"I can cut the mark off and stitch her up," Vesha said. "Rema will have a scar, though."

"Makeup will be easier," Ellie said.

"Don't you think the emperor will check?" Neco asked. "He'll see the scar or the makeup."

"And that's assuming you have the opportunity to remove the tattoo or cover it with makeup before the emperor checks," Savenek added.

Darmik stopped pacing and sat on the empty chair, facing everyone. "I'm open to ideas."

"Why don't we try to intercept Rema before she makes it to Emperion?" Savenek offered.

Darmik had already considered the possibility, but they were headed slightly north of the merchant ship. "If we're lucky enough to catch her boat, we will certainly grab her."

"Can't we arrive at the merchant port first and

wait for her there?" Vesha asked.

Darmik shook his head. "A military ship can't arrive at the merchant port—especially undetected. The army will swarm aboard, and we'll be unable to rescue her. We have no choice but to dock at the military port, north of there."

"Once we dock, can't we get off the ship and travel to the merchant port? We can try to rescue her there," Savenek said.

Darmik leaned back on his chair. He looked at each of the five faces, staring hopefully at him. "All of you need to understand something," he said. "We're entering another kingdom. They have different rules and customs. While I appreciate your suggestions, they're unrealistic. When our ship arrives, we will need to state our names and purpose for being on the mainland. We won't be able to slip away unnoticed."

"Very well," Savenek said. "We'll stick with your plan."

"I'll work on mixing some things together to make a skin-colored makeup to cover her tattoo," Ellie said.

"I'll check medical supplies for a needle and thread," Vesha added.

"I want everyone to get a good night's rest," Darmik said. "Tomorrow, we'll train, and I'll teach you proper etiquette."

Audek scrunched his nose. "Etiquette?"

"Yes," Darmik mused. "You need to know how to greet the emperor. I can't have you do something to offend him. Otherwise, he'll have you beheaded."

Audek shivered. "Etiquette it is."

Darmik's back hurt from standing so straight and stiff in the courtyard among hundreds of other soldiers. The hot sun beat down on his exposed neck, causing him to sweat in his full military uniform. The two prisoners stood on the raised platform. The first one, a boy of about twelve years old, was crying. The executioner shoved the boy onto his knees and pulled his wrists forward, locking his forearms into metal cuffs.

The warden read the charge. "This boy has been caught stealing food from the Kalmier Market. Two apples. The penalty is loss of both hands, so he will never be able to steal again."

The executioner raised his axe. Darmik's stomach twisted in pain. Surely, stealing food didn't deserve such a severe punishment. The axe came down, and the boy screamed a bloodcurdling sound. The axe went up. Darmik wanted to close his eyes; however, if he did, he'd be the one up there receiving a punishment for disobedience. The crude weapon flew down, and the boy's second hand fell off. Blood squirted everywhere. The boy lay on the ground, his arms still locked in place. He must've passed out. A soldier came out, removed the metal cuffs, and pulled him roughly from the platform.

Darmik's legs shook and his hands tingled. He couldn't pass out. He'd never hear the end of it. His vision swam.

The warden went to the next prisoner, who was covered with a bag, concealing his identity. "This one is found guilty of treason. Punishment is death."

The executioner came over and shoved the prisoner onto his knees, locking his head and arms into the equipment. The executioner grabbed his axe with one hand, removing the bag covering the prisoner's head with the other.

It was Rema.

Darmik screamed.

He sat up in bed, breathing hard, covered in sweat. It was only a dream. Memories of his time in Emperion, infused with his greatest fear of losing Rema. Ever since he boarded the ship, he'd been having nightmares.

Even though it was still dark outside, he slipped out of bed and got dressed. He decided to go up to the top deck and practice sword drills until everyone else woke up. Hopefully, the physical activity would focus his mind. He unsheathed his sword, and started running through various forms.

Barjon's angry face appeared before him. "You're doing it wrong!" he snarled. "Can't you do anything right? You're eight years old and can barely lift the sword."

"I can do it," Darmik insisted. "I just need a little more practice."

Barjon swung and hit his arm. The sword dropped to the ground with a loud clank. "I don't know why I waste my time with you. Lennek's the only one worthy." He stormed away.

Darmik bent down and retrieved the sword. Standing,

he tried the maneuver again, perfecting it. He smiled, but no one was around to see his accomplishment. Determined not to fail his father, he ran through the drill again and again, until the sword became an extension of his arm, and he didn't have to even think about the movements.

The following days fell into a routine. After breakfast, everyone went to the top deck, where they spent the morning doing physical training in order to maintain their strength. Darmik led several drills, and Savenek offered to show him some of the rebels' exercises. They were rather impressive, so Darmik incorporated them into their routine. Thankfully, Ellie caught on quickly. She and Vesha often practiced together and sparred with one another. Darmik enjoyed working with Savenek and Audek—they knew moves he was unfamiliar with and posed a greater challenge than he was used to. Neco even said he was impressed with everyone.

The afternoons were focused on Emperion protocol. Darmik explained how everything was centered on the army and war—from the structure of the city to the way their society behaved. All military members were honored, and those who didn't serve were the lowest of the low. The higher-ranking officers were Emperion's elite and noble class.

Darmik showed them how to greet one another by respectfully bowing one's head. He also told them to remain quiet at all times. Emperions discouraged individual thought and questions weren't tolerated. Everyone was to keep all emotions hidden at all times. Emperions were known for using a person's feelings against them. Darmik wanted them to present themselves as a respectful envoy from Greenwood Island, and he planned to speak on their behalf.

The brothers stood side by side, bows raised.

"Closest shot wins," Lennek said. "You go first."

Darmik focused on the target thirty feet away. He'd been practicing every day since Trell gave him the bow for his tenth birthday. He pulled back the bowstring and released. The arrow sailed through the air and landed with a thunk, dead center on the target. Darmik smiled.

Lennek grunted, and then released his arrow. It arched through the air, missing the target completely, and landing in a tree.

"I win," Darmik announced.

Lennek threw his bow on the ground. "What did you do?" he demanded. "You sabotaged my weapon, didn't you?"

"Of course not, brother." He never cheated, and it hurt his feelings that his brother would accuse him of such a thing.

"I take lessons every day. You don't. How did you beat me?"

Darmik looked to the ground, no idea what to say to appease his brother.

"Guards!" Lennek shouted, turning to face the soldiers responsible for the princes' safety. "Take Darmik to the king. Now."

"I'll go," Darmik mumbled. "You don't need to drag me there." He was escorted to Barjon's office.

"Father," Prince Lennek said. "Darmik cheated. He needs to be taught a lesson." Lennek proceeded to tell him his version of the story.

King Barjon's eyes narrowed. "Darmik won?"

"Only because he must have done something unethical," Lennek whined.

"Leave us," the king demanded.

Once alone with his father, Darmik said, "I didn't cheat. It was a fair win."

The king smiled. "Nothing is ever fair." He pulled out a leather whip. "Remove your tunic."

When Darmik wasn't having a nightmare about his father and brother, he was haunted by his time at Emperion. He always dreamt about some traumatic experience he'd tried to forget—like the time he was forced to fight a fellow cadet to the death.

"Only my ten best men from this unit can go on," Officer Gaverek announced. "That means one of you fails."

Darmik stood straight and tall at attention. He'd done well on all of his tests and challenges. Several of his fellow cadets were slower and not as qualified as he was. He should be safe from being sent home in disgrace.

"I've decided to take the two worst cadets and have you fight until someone dies. Winner stays. I won't have to *waste my time sending the loser home." No one spoke. "I've chosen Jimek—who is consistently coming in last for our runs." Officer Gaverek stopped before Darmik. "And I've chosen the soft prince, since no one likes him."*

Panic swelled inside of Darmik. This wasn't fair. He shouldn't be forced to fight a fellow cadet to the death. His hands became sweaty as he stepped forward, everyone forming a circle around him and Jimek. Only, when Darmik went to throw the first punch, Jimek morphed into Rema right as his fist struck her nose.

Awakening in a cold sweat, Darmik shook his head, trying to banish the visions of Rema screaming in pain. With shaking hands, he got dressed and went to the top deck. The air was hot and muggy, even though the sun hadn't yet come up. They had to be close to Emperion. Darmik estimated they'd been aboard the ship for two weeks. Any hope of intercepting Rema's ship had diminished. He was going to have to become the person he didn't want to be—the king's son, Prince Darmik, in order to go before the emperor. It was the only thing that could save Rema.

"Land ho!" a voice rang through the dim, gray sky of dawn.

Darmik scanned the horizon—he didn't see anything.

Several sailors ran to man the sails. One approached him. "We'll be in port soon. I suggest you tell the others to prepare."

Darmik's heartbeat quickened—this was it. He

ran to Neco's quarters, pounding on the door.

"Yes?" Neco asked, pulling open the door and squinting.

"Land has been spotted. Wake everyone. It's time."

Without waiting for a response, Darmik rushed to his berth. Emperions were all about rank, so Darmik needed to show he outranked everyone except the emperor. Opening the footlocker, he pulled out his black pants and commander's tunic. After dressing, he strapped his sword belt around his waist and sheathed his blade. Bending down, he retrieved his crown from the footlocker. He stood, staring at it. He never thought he'd wear it again. The sapphires looked almost black. Placing the crown atop his head, he felt like he was somehow betraying Rema just by wearing it. He had to remind himself that he was doing this for her. Taking a deep breath, he knew the task before him wouldn't be easy.

He went to the top deck to make sure everyone was ready. Much to his satisfaction, everyone—including the girls—wore the King's Army uniform.

"Excellent," Darmik said, coming to stand before them.

Savenek tugged at the collar. "We could have worn our uniform," he mumbled.

"No," Darmik replied. "Your uniform has Rema's crest. The emperor would have recognized it. We must bear King Barjon's colors."

Ellie fidgeted with her tunic. "Yes?" Darmik asked, knowing she had a question.

"It's just that…well…we're girls."

Audek laughed. "I most certainly am not a girl."

"Not you!" Ellie said, exasperated. "Vesha and I. Won't they know something's wrong? Girls aren't allowed to join the army."

"True," Darmik said. "But that's only on Greenwood Island, not Emperion. The emperor allows women in the army. He even allows them to fight. No one will think anything of the two of you."

"You're positive the emperor doesn't know you've defected?" Ellie asked.

"There is no way for him to know already—unless Captain has beaten us there."

Before Ellie could ask another question, Darmik continued, "I want everyone to remember what we discussed. You are all members of the King's Army. I handpicked each of you to accompany me here. You are all highly trained soldiers."

Everyone nodded.

"And remember, my position of commander and prince are equally important as me being the emperor's nephew."

Glancing out at the ocean, Darmik saw land budding on the horizon. The sky lightened, welcoming day.

"Places everyone!" Neco shouted. Audek, Savenek, Ellie, Vesha, and Neco all stood at attention along the railing of the port side of the ship. Darmik remained near the center of the deck, feet shoulder-width apart, hands clasped behind his back. Taking a deep breath, he exhaled and put on his game face—no emotion, only his bland expression, giving nothing away, as he'd been taught to do by the very people he was about to face.

The ship neared the military port. Hundreds and hundreds of small, fast-moving ships were docked there. Neco glanced at Darmik, his lips tight with concern. Neco knew they were entering a hostile kingdom with the largest army, but to see firsthand the power, and weapons, was another matter. Darmik gave a curt nod, trying to get his friend to focus. Neco faced outward again.

The crew brought the sails down, and the boat entered the port. Darmik instructed the helmsman to steer the ship directly to an open slip. As the boat made its way through the harbor, Darmik noticed several soldiers staring at them. When they neared an open slip, shouts rang through the air. Emperion soldiers swarmed the deck—already knowing something was wrong.

As the anchor dropped, Darmik glanced over the side of the boat and said, "Welcome to Emperion." More than a hundred soldiers stood below, swords drawn. While he suspected this would happen, his companions did not. He could tell they were nervous just by looking at them.

"Relax," Darmik said, "all of you. That's an order."

"But you still want us at attention, right?" Audek asked.

Darmik rolled his eyes. "Yes, at attention, but

don't look so bloody scared!"

A ramp was shoved up against the boat. Holding his head high, Darmik kept his face blank and went to the top of the ramp, prepared to face the Emperion Army.

Before the soldiers could question him, Darmik shouted, "I am Prince Darmik, son of King Barjon of Greenwood Island. I am here on a peaceful, diplomatic mission. I want to speak to my uncle, Emperor Hamen."

The soldiers stood frozen, swords pointed upward in his direction. One man, dressed in the uniform of a lieutenant, walked forward to the bottom of the ramp.

"Prince Darmik," the lieutenant said in his funny, Emperion accent. "Welcome. I was not informed of your intended visit."

"My visit was not planned in advance," he answered. "I have a message of the utmost importance from King Barjon for Emperor Hamen. Please escort me to my uncle. Immediately."

The lieutenant smiled. "Prince Darmik, or should I call you Commander?" His eyes narrowed, giving him a shrewd look. "Please forgive our inhospitality, but surely you, of all people, know I will not escort you to the emperor, unless the emperor so orders."

Darmik knew this was a possibility, the absolute worst-case scenario.

"Arrest all of them," the lieutenant ordered. "I want to know how they managed to get one of our ships."

The soldiers rushed on board. Several came at Darmik. He kept his hands clasped behind his back, knowing any sudden movement would get him a sword in the side. When he offered no resistance, a soldier pulled Darmik's arms forward and fastened metal rings around his wrists, cinching them together. His crown, sword, and daggers were removed. Glancing at his friends, he saw them all being similarly bound and disarmed.

"Take them to the main dungeon via the military route," the lieutenant ordered. Thankfully, Darmik and his friends were being kept together, for now. If they were sent to separate places, Darmik knew he'd never see them again. This was the one, and only, thing working in their favor right now.

Darmik was roughly shoved down the ramp. At the bottom, a dozen soldiers surrounded him. No one spoke as he was escorted along the dock. Stepping onto solid ground, his legs wobbled. It would take him a bit to acclimate. Focusing on his surroundings, the enormous wall enclosing the city loomed ahead, just as he remembered. It was tan stone, matching the sand-covered ground. The wind kicked up, tossing small pieces of sand at his exposed flesh. Even though it was in the early hours of the day, the sun was already hot and bright.

"Move it." A soldier slammed the hilt of a sword into his back. It almost sent him to his knees; but Darmik knew the games these men played. In order to survive, he needed to be strong and not reveal weakness or fear. Forcing himself to remain on his feet, he started walking.

Since this was the military's port, there was an entrance in the wall used strictly by soldiers entering into or out of Emperor's City. Darmik moved in that direction. When he reached the guards stationed there, they opened the locked gate without a word.

He followed the soldiers through the wall and into the city. Streets crowded with merchants and people stretched in every direction. Two-story structures, all the color of sand, lined the streets. In the distance, low, rolling hills were covered with tan stones. Not much had changed since the last time he'd been there. It was still ugly and inhospitable.

The soldiers led Darmik to one of the larger buildings across the street. Above the door was the emperor's crest. The lieutenant pushed past his men and went inside while everyone else remained outside, waiting in the hot sun.

After several minutes, the door opened and a soldier stepped out. "Will the foreigners please step forward?"

Darmik did as asked, hoping his companions all followed suit.

"First-rank officers only, escort the prisoners inside. Everyone else, return to your stations at once."

Two soldiers came toward Darmik, each grabbing one of his arms and bringing him inside.

"Use the second door," the soldier instructed as they entered the building.

At first, Darmik couldn't see anything from being in the bright sunlight. He was pulled forward and he heard feet shuffling over a hard surface, but that was it.

Gradually, his eyes adjusted and he saw that they traveled down a narrow hallway.

They came to a stop before a door with the number two engraved on it. One of the soldiers unlocked and opened it. Darmik glanced back and saw his companions close behind, each with a guard at their side. The soldier escorting Darmik shoved him through the doorway. A guard stepped next to him, holding a torch that revealed a long, narrow set of stairs, leading down. Not wanting to show any fear, Darmik quickly descended, his guards right behind him. At the bottom, a long, dark tunnel stretched out before him, no end in sight.

"Keep moving," a soldier said. Darmik recalled his studies about Emperion. There was an entire network of tunnels under the city. It allowed for not only prisoner transportation, but also evacuation of the city if need be.

No one spoke during the several mile journey. Darmik took mental notes of each turn they made. When he came to a set of stairs leading up, he quickly calculated the route in reverse, memorizing it, in case it was needed to escape. Darmik went up the stairs; though, it was only half of what he'd descended. He guessed he was still underground. A black, iron door opened, and he was shoved inside a small room. The door slammed shut, causing a loud boom to echo through the cold, still space.

He was alone.

Another door opened and two soldiers stood there, dressed in solid black. He was in the dungeon.

"Where are the members of my guard being

taken?" Darmik demanded. He needed to stay with his companions. Neither soldier spoke or indicated they had even heard his question.

A third soldier, dressed in the uniform of a prison warden, stepped into the room. "The members of your guard are going to be interrogated," the man said.

Darmik's stomach twisted in pain. He couldn't let his friends be tortured. "They are my escorts and companions. If it's information you want, interrogate me, for they know nothing of value."

The warden smiled. "We are going to interrogate you, too." He spun on his heels. "Bring the prisoner with me," he ordered.

The two soldiers seized Darmik's arms, dragging him forward.

"I am the emperor's nephew," Darmik said sternly. "I am also a prince. I demand to be treated accordingly. Take me to speak with Emperor Hamen. Now."

A putrid smell wafted through the dark, stone corridor. Darmik knew what awaited him, and he feared Vesha and Ellie would not survive. "If any harm comes to my companions," Darmik said, seething with rage, "you will answer for it."

He was furious he hadn't foreseen this outcome. He figured they might be taken into custody, but not interrogated. What purpose would this serve? They knew who he was. He did not intend to die in the dungeon without his uncle even knowing he was there. It was time to change the plan.

The warden stopped before an iron door. "Put him in there," he ordered. "Prepare him for a standard interrogation. I'll be back after I've seen to his companions."

The soldiers shoved Darmik into the room, and he fell on his side. A single table stood in the middle of the room, chains attached to both ends. The two soldiers came in, closing the door behind them. One pulled Darmik to his feet.

The soldier turned Darmik around, about to push him onto the table, when Darmik shifted his weight and slammed his elbow into his face, knocking him onto his back. The remaining soldier rushed at him. It was difficult to fight with his wrists bound together, but he'd done it several times before. The man threw a punch, and Darmik ducked. They circled one another, sizing each other up. The soldier on the ground started to stand.

He didn't have much time if he wanted to win this fight. He faked a swing toward the man's head. When the soldier lifted his arms to block the strike, Darmik side-kicked the man, hitting him in his stomach. The soldier hunched over and Darmik smashed his bound fists on his back, sending the soldier to the ground. Darmik knew the other guard was behind him, about to strike. He spun around and kicked the soldier's face, knocking him over. Darmik quickly grabbed one of the soldier's swords and hit each man on the head with the hilt, rendering them unconscious.

With both men incapacitated, Darmik stood next to the door, placing his body flat against the wall, awaiting the warden's return. He knew, all-too well, the games Emperion interrogators played. A high-pitched female scream laced with pain echoed through the dungeon. He couldn't let it affect him. If the interrogator discovered Darmik's weak spot, he'd be sure to hurt Ellie and Vesha in an attempt to get him to cooperate.

After several minutes, the door swung open and the warden ducked inside. Darmik grabbed the man's tunic, pulled his body forward, and slammed the warden's head against the stone wall. The man fell to the ground, unconscious.

In case other soldiers were near, Darmik pulled the warden up and used his body as a human shield. Stepping into the hallway, all was quiet. Darmik knew from his time in Emperion that they typically kept people arrested together near one another for interrogation purposes. His friends should be nearby. Going to the next door, he listened for noises inside. He couldn't tell who was behind the door, but he heard voices. Darmik lowered the unconscious warden to the ground. Searching the man's pockets, he found a set of keys. He fumbled with them until he found the one for his manacles. Once his wrists were free from the metal, he stood, pulling the warden up with him. Reaching for the handle, he flung the door open and rushed inside, using the warden as a shield.

One soldier held Savenek by the arm, while the other opened the manacles on the table, preparing them for use. Darmik shoved the warden's body at the guard near Savenek. Then Darmik jumped over the table, landing next to a startled soldier. A jab, reverse, and a roundhouse kick sent the man to the ground. Darmik grabbed one of the chains attached to the table and swung it at the man's head, knocking him out.

Darmik turned to help Savenek, who stood over the body of the other soldier, smiling.

"Is he unconscious or dead?" Darmik asked.

"Probably unconscious," Savenek mused. "And I thought you told us to do whatever they said."

"Well," Darmik answered, "there's been a slight change." He peered into the hallway.

"What's the new plan?" Savenek whispered, coming to stand next to him.

"Not sure. But things are too quiet. Something's not right."

The guards started to stir. "Want to lock these guys in here?" Savenek asked.

Darmik nodded. "Grab the keys in the warden's right pocket. There should be one in there that unlocks your bindings." Savenek did as Darmik said, and they stepped into the hallway, locking the door behind them. Darmik pointed to the next door, and Savenek nodded. As before, Darmik grabbed the handle, throwing open the door. They rushed inside. Savenek took one soldier down, while Darmik incapacitated the other one.

Audek lay on the table. Savenek quickly shuffled through the keys until he found one that unlocked the metal encasing his arms and legs.

"I take it things aren't going as planned," Audek said as he sat up.

"No," Darmik snapped, pacing the room.

"Well, what are we waiting for?" Audek asked. "Let's go rescue everyone else."

Darmik shook his head "We'll never make it out of the dungeon."

"So far it's been fairly easy," Savenek said.

"We have two options. We can stick together and try to rescue the rest of our group. If we do so, we run the risk of being recaptured. If they catch us, we could all be killed." He glanced into the hallway—no one was about. "Or," he continued, "we can assume capture is imminent and split up, hoping one of us makes it out alive."

"Which plan has a higher likelihood of success?" Savenek asked, coming to stand next to him.

Darmik calculated the risks of each option. Their chance of escape was slim. However, he believed one person could evade capture easier than all six could.

"I suggest we skiddattle," Audek said.

"What do you want to do, Darmik?" Savenek asked.

"I hate to ask this of you," he said, "but I think we need to split up—just the two of us. Leave everyone else here as a distraction."

"All righty." Audek laid back down on the table. "Lock me in."

Savenek rushed over and reattached the manacles. "For Rema."

"Yes," Audek said. "For our queen."

Darmik heard voices. "Hurry!" He and Savenek ran from the room.

When they reached the bottom of a flight of stairs, they heard noises coming from the top and from behind them. They were boxed in.

"I'm sorry," Darmik said.

"For what?"

"This." Darmik punched Savenek in the stomach, and he doubled over in pain. Emperion guards rushed into the corridor, surrounding them with their swords drawn.

"It's about time you arrive," Darmik said. "Detain him, and take me to see my uncle."

FIVE

Rema

Rema held on for dear life, sweat dripping down her face and back. She couldn't believe how humid it was. The closer they got to Emperion, the hotter it became.

"Excellent!" Nathenek yelled up to her. "Now slide down, careful not to burn your hands."

It was beautiful up here. Nathenek had made her climb one of the ropes attached to the mizzenmast. It reminded her of being on top of her cliff back home. The wind whipped around her body, making her feel as if she were flying. For the past two weeks, Nathenek had been pushing her harder and harder each day. The result—her muscles were tone and far stronger than before.

Keeping her legs hooked around the rope like he showed her, she began lowering herself. Four feet from the bottom, she let go, jumping onto the deck.

"Are your hands hurt?" he asked.

"Nope." She held them up to show him. Her

hands were red and calloused, but stronger than they had ever been before.

"Good, let's practice the sword work I taught you yesterday."

For the next two hours, they ran through the drill, side by side, mimicking one another, moving in perfect unison. Rema thoroughly enjoyed working with Nathenek. He was an excellent instructor, patient, and she learned a great deal from him. When they practiced together, his cold exterior melted away and he was actually pleasant to be around.

When they stopped for a water break, the captain of the ship came over.

"Land has been spotted," he informed them. "We should arrive at sunset."

Fear coursed through Rema. This was it. She'd managed to forget about her execution by focusing on training. Everything was about to change.

"Thank you," Nathenek said to the ship's captain. "We'll be in my room preparing. Let me know when we're about to dock."

The captain nodded and left. Rema kept her mouth shut as she followed Nathenek to his berth. The second she stepped foot on land, she would escape. She would need to be fully aware of her surroundings and ready to run or hide when the opportunity presented itself. Her stomach twisted in pain just thinking of what she was about to face.

Nathenek closed and locked his door. "We need

to talk." He went over to the footlocker and opened it. "When I first kidnapped you, this was around your neck." He dug around inside and pulled out her key necklace.

"That's mine!" She went to grab the chain, but Nathenek stood, raising it out of her reach.

"Where did you get it?" he asked.

"It's a family heirloom," she said. "Give it back."

"Do you have any idea what this means?" he asked.

"Yes, I do." Rema folded her arms across her chest. "I know exactly what it means. Do you?"

He lowered the necklace, placing the key on his palm. "Tell me," he demanded.

"Not that it's any of your business, but that necklace has been handed down through the generations of my family. It symbolizes the true heir."

Nathenek's eyes narrowed. "For Greenwood Island?"

"Yes, now give it to me." If Nathenek showed it to the emperor, he would know she was the rightful heir of Greenwood Island, thus making her the true heir to Emperion. He would kill her at once. Although, if he knew about the secret tattoo on her shoulder, all he had to do was look at that and she'd be condemned to death.

"The emperor wants to see me beheaded so he can verify my identity," Rema said.

Nathenek nodded, his fingers curling around the key.

"Your loyalty lies with the Emperion line? Or with the emperor?" Rema asked.

Nathenek's head jerked up. He took a step toward her, coming too close for comfort. "They are one in the same," he snapped.

"Are you sure about that?

Nathenek cursed under his breath.

"What?" Rema asked. Was he finally starting to understand her true heritage?

He shook his head.

"I want my necklace."

"I'm sorry," he said, putting it in his pocket. "I can't give this to you right now." He took a step back, rubbing his face with his hands.

"Why not?" she demanded. "It's mine."

Quick as a blink of an eye, Nathenek came at her, grabbing her upper arms. "Listen to me," he said, in a voice that was cold and hard, sending chills through her body. "Keep your mouth shut about the key, or I'll kill you."

She felt something pierce her side. Glancing down, Nathenek had let go of her arm, unsheathed his dagger, and dug it into her side just under her ribs. She never even saw him move. Rema nodded, afraid to say anything at all.

He let go, putting his knife away. "Now listen closely," he spoke. "When we arrive, we'll be disguised as merchants as we travel through the city to the palace. Then I will take you in through the servants' entrance and inform the emperor you're there."

Rema wondered why he told her his plan. "And

then I'll be executed?" Rema whispered.

"Yes."

"By you?" she asked.

Nathenek's eyes darkened. "I'm an assassin, not an executioner. He'll either have me kill you immediately and, if that's the case, I promise to do it swiftly and as painlessly as possible. Or, he'll have you publicly executed before the city. That occurs the first day of every new week."

There was a knock on the door. "Captain told me to tell you we're coming into port."

"Thanks," Nathenek yelled, loud enough for the sailor to hear through the closed door. "We don't have much time," he said to Rema.

She was well aware how little time she had to escape. Could she jump off the boat and swim to shore? Or should she wait until they were on the dock to get away?

Nathenek pulled out a brown cape. "Put this on," he instructed.

The air was hot and sticky—unlike anything she'd ever experienced before. The last thing she felt like doing was putting on a heavy, warm cloak. Besides, this would make it impossible for her to swim.

"Trust me," Nathenek said. "Not only is the sun hot, burning exposed skin, especially white skin like yours, but the sand is severe. You'll need it for your protection."

Rema reluctantly took the cape, draping it over her shoulders. There was fabric around her neck and she pulled it out, thinking it was a hood, but the material was too long.

"That's for your face," Nathenek said as he put on his own cloak. "If a sandstorm picks up, wrap the fabric around your head to protect your ears, nose, and eyes."

A sandstorm? As frightened as she was with the need to escape, she was equally intrigued by the fact that she was about to step foot on foreign soil.

"Fix your cap so your hair is completely concealed."

While Rema adjusted her hat, Nathenek closed and locked his footlocker. He picked it up, lifting it above his head. "Let's go."

Rema followed him to the top deck, where a flurry of activity was going on. The sails were being lowered and men ran around, yelling commands she didn't understand.

"Wait here," Nathenek instructed, leaving her next to the door, out of everyone's way. He hurried over to a man dressed in a long, brown cape, his head concealed by a large hood. She wondered if it was Trell, and if so, what the assassin planned on doing with him.

Nathenek set his footlocker down and handed the man a small bag and some papers. The man nodded, briefly glancing her way. Nathenek returned to her, leading her toward the front of the ship, and away from the mysterious man.

"What's going to happen to him?" she asked, assuming it was Trell.

"That is none of your concern," he said in a harsh

tone, making her flinch.

They stopped next to the railing on the starboard side of the ship. There were several docks jetting out from a larger pier, all filled with ships of various sizes. Beyond the port was a massive, tan wall lining the beach in each direction for as far as she could see. A large opening stood in the wall, and all traffic seemed to accumulate in that gateway.

Past the wall, flat land covered with rows and rows of structures so numerous, Rema didn't see any spacing between the buildings. In the far distance stood bare, rolling hills.

The sun beat down, sizzling hot, and the air felt heavy. Rema swayed, lightheaded. Nathenek grabbed her arm. "Are you well?" he asked.

"I'm fine," Rema snapped, pulling away from his grip. "Just nervous about my death."

The boat came into an empty slip. Sailors pushed the massive anchor over the side and into the water. Nathenek drew her away from the railing.

"I know you want to see," he said, "but I can't have anyone recognize me." He wrapped the fabric around his face, leaving only his blue eyes exposed, concealing his identity. "When we descend the ramp, keep your face down and don't speak to anyone. Understood?"

Rema nodded. "Where's the emperor's palace located?" She wanted to make sure that once she escaped, she didn't head in that direction.

"We must travel through the city a couple of miles.

It's on the backside."

That would give Rema plenty of time to escape. The thought of being alone in a foreign country, especially one as hostile as Emperion, was terrifying. Still, she knew she could get away and survive on her own.

"Let's go." Nathenek took Rema's elbow, guiding her toward the exit.

Several of the crew members carried crates down the ramp, stacking them on the dock.

"Grab one," Nathenek ordered. "Put it on top of your head. Be careful to keep your balance when you descend."

Now was not the time to make a run for it. She needed to wait until she was among all those people working on the wharf and could easily blend in and disappear among them.

Rema wondered what was inside the crates. Food? Supplies? Whatever it was, King Barjon had no right exporting products while so many in the kingdom suffered from a lack of food. Grabbing a crate, she did as instructed. Luckily, it wasn't too heavy, and she made it off the ship and down the ramp with ease.

After setting the crate on top of another, an atrocious odor almost made her gag. It smelled like a dead, rotting animal. Rema pulled the wrap around her face, trying to block the foul stench. The dozens of people about, unloading the merchant ship, seemed unfazed by the stink. Before she had a chance to get lost among the chaos, Nathenek snatched her arm, pulling her away from the dock and toward the entrance in the wall.

"Keep your head down," he instructed, holding onto her arm with an iron grip. They stepped off the wooden pier and onto solid ground. Rema swayed, but Nathenek held her tight. "Walk fast and with purpose, and whatever you do, don't leave my side." Rema couldn't help but laugh. "You think this is funny?" Nathenek leaned down, close to her face.

"You act like you're trying to protect me."

"I am."

"By taking me to the emperor to be executed? I don't think so. I'll take my chances here if afforded the opportunity."

Nathenek shook his head. "Death by execution is a mercy compared to what will happen if the army gets ahold of you."

"After spending two weeks with me," Rema said, "I thought you'd know me better than that." She refused to be led to slaughter like some animal. She would fight, and she would get away.

Nathenek stopped walking. Dozens of people moved past them as if they weren't even there. Everyone wore cloaks that covered their entire bodies, including heads, leaving only their faces exposed. No one looked Rema in the eyes. It was as if everyone were afraid of something.

"The army is ruthless," Nathenek whispered in her ear. "They beat you down in order to break you—make you obedient. Yes, I know you well enough to know you would survive. But you wouldn't be *you* anymore. And I can't let that happen."

He pulled back slightly, looking at Rema. He raised his eyebrows, waiting for her response. She had none. Why did he care what happened to her now? He was taking her to her death, why show her mercy? It didn't make any sense.

Nathenek nodded toward the wall's entrance. "Let's go." He released her, taking a step back. If she turned and ran, would he catch her? Could she get lost in this crowd? Her foot inched its way back, putting her out of arm's reach. "If you run," he said, "they'll shoot you." He pointed to the top of the wall, where archers stood with bows at the ready.

Rema had absolutely no intention of dying or letting the army get their hands on her. Her best bet would be to enter the city and find an elderly person or a mother—someone who would be sympathetic to aid in her escape. Then she could hide in their home, acquire supplies, and board a merchant ship voyaging to Greenwood Island. She would return to *her* kingdom, to *her* people, and to *her* Darmik.

There was no way her destiny could be so cruel as to take everything away from her—her entire family, her love, her life. She refused to allow it. Rema would fight with every ounce of her being.

He grinned and turned away from her, walking directly toward the wall's opening. She hurried after him, knowing he would see her safely inside. Dozens of soldiers guarded the entrance, checking everyone's papers who entered.

Nathenek stopped before a younger-looking soldier, handing him two pieces of paper. "For me and my wife," he said in a rough voice. The soldier glanced over the documents and waved them through. Nathenek took the papers back, shoving them inside his cape.

Rema kept her mouth shut, following meekly behind him. Why didn't he declare that he worked for the emperor and was transporting a prisoner? Did he want to keep his identity concealed from everyone? Once inside, Nathenek slipped his arm around her waist, keeping her close by.

Traveling through Emperor's City was beyond anything Rema had ever imagined. She felt as if she were dreaming and kept waiting to wake on board the ship or in her bedchamber at the rebel fortress.

Buildings lined both sides of the narrow streets, and people walked shoulder to shoulder. The two-story structures, made of rough-looking stone blocks, were all light brown, matching the sandy ground. It was ugly. No greenery, no living plants, and no color.

"Stop gawking," Nathenek hissed in Rema's ear, causing her to jump. "Keep your head down and walk faster."

Someone bumped against her shoulder.

"Sorry," she mumbled. The stranger hurried away, too busy to respond.

Nathenek growled, shaking his head, his lips

pulled tight, as if he were furious. He shoved her down a dark alley, pushing her up against a wall.

"Stop talking," he demanded, placing his hands on either side of her head. His entire body shielded hers, and he leaned in, as if he were going to kiss her. Anyone passing by would think they were two lovers embracing one another. "You have a ridiculous accent," he hissed.

"Sorry," she whispered.

"We need to get through the city unnoticed." His eyes focused on hers, as if pleading with her to cooperate. "Stop looking around, walk right next to me with your head down, and act like you have a purpose."

"A purpose?" she questioned him.

"Yes," he said, resting his forehead against hers. "Like you know where you're going and what you're doing, so you don't stand out."

Rema leaned her head back against the rough wall behind her, away from him. She did have a purpose—to find someone sympathetic who would help her.

Nathenek sighed. "If you don't cooperate and do *exactly* as I say, I'll drug you again."

"And drag my body to the palace?"

His eyes narrowed. "If I have to."

Shoving against his chest, Rema said, "Fine, let's go." She decided to play along, doing as he said, while keeping her eyes open for opportunities to seek help or get away.

"My sister never does what I ask either. She always has to make things difficult, instead of trusting me," Nathenek mumbled, while taking ahold of her arm. "So obstinate."

They entered the busy street again, traveling quickly among the hordes of people. Rema kept pace with him, her head down, like she'd been there a thousand times before, and knew exactly what she was doing and where she was going. About half the people they passed also wore brown capes similar to the one she had on. The rest of the people sported long brown pants and plain tunics, even the girls. Every single person had either a scarf or fabric wrapped around his or her neck. Very little skin was exposed. Everyone appeared to be in their late teens to early thirties. There weren't any elderly people or children about.

Even though the bright sun was about to set, Rema was covered with sweat. She felt as if she were a candle on fire, wax dripping down her sides. How could people stand this heat?

Nathenek cursed. Rema glanced up and saw dark clouds in the distance, rapidly moving toward her. The clouds covered the sun, giving momentary relief from its hot rays.

People started running as a low *bong* sound rang throughout the city. Doors slammed shut, and people covered exposed windows with wooden boards.

Nathenek started sprinting, dragging Rema behind him. "Hurry!" he shouted.

"What's going on?" Rema asked, trying to keep up with his long strides.

"A sandstorm is coming."

Rema had no idea what that was, but it didn't sound good. Darkness descended over the city, and the streets became eerily devoid of people.

"Where are we going?" Rema yelled. The wind kicked up, tossing her cape violently around her body. Little pieces of sand flew in the air.

"Use your scarf!" Nathenek shouted. A loud, rumbling noise resonated through the streets, filling Rema with panic. She tried covering her face, but the wind was so strong that she couldn't wrap the fabric around her mouth and nose. She ended up holding it against her face with her free hand.

"Almost there!" Nathenek cried, hauling her alongside him.

Rema was thankful for all of the running Savenek had forced her to do around the fortress. Sand bounced against the walls of the nearby buildings, stinging her body, even slicing through her clothing, as it whipped by. She didn't think they could last much longer. They rounded another corner, running down the street at full speed.

Nathenek threw himself against a door on the left, pounding hard. It opened a couple of inches, and he shoved Rema inside, slamming it closed behind him. Rema blinked, taking in her surroundings. She stood in a long, empty hallway, a young child before her.

"Thank you," Nathenek said. "No one else is about. You can go to your room now." The boy nodded and left without saying a word.

"Where are we?" Rema whispered. After the howling wind outside, it was utterly quiet in there.

Nathenek's eyes sliced over to her, and he scowled. She forgot she wasn't supposed to talk. She didn't know why he was upset; she didn't speak loud, she'd whispered, and no one was about to hear her.

She mouthed the word "sorry," and followed him into the dark corridor. Halfway down, he stopped before a door, pulled out a key from his pocket, and unlocked it. Rema stepped inside the pitch-black room, unable to see a single thing. She heard the door close and lock. There was a shuffling noise, and light appeared before her. Nathenek stood there, holding a small candle.

"Where are we?" she asked, hoping she could speak now.

"My home," he answered, not looking her in the eyes. Nathenek turned and lit several more candles throughout the small room.

The space reminded her of the berth aboard the ship. "You live here?" she asked in disbelief. There was a cot, dresser, and a desk. No fireplace, no kitchen, and no privy.

"Yes," he answered, sitting on the edge of the bed. "I'm not often home." Nathenek removed his boots. "I'm either at the palace working, or on assignment. The only time I'm here is for a few hours of sleep."

There weren't even any windows. She didn't know how he could stand to live in a place that felt like a cage.

Rema swayed. Now that she stood still, she felt herself moving up and down, causing her stomach to roll in discomfort. "Why does it seem as if I'm still on the ship?" she asked, sitting on the stone ground. She ripped off her cap and clutched her head in her hands, wishing the sensation would pass.

"I'm surprised you lasted this long," Nathenek gently said. "You'll adjust. It'll take some time, though."

"Funny coming from you—considering I have little time left." The brown stone floor was cold, and she started shaking uncontrollably.

She felt her body being lifted, the rocking motion increased, and then she was placed on the soft bed. Nathenek knelt beside her, his eyebrows bent in worry. "Would you care for some water?" He covered her with a blanket.

"No," she whispered, afraid if she ate or drank, she would vomit. She closed her eyes, wanting the sickening feeling to pass.

"I hadn't planned to come here," he mumbled. "Since we did, go ahead and sleep for a bit while I come up with a revised plan." He pushed the hair off her forehead.

"I don't understand," she said.

"We can't go outside until the storm has passed. We're stuck here for at least a couple of hours." His hand rested on her head.

"No." She opened her eyes, staring at him. "I mean, why are you being so kind?"

He snatched his hand away from her. "I…uh…

I'm not. I simply need you strong enough to walk the three miles to the palace."

"So you're not going to poison me if I take a nap?" she mumbled, her eyelids feeling heavy.

"No, I'm not going to hurt you. There is nothing to fear."

She drifted off to sleep.

When Rema woke, her body still felt as if it were on a boat, rocking up and down; but the sensation was tolerable now. Glancing around the candlelit room, Rema saw Nathenek sitting on a wooden chair, hunched over, staring at something in the palm of his hand. She lay there, watching him. He sighed and leaned back, a gold chain slipping through his fingers.

"Is that my necklace?" she asked, sitting up on the bed.

His eyes darted over to her. "You're awake." His fingers curled over the key as he stood and slipped the necklace into his pocket. "We should leave."

Nathenek blew out the candles, the smoky smell engulfing the room. Rema stood, unable to see a single thing.

A hand encircled her upper arm. "We have to talk," Nathenek whispered in her ear. "I need you to trust me. From here on out, do exactly as I say."

"You want *me* to trust *you*?" Was he playing her

for a fool? Trying to get her to have faith in him in order to make his job easier? She didn't understand Nathenek. One minute, he was kind and helping her; the next, he was cold and harsh. Who was the real Nathenek? The only thing she knew for certain was that he was an assassin—and she didn't want to die.

Nathenek exhaled, his breath blowing the stray hairs by her ear. "Never mind," he said. "Let's go."

He jerked her hands forward, wrapping something rough around her wrists. "What are you doing?" she demanded, unable to see in the dark room.

"I have to bind you. I would never deliver a prisoner to the emperor any other way." He gently pulled her forward, guiding her through the low doorway, down the hall, and out into the dead of night.

The streets were empty. A half-moon was the only light out. Nathenek kept hold of her arm as they made their way to the main street. Walking at a brisk pace, Rema's chest tightened. How was she going to beg anyone to help her when no one was around? Her only other option was to break free from Nathenek and make a run for it.

Something moved up ahead. Two figures stepped away from one of the buildings. Nathenek's hand squeezed her arm as he roughly dragged her along.

"It's after curfew," a deep voice said. "State your business." The moonlight shone on the people, revealing two soldiers, swords drawn.

"I am following orders of His Royal Majesty,

Emperor Hamen. I'm transporting a prisoner of the utmost importance."

"Your name?"

"Nathenek, of the Elimination Squad, First Division."

"We'll escort you the rest of the way, so you won't be stopped again." The soldiers abruptly turned and walked down the middle of the street, Nathenek pulling her along behind the men.

How in the world would she escape now? She couldn't possibly outrun three armed men. Yet, her only other option was to be taken to her death. She had to try. When they turned a corner, Rema reached up and shoved Nathenek toward the side of the building. He released her and she spun around, running as fast as she could.

Something long and hard hit her legs, tripping her. Raising her bound wrists, she prevented her face from smashing into the ground. A hand grabbed the back of her cape, lifting her as if she weighed nothing. Nathenek held her suspended in air, the two soldiers right next to him. One bent down and retrieved Nathenek's longsword, handing it to him. Nathenek dropped her to her feet and sheathed his sword. He looked furious. "You do that again and I'll throw a dagger in your back, and then let you rot in the street. The vultures can pick away at your body for all I care."

"It doesn't matter to me," Rema said, seething with rage. "I'm going to die anyway. Might as well at least try and get away instead of being taken meekly to the emperor."

The two soldiers turned around and resumed walking. Nathenek grabbed her arm, tugging her forward. "Let's go."

As they traveled toward the palace, Rema never saw a single person along the way. Yet, she felt eyes on her, especially when Nathenek became extra rough by pushing or shoving her. He even made her fall a couple of times. Rema had no doubt someone was watching.

After traveling a good hour, the buildings abruptly ended, leaving nothing but open land before them.

"Where are we?" Rema asked, wondering if the palace was near.

One of the soldiers glanced back at her. "You're not from around here, are you?" he asked, noticing her accent.

"That is none of your concern," Nathenek answered.

Rema didn't see anything but smooth, brown, rolling hills. They walked for another fifteen minutes in silence before Rema realized there was an enormous wall up ahead. They arrived at massive iron doors, easily five times her height and width.

"This is as far as we go," one of the soldiers said.

Nathenek nodded. "Thank you for the escort. I will deliver the prisoner from here."

After the soldiers left, Nathenek knocked on a small, wooden door off to the side that Rema hadn't noticed before. He mumbled a few words to someone and the door opened, granting them entrance.

Rema stepped through the doorway, and a burlap sack was immediately shoved over her head. She reached up and tried pulling it away, but someone smacked her hands. Another person roughly felt around her body.

"She's clean," Nathenek said, a hard edge to his voice.

"Standard protocol."

"Let's go," Nathenek growled, yanking her along.

"Get this off my head," Rema demanded. Not being able to see caused her heart to beat erratically, and she started shaking.

Nathenek chuckled. "All prisoners are hooded." His voice was cold and malicious, sending chills down her spine. He grabbed her wrists much rougher than before, yanking them up. He did something with her bindings, and then he let go. She fumbled around until her fingers came across a rope attached to her bound wrists, like a lead rope used on horses.

The assassin's hands went to the burlap bag covering her head. He cinched the fabric around her neck and started wrapping something around it to keep it closed.

"What are you doing?" Rema panicked. She tried to raise her hands to feel what was going on, but she couldn't lift her arms. Nathenek had to be standing on the rope attached to her.

He tied off the rope, or whatever it was he'd used around her neck. It was difficult to breathe. Rema had a rope around her neck—again. She was going to die.

She thrashed her arms about, wanting to tear the bag off. Someone laughed and the rope she was attached to jerked, making her stumble to the ground.

"Get up," Nathenek growled.

Tears slid down her cheeks, soaking into the bag. She didn't want to cry or show weakness—not that anyone could see her face. She needed to be strong and fight her way out of this.

She stood, willing herself to calm down and focus. She couldn't afford to lose it now. They walked in silence for several minutes.

"Captain Nathenek," a voice said. "Good to see you."

"I assume Emperor Hamen is asleep?" Nathenek said, coming to a stop.

"He is, although I have specific instructions to wake him upon your return."

Rema was yanked forward, and she fell to her knees. Fingers dug into her right shoulder, pinching her skin, making her cry out in pain. "Then summon the emperor. Let him know his package has arrived."

Six

Darmik

The ring of guards surrounding Darmik and Savenek parted as a robust soldier bedecked with medals glided forward.

"Darmik," the man said, "we meet again."

Darmik pushed the hunched-over Savenek, still clutching his stomach, to the ground, wanting him to remain quiet. Standing tall, Darmik faced his old mentor—the one who had ordered his beatings numerous times, trying to tear him down.

"Gaverek, good to see you." Darmik used every ounce of energy he had to remain composed. No one could know how much he hated and feared his old instructor.

Gaverek stood there, assessing the situation. "Still causing trouble, I see."

Savenek moved to stand, but Darmik put his foot on his back, pushing him to the floor.

"I'm trying to understand the lack of respect I'm

receiving. I am a prince and commander, here to see my uncle. Locking me in the dungeon is not a very wise move on your part. I suggest you inform Emperor Hamen that I'm here with vital information."

Gaverek chuckled. "Of course the emperor knows you're here. While he is interested in the information you claim to have, he is also concerned by your unannounced visit." Gaverek pointed to Savenek. "Get him back into his cell," he ordered his men. "Release the guards that are in there."

Two soldiers grabbed Savenek, dragging him down the corridor. Darmik kept his focus on Gaverek, trying not to show any interest or concern for his friend.

Gaverek came closer. "I can't take you to the emperor until I know you'll behave." Cold fear shot through Darmik. These Emperion soldiers weren't going to interrogate them; instead, they were going to be tortured. Darmik would survive—after all, he'd been through it before and knew what to expect. But Ellie and Vesha? He forced his face to remain expressionless. Gaverek was probably already testing him.

"Sir," a guard said. "The prisoner is strapped to the table." The warden and injured guards stood behind him. The warden pushed the guard out of the way and came at Darmik, swinging his fist. Darmik ducked.

"Enough," Gaverek ordered. He pointed to the men Darmik had managed to overpower. "You all are demoted for your incompetence." Turning to Darmik, he said, "Come with me."

They walked down the hallway in silence. Once they were out of sight from everyone, Gaverek abruptly stopped. "Why are you here?" he demanded.

"I'm not at liberty to discuss that with you."

"You're not going before the emperor until I know."

Darmik stared at his former instructor. Was he testing him? "Have you forgotten that I outrank you? You are out of line."

Gaverek leaned forward. "No one knows you're here. I can make you disappear."

"An entire platoon of soldiers knows I'm here," Darmik said. "And I sincerely doubt you want to be the reason our kingdoms go to war. If you injure me, I will personally see you destroyed."

His former instructor turned and headed down the hallway. Two soldiers stood on either side of Savenek's door. Gaverek said, "Restrain Darmik. I want him guarded by the both of you."

"Sir, do you want him in a cell?" one soldier asked.

"No," Gaverek responded. "I want him with me. He's going to watch his companions be interrogated." He smiled. "You're easy to read and predictable," he sneered.

Darmik stood in a cell, his arms bound in front of him. Vesha lay strapped to the table. He'd already witnessed Savenek and Audek's interrogations. While they hadn't been fun to watch, Darmik had been privy to many such events in the past. He knew how to emotionally shield himself from what was happening.

Vesha was different.

He hadn't seen a female interrogated since his time in Emperion. Although Vesha was a trained soldier and knew how to fight, she knew nothing of what she was about to face. Darmik hoped she was strong enough.

"Let's begin," Gaverek said.

Darmik looked at the situation objectively—once this was over, Neco and Ellie were the only two remaining. Then Darmik could see his uncle and hopefully save Rema.

Two soldiers released the levers, flipping the top of the table upside down. Much to Vesha's credit, she didn't scream. Still strapped to the table, she lay parallel three feet off the ground. A bucket was slid under her. A soldier released a different lever, tipping the table forward. Vesha's head was submerged in the bucket filled with ice-cold water.

The trick was to remain calm. Darmik found it most effective to hold his breath, and then slowly release the air out in gradual intervals. If he panicked, breathing in water was quite painful.

Vesha balled her hands into fists, her legs twitching. She wasn't going to last much longer, and it had only been ten seconds. Emperion soldiers were trained to dunk a person's head under water in thirty-second increments. Her entire body jerked. She tried lifting her head, but was unable to move since she was strapped to the table.

The table was straightened, raising her head out of the bucket, but her stomach was still parallel to the floor. Vesha's hair dripped water onto the ground. She turned and looked at Darmik, horror showing in her eyes. She vomited, most of it splashing into the bucket.

Gaverek knelt beside her. "Tell me why you're here," he demanded.

Heaving in deep breaths, Vesha responded, "I…I'm accompanying Prince Darmik."

He was thankful they'd rehearsed these answers. He assumed the emperor would be the one asking, not an interrogator. Nonetheless, at least everyone was giving consistent responses.

"Yes," Gaverek said, "but why is Prince Darmik here?"

"He…he…has a message for the emperor."

"What is that message?"

"I…I don't know. He ordered me…to accompany him, and I did."

"How did you acquire one of our military ships?"

Darmik wondered if there was a record of Captain leaving with the ship. Vesha glanced at Darmik.

"Dunk her again."

"No!" she screamed as the table tilted again, submerging her head in the filthy water.

Knowing she wouldn't last long, Gaverek raised his hand, giving the command to right the table. "Flip her face up," he ordered.

Vesha's chest heaved up and down, her hair and face covered with her own vomit. "Why are you doing this?" she cried, her eyes wide with fear. "I don't know anything of importance."

"I'll be the judge of that." Gaverek stood before Darmik. "What do you suggest?" he asked. "The cane? Or the knife?"

Both weapons were painful. He'd witnessed Savenek and Audek's canings and had no desire to see Vesha abused. He wished the entire ordeal were over. "I don't care," Darmik answered. "I am here simply to witness your barbaric behavior. I had forgotten how... unrefined your empire is."

Gaverek studied him for several moments. "You're from Emperion. We put you in power. We are the strongest and largest empire in the world. Do not forget that."

Darmik took a step toward him. "The strongest empire?" He cocked his head to the side. "You're beating up on a girl, simply to prove your power. That doesn't make you strong. It makes you pathetic."

Gaverek punched Darmik in the stomach. "I'm pathetic?" His knee flew up, slamming into Darmik's jaw. "You're the soft prince who's locked in a dungeon. You're the pathetic one, not me."

Darmik sucked in a deep breath, trying to work through the pain.

"I knew you had a soft spot for your companions. You're so predictable."

Darmik pushed himself up on his knees. "Has it ever occurred to you that my uncle might actually want to hear what I have to say? That you are jeopardizing your position by keeping me here?" He was running out of time.

"Move him into his own cell," Gaverek demanded.

Darmik stood, thankful he didn't have to witness anymore of this brutality.

Neco's scream pierced the air. Darmik had never heard that kind of pain from his friend before—something was wrong.

Gaverek smiled. "I think I'll go join that interrogation. It's always fun to witness lovers being tortured in front of one another."

Darmik wanted to tear Gaverek apart, but he maintained his position, knowing his old instructor was simply goading him. If Darmik showed any emotion or attempted to fight back, whatever horrors Neco and Ellie faced would be multiplied tenfold.

Darmik woke up in a cold, damp room. He was lying on the ground, his arms still bound in front of him.

The door opened, and a small amount of light pierced the darkness. "Get up, you filthy piece of trash," the soldier said. "The emperor is ready to see you."

Darmik had managed to make it without being interrogated, but watching his friends get tortured was worse. Hopefully, it was all worth it now that they were going before Emperor Hamen.

Darmik stood, stretching his stiff limbs. The soldier took him to another room where all of his companions were waiting.

"Put these uniforms on," a soldier said. "Once everyone is dressed, I will escort you from the dungeon. If any of you make a single move against me, or any other soldier, you will be killed on sight. Understood?" Everyone nodded. Darmik's bindings were removed, and the door slammed shut.

"Everyone change," Darmik demanded, "quickly." They all faced outward, toward the wall, while they dressed. "These are Emperion uniforms, what the cadets wear, as in the lowest-ranking uniform possible." Darmik pulled off his pants and tunic, putting on the Emperion Army's uniform. It made his skin crawl—he never thought he'd wear these clothes again. "In other words," he said, still facing the wall, "even though we're being taken out of the dungeon and to the emperor, they want us and everyone who sees us to know that we're insignificant and have no rights."

Once everyone was done, Darmik surveyed his friends. He'd witnessed Audek and Savenek's interrogations, watching both men dunked underwater and caned. "Did anything else happen to either one of you after I left?" Darmik asked.

"Nope," Audek said. "After they were done playing with me, they left me there."

"Same here," Savenek said, his voice harsh.

"What about you, Vesha? Are you well?" Darmik asked.

She nodded. "I'd really like to find Rema and get out of here." Her coloring was pale, and he hoped she wasn't getting sick.

Darmik had no idea what Neco and Ellie went through. He looked to his friend, afraid to ask.

Neco wrapped Ellie in his arms, hugging her. "They did exactly what you said," Neco whispered. "They figured out what matters most to me, and then they used it against me."

Ellie glanced up into Neco's eyes. "I'm sorry you had to see that," she whispered. "I don't want to be your weakness."

"You're not," he responded. "You are my strength." He kissed the top of her head.

Darmik hated to interrupt the couple, but he needed to make sure they were physically well. He cleared his throat, getting everyone's attention. "Are you hurt? Savenek and Audek were both caned."

"We're fine," Neco answered. "They were mentally toying with us, trying to drive me mad. They hit Ellie a few times, but that's all." Ellie's eyes glossed over with tears.

"Good," Darmik said. "I want everyone to remember what we discussed on the boat about how to behave. No matter what happens, do not fight back when we leave this room. They won't hesitate to kill all of us."

The door opened and a soldier waved them out into the corridor, where a squad of armed men waited for them. The soldiers escorted everyone through several stone hallways and up a steep flight of stairs. They exited into a small courtyard, surrounded by a tall, brown wall.

Gaverek entered through another doorway and came to stand before Darmik. "I see no need to take such a large party of barbarians to the palace."

This was what Darmik had feared—being separated from his friends.

"Like you've said, I'm soft," Darmik replied. "Surely you don't expect me to see the emperor alone? Who will assist me when I'm tired or need help?"

Gaverek stared at him. He finally said, "You may take one to attend you. That way if you do something I don't like, I have leverage."

Darmik quickly thought. Ellie and Neco should remain together. Vesha needed someone strong to watch her back. That left Audek and Savenek. Of the two, Savenek was the stronger fighter. Would it be more beneficial to have Savenek with Vesha, or accompanying Darmik?

Gaverek raised his eyebrows, awaiting his answer.

"Makes no difference," Darmik said. "Audek, why don't you accompany with me?"

"Uh, yeah, sure," Audek said. Darmik glared at him, and he snapped his mouth shut. Maybe choosing him wasn't the best of ideas.

"Excellent," Gaverek said. "You two come with

me."

"Where will the rest of my companions be?"

Gaverek walked toward the door, not bothering to answer.

"He's quite friendly," Audek sarcastically said. "This should be loads of fun."

Darmik grabbed Audek's elbow, dragging him along after Gaverek, a dozen soldiers following. "What part of *keep your mouth shut* are you not understanding?" he hissed.

"It's shut! I'll be quiet now, I promise."

They went through the doorway, down a short hallway, and then stepped out into the bright sunlight.

"Oh boy, how do you people stand this heat?" Audek asked the soldiers surrounding them.

Shaking his head, Darmik hurried after Gaverek, ignoring Audek completely.

"I can see you are an effective leader and commander. Your subjects are quite obedient," Gaverek said.

Darmik didn't respond. Instead, he looked around, trying to get his bearings. They were in the outskirts of the city near the military compound, which was directly north of the palace. Glancing east, he saw the training facility, nestled among the hills in the distance, where he'd spent most of his time.

"Where's the color?" Audek asked, jogging to catch up. "This place is so… blah."

Darmik ignored him. He should've brought

Savenek instead.

Gaverek looked at Audek. "Everything is functional and serves a purpose. It obviously works, seeing as how we're the largest known empire in the world."

"Naw, that's not what I meant," Audek said.

Gaverek stopped and turned to face him.

"I…uh…meant that the place," Audek frantically waved his arms, pointing to the dry, brown hills and the garrison nearby, "is…uh…rather limited in color."

Gaverek cocked his head to the side, studying Audek.

"You know…'cause everything is brown."

"If you don't shut your mouth and refrain from talking," Gaverek said, "I'll chop off your tongue. Understood?"

Audek nodded.

"Good," Gaverek said. "Let's continue—in silence."

Darmik balled his hands into fists. He wanted to punch Audek. What was the point of teaching him how to behave in Emperion if he was going to ignore everything Darmik had said?

They passed the garrison and traveled directly toward the emperor's home, approaching the twenty-foot wall surrounding the palace. Armed soldiers stood on top of it and in lookout towers. After being roughly searched, they were granted entrance. Once inside, Darmik had a clear view of the pristine palace.

The sight was astounding and unlike anything on

Greenwood Island. The walls were made of shiny white stone tiles, while the roof was covered in gold. Several round towers stood throughout the massive structure. Even more intriguing were the vibrant, colorful gardens surrounding the entire place, a stark contrast to what was outside the wall.

Audek huffed, about to say something, but Darmik clasped his hand over his mouth to prevent him from speaking. Audek's eyes widened when he realized what he had almost done.

They walked along a cobblestone pathway toward the emperor's home. Darmik had been there once before—when his uncle wanted to meet him when he first arrived at the mainland for military training. After that one time, he never stepped foot in the palace or saw his uncle again.

They went through a golden doorway, at least fifteen feet tall. Inlaid on each door was the royal crest of Emperion, along with a large key. Audek grabbed Darmik's arm, pointing to the doors.

Darmik doubted it was a mere coincidence that Rema's key necklace matched the shape of the keys on the doors. "Permission to speak?" Darmik asked. "I'd like to make sure my man behaves properly."

Gaverek gave a curt nod. "Fine. Just keep your voices low since we are inside the palace now."

Leaning toward Audek, Darmik whispered, "This building has been here for centuries. It was constructed when Emperion was first formed over six hundred and fifty years ago." Rema's key was no simple heirloom passed down through the rulers of each generation—it had ties all the way back here, to Emperion. It would, beyond a doubt, prove her to be the true heir to the Emperion throne.

The hallway before them was adorned with gold-framed pictures covering the white walls, richly colored rugs atop the marble floors, and large, ceramic vases filled with fragrant flowers. The ceiling was covered with paintings.

"This is…it's…" Audek mumbled.

"Yes," Darmik agreed. "Please remember to show the utmost respect before the emperor. Do you remember how to bow and properly greet him?"

Audek nodded, his focus on the ceiling. Darmik followed his line of sight. The ceiling had a painting of a beautiful girl with long, dark hair. In her hands lay a key—the exact replica of Rema's.

"Try not to gawk," Darmik said. "It makes us look like simpletons." He hoped no one noticed them observing all the keys. Darmik thought back to his studies when he was here before. He didn't recall anything about keys being a symbol or having meaning, yet they obviously did, seeing as how they were everywhere.

Gaverek stopped before a large door with a key-shaped handle. "The emperor is in his receiving room." He pointed to the door. "When we enter, keep your head down, wait to be presented, and then bow. Once he acknowledges you, you may rise. If you do anything disrespectful, I'll run my sword through you."

"But there would be blood everywhere. Would the emperor want you ruining his room?" Audek asked in mock horror.

Gaverek's gaze darkened. "You wouldn't last a day under my command."

"Then I guess it's a good thing I'm not under your command. Now, are we going to do this? I'm ready to meet the all-powerful emperor." He clasped his hands together. Darmik was on the verge of running his own sword through Audek, just to get him to shut up.

"Excuse me," Darmik addressed the servant passing by. "May I please have the sash around your waist?"

The girl looked confused, but she complied. Darmik took the fabric and tied it around Audek's head, covering his mouth.

"You're going to get us both killed. Keep your mouth shut."

Gaverek chuckled and opened the door. Darmik stepped into the receiving room. Walking down the center aisle, he glanced around. There were several velvet-covered sofas and goldwood chairs throughout. In one corner stood some sort of tall, stringed instrument. The walls were adorned with framed portraits of all the emperors who ruled through the years. At the end of the aisle was a raised, marble dais with two intricately designed golden chairs. Looking closer at them, Darmik saw there were keys engraved in the gold—keys that

matched Rema's necklace.

Other than their party, the room was empty. Gaverek instructed Darmik and Audek to wait by the dais. There was a door off to the side, and Darmik suspected the emperor was behind it.

Gaverek knocked on the door, mumbling something that Darmik couldn't hear, and then he straightened and announced, "His Majesty, Emperor Hamen."

A regal man with fair skin and black hair entered the room. He wore an emerald-green tunic embroidered with the Emperion crest. A gold crown embedded with emeralds sat atop his head.

Darmik dropped to his knee, bowing his head in submission.

"Rise," the emperor commanded in a deep, authoritative voice.

Darmik stood and looked at the man before him.

"I didn't think I'd see you back here," Emperor Hamen said.

"Uncle, I didn't expect to be back here either."

The emperor smiled, catching Darmik's familiar use of wording.

"I assumed I'd receive a…" Darmik searched for the right word—not *warm* exactly, "a more hospitable greeting—one befitting of my station."

The emperor crossed his arms, his broad shoulders pulling his tunic. "Everyone out."

Darmik kept his focus on his uncle. He felt

Audek's questioning stare, but he refused to take his eyes off the man before him.

When the room was completely empty except for the two of them, the emperor asked, "Why are you here?" His eyes appeared tight with concern.

"You sent an assassin to my kingdom," Darmik answered, trying to ascertain if Rema had already arrived or not.

"Greenwood Island is not *your* kingdom," the emperor said, moving to the window. "What have you done with my man?"

"Nothing," Darmik said. "But he has taken something of mine."

"Oh?" The emperor stared outside, his back to Darmik.

"Yes. And I'm here to get it back."

Emperor Hamen turned around to face him, his eyes cold and hard. "And what is the item you *think* my man took?"

"The woman I am going to marry."

The emperor's eyes narrowed as he stood there facing Darmik, studying him.

"You're a hard one to read," he said, rubbing his chin. "I have you and your companions thrown into the dungeon, you watch your friends' interrogations, and you don't fight back. Why? Simply to be granted a meeting with me?" He turned and faced outside again. "I thought it had something to do with a piece of important information you may have…accidentally…stumbled upon. But that's not the case. You're here because of my assassin." Emperor Hamen went to one of the velvet chairs and sat down, tapping his fingers on the armrest. His eyes roamed over Darmik as if he were dissecting him. "Stop standing there and sit."

Darmik did as requested, taking a seat on the sofa opposite him. He kept his mouth shut, waiting for his uncle to continue.

"Tell me what you know of the assassin's mission."

Now was the time to tread very carefully. Darmik decided to fabricate a story. "The assassin was looking for Lennek's fiancée, Rema, who was sentenced to be executed."

The emperor nodded, knowing all of this already.

"Greenwood Island has a small band of rebels who try to undermine the king whenever an opportunity presents itself. In an attempt to flush out these men, I put a decoy on the gallows. The real girl was executed, and the decoy was rescued by the rebels. I used her to follow them to their base camp. Your assassin took my decoy."

"And this decoy, as you call her, is your fiancée?"

"She is."

The emperor leaned back on his chair, a hint of a smile across his face. "Why so careless with the ones we love?" he asked, staring at Darmik.

Darmik didn't know how to respond to his uncle, but he got the distinct impression he was missing a vital piece of information.

"I'm going to be honest with you," Emperor

Hamen said. "I find it hard to believe my assassin made a mistake."

"I tried explaining the situation to him, but he wasn't interested in reason."

"Well," the emperor mused. "It seems we have a problem, don't we?"

Darmik's heartbeat quickened. Was Rema already dead? Was he too late to save her?

"My assassin hasn't returned yet."

Relief coursed through Darmik, and he suddenly breathed easier. If he was smart about it, he could save her.

"You will stay here until he does," the emperor continued. "When my man arrives, I will verify the girl's identity. If you are lying to me," Emperor Hamen said as he stood, "I'll have your companions executed."

Interesting that the emperor would threaten the lives of his friends, but not Darmik himself. Why couldn't Darmik have a single normal, decent relationship with a family member? Why did everyone treat him like dirt? Go out of their way to degrade him?

Emperor Hamen turned to go.

"Uncle," Darmik said, just as the emperor reached the door. "Why isn't me telling you that this girl is going to be my future wife not enough of a reason to spare her life? Do you think so little of me?"

"No," the emperor said, turning around to face Darmik. "But let me ask you this, do you think so little of me? Do you actually think I would sit back and allow

you to marry her? Surely, you know what I do to anyone who poses a threat or challenges my authority. So don't stand there and disrespect me by claiming something so trivial as love. This has nothing to do with love—and everything to do with power."

Did the emperor think Darmik only cared for Rema because of her lineage? Did he fear he would try and overthrow him?

"I just want to take my fiancée and return to Greenwood Island, where we can be married and live in peace."

At the door, Emperor Hamen said loud enough for Darmik to hear, "You're not as good of a liar as you think." Their eyes met for a brief moment. "Let's not forget, I personally oversaw your training when you were here. I know everything about you." And with that, he turned and left.

Seven

Rema

Rema sat on the cold, stone ground with the burlap bag over her head and her hands tied before her. After what felt like hours, she heard a man say, "Emperor Hamen is ready for the prisoner."

The rope attached to her bindings tugged her forward, and she scrambled to her feet. Rema was taken through various twists and turns. Not being able to see anything only added to the panic swelling within her. Someone squeezed her elbow, bringing her to a stop.

"Your Majesty," a man said, his voice echoing. "Captain Nathenek of the Elimination Squad, and his prisoner."

Someone pulled her forward. It sounded like two heavy doors closed behind her. "Your Majesty," Nathenek said. It felt like he knelt beside her.

"Rise," a dignified voice commanded.

"May I present to you Amer of Greenwood Island," Nathenek said.

"I'd like to see the face of the girl who's been causing so much trouble."

Nathenek fumbled with the rope around her neck, and the burlap bag was pulled off in one swift motion. Rema squinted against the bright light, blinking several times as she took in the sight before her.

A handsome man in his early fifties stood in front of her with a look of curiosity on his face. He wore simple black pants and a tunic. Rema would never have known he was the emperor were it not for the emerald crown atop his head.

Rema scanned the ornately decorated room. Gaudy gold covered the walls along with pictures of the emperor, his wife, and daughter. One of the portraits must have been painted recently because the emperor looked as he did in person. His wife stood next to him. She had beautiful chestnut hair, fair skin, and appeared to be of similar age as the emperor. Between them sat a girl of about fifteen years. Her skin was unusually white, and her eyes were sunken, giving her a sickly look. Peeling her eyes away from the picture, Rema saw large windows situated behind the emperor, the dull gray of the early morning light allowing her to see the lush green gardens outside, a stark contrast to what she'd observed of the city.

The emperor tilted his head to the side, and his eyes narrowed, assessing her. Rema tried to decide the best course of action. Play dumb and innocent? Or claim her birthright? She quickly glanced over at Nathenek, trying to ascertain the situation. His chin pointed toward the ground, meek and obedient.

She focused back on Emperor Hamen. He had thick, black hair, chocolate-brown eyes, and a jawline that distinctly reminded her of Darmik. She knew the emperor was Darmik's uncle, but the similarities between them were uncanny.

She cleared her throat and raised her chin in the air. "I am Queen Amer Rema of Greenwood Island."

"Excuse me?" Emperor Hamen asked.

"My name is Queen Amer, and you will address me as such."

He laughed loudly, the sound echoing in the room. "I've heard a lot about you," he said, clapping his hands together. "You are a piece of work."

He moved to a chair and sat down, crossing his legs. "The question is what to do with you," he mused, tapping his fingers on the armrests.

"Let me return to my island. I will keep trade open with you. We can peacefully co-exist."

Emperor Hamen chuckled. "You're delusional. When I said, *what to do with you*, I simply meant do I have Nathenek kill you now? Or do I have you beheaded in front of the city for all to see?"

Rema suspected he would do the opposite of whatever she wanted. "I've been sentenced to a public execution before. It didn't go so well. I suggest you kill me now, so you don't regret it."

The sound of steel rang through the air as Nathenek unsheathed his sword, making Rema jump.

She tried to appear calm, even though her body shook uncontrollably. She stared at Emperor Hamen, daring him to order her death.

He shook his head. "You're disgusting. Just look at your blonde hair and blue eyes. You look like a filthy commoner." He stood and came before her. He had the same height and build as Darmik, and it unnerved her. "Are you positive you've captured the correct person?" he questioned Nathenek.

"I am," the assassin said. "Not only is she the only one on Greenwood Island with that hair and eye color, but she bears the royal mark you spoke of."

How did Nathenek know of her tattoo? Did he check for it when he drugged her and brought her down the mountain?

"Show me," the emperor demanded.

Rema shrank back, away from him.

Nathenek sheathed his sword. Taking a hasty step toward her, he squeezed the back of her neck, causing a shooting pain to radiate down her spine. With his free hand, he tugged the neckline of her tunic off her shoulder, exposing her one inch wide, circular mark. It was pale, almost a soft gray, with delicate lines of red interwoven into a complex symbol, looking like a unique piece of jewelry.

The emperor leaned in. "It's true," he whispered in disbelief. "Tell me, how did Barjon miss this one?"

The assassin released her, and she quickly covered herself. "After the entire royal family was disposed of,"

Nathenek said, standing tall before the emperor, "King Barjon gathered his proof. He collected the head and tattoo of each individual. At that time, he discovered that Princess Amer, who was only a few months old, didn't bear a royal mark. Barjon mistakenly assumed the island didn't tattoo their children until age one. Trell, whom I'm sure you remember as your previous chief battle strategist and King Barjon's father-in-law, tried to tell him that wasn't the case. Barjon refused to listen. Trell has been hiding in exile ever since."

Rema was stunned. Trell was Darmik's grandfather? Neither Trell nor Darmik had hinted at any sort of relationship with one another.

Emperor Hamen crossed his arms. "I don't suppose you managed to locate Trell while you were at Greenwood Island?"

"I found him near her." Nathenek jerked his chin in Rema's direction. She kept her mouth shut, curious to hear what the assassin had to say. "Trell discovered Rema's true identity and was about to kill her."

"What?" Rema asked, shocked. The old man had seemed so sincere when he said he wanted to join her cause and place her on the throne. He only did that to get close to her? In order to murder her?

"Where's Trell now?" the emperor asked.

"Here," Nathenek said. "I brought him with me."

"Excellent work, as always." Emperor Hamen went to the window, gazing outside. "Very well, she'll be publicly beheaded."

"Yes, Your Majesty," Nathenek said. "Next week with the others?"

"No," Emperor Hamen said, "today. We'll hold a special execution. Now, if you'll excuse me, I have duties to attend to." He turned and left.

"He's not what I expected," Rema said. She had assumed the emperor would be volatile like King Barjon.

Nathenek shook his head. "That's why he's so frightening. He is always calm and in control, but lethal and unforgiving at the same time. He's not someone you ever cross and expect to live." Nathenek turned to leave. "Let's go."

Rema started to follow him when she saw the handles on the golden doors were in the shape of keys. She froze, studying them in greater detail. They were the exact shape and had the same features as her key necklace.

"Rema," Nathenek said, recapturing her attention. She felt an overwhelming sense that she belonged here. Her key necklace was more than a family heirloom passed down through the generations—it tied her to this strange land. Never before had she wanted anything to do with Emperion. Now she was beginning to understand it wasn't simply a choice, but rather a duty to her people. These keys unlocked the secrets of her past, revealing a destiny she'd never imagined.

Emperion was hers.

She hurried from the room. "Are you going to cover my head again?" she asked, wondering where the burlap bag had disappeared to.

"No," Nathenek replied. "I'm taking you directly to the Execution Tower, where we keep those who are sentenced to die." He grabbed the rope, leading her along like an animal. "Hopefully, there will be an empty cell for you," he mumbled under his breath, barely audible.

Walking down the hallway of the palace, Rema became intrigued with the idea that her ancestors had walked down this very corridor. The rounded ceilings were covered with intricate paintings. Rema examined the beautiful artistry above her. Between two black horses was a picture of a key—an exact replica of her necklace. What did the key symbolize in the Emperion culture? There had to be a way to discover its true meaning.

Nathenek jerked the rope, and Rema flew forward, almost losing her balance. He led her out of the palace to a dirt path that was surrounded by vibrant green grass and lined with rose bushes. The walkway went directly to the wall encircling the grounds. The guards opened a small wooden door and Rema quickly passed through. On the other side of the wall, a bleak, dry landscape covered in sand greeted her. In the distance stood Emperor's City.

"I can't believe the sheer number of buildings," Rema observed, looking ahead to their destination. "There has to be thousands of people living there." The idea of so many crowded together, living on top of one another, was astounding. "There's open land over there." Rema pointed to the dry, brown hills outside the city wall, behind the palace. "Why don't people spread out?"

Nathenek chuckled. "You are young and naïve."

"But why is everyone so crammed together?" There was a lot of empty space surrounding the emperor's palace and the military compound.

"This entire area," Nathenek pointed to the open land surrounding them, "used to be covered with buildings as well. When Hamen married Empress Eliza and ascended to the throne, he ordered all structures within one mile of the palace be torn down and removed."

"What's on the other side of the wall surrounding Emperor's City?" Rema asked, pointing to the area behind the palace.

"Those hills are used exclusively by the army. Not only is the training facility located there, which houses all cadets and classrooms, but the nearby land allows instructors to run various exercises or officers to run practice drills."

"What's beyond that?"

"There's nothing but dry, open land for several miles. Then, eventually, small villages and towns are scattered throughout."

"Is all of Emperion so dry and brown?" she asked.

"You are full of questions today," he said, glancing sideways at her. "Why the sudden interest?"

"I'm simply curious," she said. "And I find talking helps pass the time."

Nathenek smiled. "Fine, I will answer all that you ask until we reach the city." Looking around, he shook his head and said, "No, the rest of Emperion is not like this. Emperor's City sits on the southernmost tip of the mainland. The further north one travels, the higher the land becomes. The increased elevation brings cooler weather, more rain, and lusher landscape. Granted, it's not like Greenwood Island, but it's not a desert either."

Rema scrunched her nose. "Why does the emperor live here instead of further inland?"

Nathenek shrugged his shoulders. "Security, I suppose. There are nine palaces throughout Emperion, and the emperor will spend time at each of them. He chooses to maintain this one as his main residence because it's close to the empire's largest military garrison, it's near the ocean, and the city is well protected."

That shocked Rema. *Nine palaces.* Were all the emperor's homes as luxurious as this one? She wondered how he could afford so much, including maintaining such a large army.

"Enough questions," Nathenek said in a clipped tone, glancing up ahead. His entire body went rigid.

Rema followed his line of sight. A squad of soldiers jogged in their direction. As the soldiers neared, Rema moved to the side of the dirt road, giving them room to pass. Instead, the squad halted five feet before them.

"Captain," a man said, stepping forward, out of formation.

Nathenek slowly pulled the rope, bringing Rema closer to him. "Yes?" he said, his voice hard and deadly.

"We were sent to guard the prisoner. When we arrived at the Execution Tower, we were informed you hadn't delivered anyone yet." The soldier glanced back to his men. These soldiers made her nervous. Rema wanted to be on her way. "We will escort you."

She wondered how these men knew she was being transported for execution. After all, the emperor had only just sentenced her. It was almost as if they'd known she was here…but how was that even possible?

"It's not necessary," the assassin said. "I can take her to the holding cell easier without the notice of so many guards accompanying us."

Rema prayed Nathenek outranked these soldiers and got his way. If the squad surrounded her, she would have no chance of escaping.

"Of course, Captain," the man replied. He slid back into formation, and the group continued in the direction of the military compound. As the squad passed, Rema realized several of the soldiers were female.

"Come on," Nathenek mumbled. He pulled the hood of his cape over his head. Rema did the same, shielding herself from the harsh sun and unwanted eyes. They traveled the remaining distance to the city in silence.

Walking down the narrow street, tall buildings lined both sides, situated so closely to one another they touched. People were also about, quickly walking with their heads down, paying no attention to Nathenek or Rema, even though he pulled her by a rope.

There were enough people that if she could manage to untie her bindings, she'd have a decent chance of disappearing among the crowd.

Very slowly, she slipped her hands under her cape, concealing them from sight. She had to walk a little closer to Nathenek so he didn't notice the rope wasn't as slack as it had been.

Turning a corner, something hooked around Rema's ankle, making her fall. She hit the ground hard, unable to catch herself. Nathenek leaned down. She thought he was going to help her up; instead, he took a small piece of rolled paper out of his boot, placing it on the ground, and then fixing the laces of his boots. Another man stopped and helped Rema to her feet. The man smiled and walked away, slipping the rolled paper up his sleeve.

Nathenek stood and jerked the rope, pulling her down the street once again. She was about to ask him what had just happened when his head shook ever so slightly. There was someone watching them. She could feel it. Instinct told her to play up her part of the prisoner, so she tried yanking away from her captor. When he pulled her back, she wiped her cheek as if she had been crying.

A few streets later, a man bumped into Rema's shoulder, throwing her off balance. Nathenek reached out, pushing the man away from her. She could have sworn she saw the guy take a small piece of paper from Nathenek.

"I want to know what's going on," Rema demanded.

"You know I'm a member of the emperor's Elimination Squad." Rema nodded, listening carefully to his words. "I took an oath, and am dedicated to preserving the royal line."

Did that mean he was on another assignment right now? Were the men he'd exchanged something with also assassins? Did he intend to deliver her to the Execution Tower so he could get onto his next kill? If he truly cared about the bloodline, then he should want to put her in power, and not support Emperor Hamen. But he'd sworn an oath to the emperor, not her.

They turned a corner and onto another crowded street. Several food carts piled high with brightly colored fruits and vegetables lined one side, while carts filled with wares and goods lined the other. People shopped, hovering under canopies, trying to avoid the scorching midday sun. Rema had never attended the market in her hometown of Jarko; yet, she suspected it was similar to this one. She observed people shopping for leather belts, candles, and eating utensils. Her stomach growled from the smell of smoked meat up ahead.

There was enough activity going on that Rema thought she might be able to escape. She fumbled with the knots around her wrists, loosening them. Four soldiers stood up ahead, asking for people's papers. She was about to ask what the papers were for when Nathenek stepped to the left in order to pass by the soldiers. Rema hurried and moved behind him, so he wouldn't suspect she'd untied her bindings. She slid the rope from her wrists, holding it, waiting for the perfect opportunity to run. The soldiers nodded to Nathenek in acknowledgment, letting him pass without question.

There was a narrow space between two food carts that led to an alleyway. Rema dropped the rope and casually stepped between the carts. When no one seemed to notice, she took off, sprinting down the alley. A ladder was attached to one of the buildings and she grabbed on, climbing as quickly as possible. She dared not look back to see if Nathenek followed.

She sprang onto the rooftop and ran, removing her cape and tying it around her waist. At the edge of the roof, she jumped, flying through the air and landing on the adjacent rooftop three feet away.

"Stop!" Nathenek shouted. She heard the sound of footsteps quickly approaching.

When she reached the next ledge, she noticed another ladder, so she descended, knowing Nathenek followed closely behind.

Running to the main street, she spotted a man sitting on the ground with a gray fabric draped across his legs. She grabbed the man's cape, throwing hers back at him as she sprinted away. As soon as the cloak was on her shoulders, she forced herself to walk in order to blend in. Several people wore their hoods up, so Rema slid hers on in order to shield her face. Unfortunately, the cape was a little long. With any luck, Nathenek wouldn't think to look for her in a different color.

Stopping at a cart, Rema examined the various woven baskets, as if in the market for one. Holding a basket up, she pretended to inspect the bottom, while secretly glancing down the street, searching for Nathenek. She didn't see him anywhere.

Putting down the basket, Rema slowly walked away. Her best bet was to head toward the merchant port to try and board a ship unnoticed. She stopped at a cart selling leather boots. Examining a pair, she casually asked which direction the docks were.

The man selling the goods squinted, looking at her funny. "You're not from around here, are you?"

She'd forgotten about her accent. "No, I'm not." She couldn't afford to bring attention to herself. Savenek always told her to tell a believable lie. "I am with my father on a merchant vessel from the southern islands. We stopped to unload goods. I must get back before he notices I'm gone."

The man smiled. "The merchant pier is that way." He pointed behind her.

She hurried away, eager to distance herself from the assassin. Looking at the position of the sun, Rema tried to get her bearings so she'd travel in the correct direction. Forcing herself to walk at a slow pace, she headed toward the ocean. After three blocks, there were no longer any vendors and the crowd thinned. Rema felt exposed, so she kept her hood on, head down, and pretended to walk with purpose.

Five men dressed in army uniforms headed toward her. Since there weren't any side streets, she kept on course, desperately praying they wouldn't ask for her papers. She recalled Nathenek passing on the left, so she moved over in order to pass them on the correct side. The men talked and laughed, not appearing to be in any particular formation. Perhaps they were off-duty.

Her heartbeat quickened as she neared the group. Forcing herself to stay at a slow, steady pace, she kept her eyes averted, hoping to walk by avoiding any incident. Once the men were behind her, Rema relaxed, thankful to have passed by without notice.

"Rema!" a male voice called.

She glanced about, looking for who said her name. Not seeing anyone, she turned around. All five soldiers stood staring at her, smiling. It felt as if a cold bucket of water had been tossed on her head. They knew who she was.

Taking a step back, Rema wondered if she could outrun them.

"Someone's looking for you," one taunted. The men spread out, blocking the entire street, leaving her no choice but to go the other way. What if another group of soldiers stood waiting for her? She unclasped her cloak, needing her legs free and uninhibited. Her only option was to run and hide.

"Why don't you make this easy on yourself and come here," the taller man in the middle suggested.

"Fine," Rema said, making her voice quiver as if she were weak and scared. "Just don't hurt me." Her shoulders slumped in defeat. When the soldiers laughed, perceiving she wasn't a threat, she dropped her cloak, spun around, and took off running.

Several shouts echoed behind her, but she ignored them and turned down a side street. Tan, rectangular buildings lined the road, offering no opportunities to hide. She continued running, her lungs burning, but she dared not slow down. She heard boots pounding on the street behind her as the soldiers drew nearer.

A few people loitered up ahead. Rema ran around them and spotted a dark alley on the left. She rounded the corner and sprinted down the narrow path. When she came to the end, she was back on a main street, and people were everywhere. She dodged around a group, almost losing her footing. Glancing back, all five soldiers were gaining on her. As Rema ran past a cart piled high with apples, she shoved the fruit, causing them to topple down to the ground.

Turning down the next street, she hoped to find a place to hide. There were several doors, but she didn't have the time to stop and check to see if any were unlocked. There had to be a heap of trash or a feed barn somewhere to hide in. The soldiers were almost upon her.

Rema knew she couldn't keep this pace much longer. She flew onto the next main street, hoping to hide under a merchant's cart. She kept close to people, shoving a few, wanting them to get in the soldiers' way and slow them down. Glancing back, the men still pursued her. She couldn't gain enough of a distance to buy her time to hide.

Someone grabbed her arm. Without thinking, she swung, punching her assailant in the stomach. He doubled over and she brought her knee up, slamming it into his face. He released her.

The remaining four soldiers formed a circle around her. She looked to the merchants and citizens for help, but they avoided eye contact and moved away from her.

Four soldiers. How could she fight four men at the same time? Savenek had always told her to hit and run away. Darmik had taught her to use her size and femininity to her advantage. Nathenek had expressed the importance of being confident and believing in herself.

Taking a deep breath, Rema squared her shoulders and prepared to fight. The soldiers closed in, tightening the circle. Keeping her hands at her side, she tried to appear small and harmless. All four of them were at least a head taller than she was, with two times as much muscle. She knew she was nowhere near as strong, but she was flexible and fast.

The first soldier went to grab her wrist. She pulled her arm back and broke away, adrenaline rushing through her body. She was determined to get away. Aiming straight for his knee, she threw a powerful kick. The soldier yelled from the sharp pain as his knee buckled beneath him, and he fell to the ground, clutching his injured leg.

The soldier standing behind Rema didn't hesitate to reach for her. She spun around to face him. Using her momentum and strength, she landed a punch right to his nose. He stood there, stunned, as blood poured from his face and his vision blurred from the hard hit.

The two remaining men rushed to seize her. She dodged one, but the other grabbed her from behind, trapping her arms at her sides. Rema wasn't ready to give up. She shifted her weight backwards, lifted both legs as high as she could, and kicked the other soldier's stomach and head repeatedly until he fell to the ground. The soldier who held her tightened his grasp, but she quickly elbowed his stomach and groin using both arms. She was able to create enough space to loosen his grip. She faced him, pulled him down, and kneed his groin until she was able to break free.

She started running. One of the soldiers had already recovered and he sprinted after her, tackling her to the ground, smashing her face into the dirt. She rolled over to escape, but he was already on top, punching her stomach and ribs to weaken her. Rema lay there in pain as she gasped for air, trying to catch her breath. Filled with anger and frustration, she used every ounce of strength she had left and threw punches to his body, hoping to escape, but he had already defeated her. He rolled her onto her stomach, forcing her hands behind her back.

"Go tell Captain we've got her!" the man said, wrapping a rope around her wrists while his knee dug into her lower back. Rema turned her head to the side, spitting out dirt. Two soldiers hurried away to get Nathenek.

They were on a busy market street, yet, all the citizens studiously ignored them. Rema wondered if this sort of thing was a normal occurrence.

A soldier lifted her to her feet. "I was wondering how Nathenek lost you. Now I know. You're a squirmy one."

She glanced at a woman passing by, but the woman refused to acknowledge her. The soldier dragged Rema down the street, the remaining two following close behind. People quickly moved out of their way, going about their business.

She tried wrenching free, but his grip on her arm was too tight. "Release me," she demanded. "How dare you treat me in such an undignified manner?" She spit out more dirt.

"This isn't undignified," the soldier said, chuckling. He grabbed her by her tunic and slammed her body against a nearby building, her head smacking against the stone, sending pain radiating through her. The soldier kept Rema pinned against the wall, her feet dangling two feet above the ground.

"Now this is undignified," he smirked. Since her hands were tied behind her back, she couldn't fight him. Tears filled her eyes as his lips slammed down on hers. Revulsion consumed her and Rema bit his lip, drawing blood. The soldier screamed and dropped her to the ground. She rolled to her stomach. As she started to stand, he kicked her side, knocking the wind from her body. An enormous amount of pain shot through her. She couldn't breathe. It reminded her of when she'd been thrown from her horse, Snow, and he'd accidentally stepped on her ribs. The soldier yanked her hair, forcing her to stand. Her vision swam from the immense agony.

"You're lucky I have orders to capture you alive," he said, holding his free hand to his mouth where blood trickled from her bite. He released her hair and stepped away.

Nathenek stood behind the soldiers, the hood of his cape low on his face, making him look menacing. Not uttering a single word, he stepped past the soldiers and stood before her. His eyes narrowed, making him appear furious.

"Let's go," he said. "Two of you will escort her, two of you behind her. And you," he said to the soldier who had assaulted her, "walk next to me."

The men formed a box formation around her and started down the street. Rema felt something wet and sticky dripping down the back of her neck. Breathing was laborious, and her vision blurred. The soldiers on either side of her held her up.

"I...I...don't think...I..." Her voice trailed off.

Nathenek spun around, his eyes scanning her body. "Is that blood?" He pointed to her head.

"Yes," one of the soldiers answered.

"She can't die before her scheduled execution," Nathenek murmured. He walked over and released the bindings around her wrists.

"Aren't you afraid she'll make a run for it?" a soldier asked.

Maybe if she sat down, she'd feel better. She tried

to sit, but Nathenek picked her up, cradling her in his arms.

"Let's go," the assassin commanded.

Rema turned her head toward him. If only she had managed to get away. Instead, there she was, captured, and her body felt broken. Resting her cheek against his torso, she felt something hard under his clothing. It was her key necklace—she was sure of it. Why did he have it on? She was about to ask when darkness consumed her.

She awoke as they entered a tall, brown, three-story structure.

"I have a prisoner for execution," Nathenek said, his voice rumbling in his chest.

Rema closed her eyes, hoping the overwhelming pain would go away if she managed to fall asleep.

"Put her with the others, down the hall."

"No," Nathenek responded. "She is injured and I need to ensure her survival until her scheduled execution. The emperor would be upset if he didn't have the pleasure of watching her die."

"Very well," the man answered. "Second level, third door."

Rema felt Nathenek climb a flight of stairs. She heard a door open, and then her body was laid down on a hard, cold surface.

"Are you awake?" the assassin asked, his voice soft.

"Yes," Rema croaked.

"Tell me what's wrong."

"Everything," she replied.

Nathenek sighed. "Let me see the back of your head."

Rema rolled onto her side, allowing him to investigate the wound on her head.

"What happened?" he asked.

"The one soldier threw me against a wall, and I banged it. That's all."

His fingers moved her hair aside, examining the wound. "There's blood, but it doesn't look that bad."

"My stomach," she said, pointing. "I was kicked. It hurts to breathe."

"What were you thinking?" Nathenek asked, lifting the bottom of her tunic to look at her wound. His fingers pushed on her ribs. It was painful, but manageable.

"I was thinking that I needed to get away from you so I could avoid my execution."

The assassin shook his head. "I meant what were you thinking to take on five soldiers? Five."

"I wasn't," she murmured.

"Obviously," he said, lowering her shirt. "Definitely bruised, but not broken."

"I just wanted to get away," she admitted.

Nathenek sat cross-legged before her. "Those men have trained the majority of their lives. You've trained for what? A few weeks?"

"I had to try." Tears filled her eyes. She would

be hauled out to her execution broken. She'd never see Darmik again. She was unsuccessful as a queen and leader. She had let everyone down. "I failed," she whispered.

"Wait here." Nathenek left and returned several minutes later with a basin of water and a small towel.

He sat next to her. "I need to clean your wound to make sure it isn't serious." Rema nodded.

Nathenek gently moved her hair up, away from her neck. His fingers carefully felt around the back of her head. "It looks worse than it is," he said, immersing a cloth in the basin of water. "I'm going to wash the blood away." He began wiping the back of her neck.

She closed her eyes, having no energy to argue with her captor. What was the point in tending to her wounds when she was about to be killed?

"The cut on your head has already stopped bleeding."

The water was cold, making her shiver.

Rema heard several voices talking, some of them seemed angry or upset. It sounded like the commotion was coming from outside the tower. "What's going on?" she asked.

Nathenek ignored her question. "Here," he said, pulling something from his pocket. "Eat this."

"I'm not touching anything from you."

"It'll help control the pain."

Rema grabbed the small, brownish lump from his palm and ate it. It was bitter, but she immediately felt better.

It sounded like a crowd had gathered outside her window. "Are those people here to watch my execution?" she whispered.

He shook his head. "No, your execution isn't until later." He stood and went over to the small window, looking outside.

"What is it?"

Nathenek rubbed his face and sat down, leaning against the stone wall of her cell. No longer feeling dizzy, Rema stood and went to the window. Below was a large courtyard, packed with people. Everyone stood facing a platform. There was a young boy, ten years old perhaps, standing there.

"What's going on?" She demanded. He didn't answer. "What is going on?" she asked again, looking down at the assassin. He was sitting with his head between his knees, his hands atop his head.

Focusing back at the courtyard, she saw two soldiers tie the boy's arms to a post, ripping off his shirt, and tossing it to the ground. Another man came out dressed all in black, carrying a long stick.

The courtyard went silent.

"No!" Rema screamed, realizing what was about to happen.

A few heads turned in her direction.

"He's only a child!" she yelled. "Please don't hurt him!"

The cane went up, sliced through the air, and wacked across the boy's back. The sound of the cane tearing into the boy's flesh was utterly disgusting.

"Stop!" she cried. "Please! I'll take his place! He's only a child."

Strong arms wrapped around her body, pulling her away from the window.

"Don't watch," Nathenek whispered in her ear.

Tears streamed down her face. What kind of sick, twisted place was this? How could they harm a young boy? Rema buried her face against Nathenek's chest, sobbing.

EiGHt

Darmik

The door closed behind the emperor. What did he say? *I personally oversaw your training when you were here. I know everything about you.* That seemed impossible. Darmik had only ever met his uncle that one time. Perhaps the emperor was simply trying to rattle him. After all, when he said, *You're not as good of a liar as you think,* that certainly frightened him. His uncle must know he wasn't telling the truth about Rema.

Darmik needed to return to his friends, and they needed to come up with another plan to rescue Rema. At least she hadn't arrived yet. Exiting the room, he found Audek, Gaverek, and the remaining soldiers standing in the hallway waiting for him.

"My orders are to escort you to the military compound where you will remain with your companions until the emperor decides your fate," Gaverek said.

"Interesting," Darmik mused, trying to figure out why they were being taken to the garrison instead of the dungeon.

"Yes," Gaverek said, staring at Darmik with an expression of hate. "The emperor wants you locked up, but not mistreated. It seems he is acknowledging your title and family connection; otherwise, you wouldn't be handled so kindly." He turned and walked at a brisk pace down the pristine corridor, Darmik and everyone hurrying to catch up.

Since the sash was still tied around Audek's mouth, he remained quiet as they exited the palace.

If Darmik and his friends were sequestered at the military compound, he wasn't sure how they would intercept Rema. But he would find a way—no matter the cost.

They left the lush grounds of the emperor's palace and headed north, to the stark, functional military compound. Since he wasn't cuffed, Darmik considered trying to escape. However, the area around the palace and garrison was flat for a reason—so the guards on patrol could easily see what happened at all times. That meant that if Darmik started sparring with these soldiers, someone would see and come to their aid. The best bet was to go with them and be reunited with his friends. Then, together, they would figure out what to do.

Arriving at the military compound, Gaverek led Darmik and Audek between two buildings, through the empty courtyard, and inside a small, two-story structure.

There was a short hallway lined with iron doors. Gaverek unlocked one and motioned for them to enter.

Audek went in, Darmik following right behind him. Inside, Ellie, Savenek, Neco, and Vesha all sat, looking grim. The door slammed shut and Darmik held his hand up, indicating for everyone to remain silent. He scanned the room, noticing only one small window, high on a wall facing the courtyard, allowing light in. Since they hadn't climbed any stairs, their room was on the ground level and, feasibly, someone could stand outside that window, listening to their conversation. He pointed to the window and then his ear, trying to convey his concern to his companions. They nodded in understanding.

Vesha started laughing. He glared at her and she mouthed, "Sorry," pointing to Audek. She must have found the sash tied around his mouth funny. Audek unknotted the fabric, throwing it at her.

Shaking his head, Darmik motioned for everyone to come toward him. When they were shoulder to shoulder in a tight circle, he whispered, "Rema isn't here yet. We need to find a way to escape."

"Any ideas?" Savenek asked.

"No, but be prepared. When an opportunity presents itself, we'll take it." Darmik went over to the iron door and tried to open it. It was locked. Most likely, there were soldiers standing on the other side.

Neco squatted, and Ellie climbed onto his shoulders. He carefully stood and moved to the window. Ellie was high enough to see outside. She gave a thumbs-up signal, and Neco lowered her to the ground.

"How many?" Darmik whispered.

She held up two fingers. Darmik paced around the room, trying to figure out what to do.

Savenek came over to him. "What happened with the emperor?"

"Not much," Darmik answered.

"Why are we here instead of the dungeon? Something is off."

Darmik agreed—something didn't make sense. He went over everything that the emperor had said or implied. What was he missing?

"How do you know Rema isn't here?" Savenek asked.

"My uncle said his assassin hasn't returned yet."

"And you believe him?"

Darmik replayed the encounter in his mind, searching for signs the emperor was lying. When he had said his man hadn't returned, he was sitting in a chair, his eyes focused on Darmik. In training, Darmik had been taught to always look a person in the eyes when lying in order to make the lie believable. "No," he said, "I don't."

"How can we discover the truth?" Savenek asked.

They had to find a way out of their holding cell. What if Rema was sitting in the dungeon right now? Last time she'd been imprisoned, he had done nothing to save her. He couldn't fail her again. Thinking logically, if Rema was in Emperion, locked in the dungeon, then the emperor would likely order Darmik and his companions be held at the military compound, in order to keep them from crossing paths.

"What time is it?" Darmik demanded.

"I'm not sure," Ellie said, "but if I had to guess, I'd say midday based on the position of the sun."

"Why?" Savenek asked Darmik.

"All executions are held at sunset."

Everyone remained quiet, lost in thought.

"Uh," Audek whispered, "are we concerned that we're all going to be executed? Or are we talking about Rema?" He glanced around at everyone, his face white.

"Both," Darmik said. "I have a feeling they're only keeping us alive until she's killed."

No one spoke.

"We knew coming here was a long shot," Savenek said. "At least we tried."

"We haven't tried," Darmik said, his voice harsh. "We're only getting started."

They sat cross-legged in a circle, heads bent inward, "Our best bet is to get someone to open the door to check on us," Darmik whispered. "Then we can try to escape."

"How do you suggest we do that?" Neco asked.

"One of the girls can scream, pretending to be injured. Hopefully, someone will open the door to see if we're okay," Savenek suggested.

Darmik thought it was a decent plan. He just

hoped the scream wouldn't cause several guards to check on them. They could handle a couple, but if too many armed soldiers came, their plan wouldn't work—and they'd only have one shot at this.

Getting into position, Darmik and Savenek stood on either side of the door. Neco and Audek waited by the window, ready to run forward and fight when necessary. Darmik nodded at the girls sitting in the center of the room, indicating it was time to put their plan into action.

Vesha screamed.

They all waited. Nothing happened. Darmik held up his finger, indicating that they should give it a few more minutes. His muscles were tight, adrenaline rushing through him. This plan had to work.

It sounded as if there was some sort of commotion on the other side of the iron door. Darmik held up his fist—his signal to prepare to fight. Vesha grabbed her leg like she was hurt, while Ellie sat by her side, comforting her.

The door opened outward, and a soldier entered with his weapon drawn. Darmik tackled the man, knocking his sword from his hand. Ellie reached out, grabbing it. Darmik twisted, throwing the soldier to the ground. Several additional guards rushed into the room. Darmik pinned down his opponent and glanced about the space.

Savenek and Neco each managed to disarm and restrain a soldier. However, guards stood behind Audek, Ellie, and Vesha, holding daggers to their throats.

A man, covered head to toe in a black cape, glided into the room, his face concealed under his hood. "Release my men," he ordered.

Darmik contemplated his options. If he refused to comply, his friends would be killed. Nevertheless, would it be enough to buy him an opportunity to escape? Were there additional soldiers in the hallway? Could he sacrifice the lives of his companions to save Rema?

Darmik glanced into Neco's eyes. Neco nodded, as if he understood what Darmik was thinking, and he agreed. Sacrifice a few for the good of the many. This is what Emperion had taught him, and what he'd practiced as commander. Yet it was not how Rema operated. She would never sacrifice a few to save others. She would fight to save everyone.

Darmik growled in frustration and reluctantly released his opponent, Savenek and Neco following suit. Six additional soldiers swarmed into the room. One held Darmik, while another tied his hands and feet together.

Once Darmik, Neco, and Savenek were all bound, lying on the ground, the man in charge ordered, "Everyone out. I want six of you stationed outside the door. The rest of you are to report to the fifth sector for additional patrols. Dismissed."

The soldiers exited and the iron door slammed shut, leaving the man in the cape alone with Darmik and his friends. "I want all of you lined up against this wall." The man pointed to his left. Darmik shimmied his body over and used the wall as leverage to prop himself up to a sitting position. Everyone else did the same.

"I'm surprised you surrendered so easily," he said, his cape still concealing his identity. "Why?"

There was something slightly familiar about his voice. "I saw no need," Darmik answered.

"No need to escape? Knowing full well you're all going to die? Why not at least try?"

"I couldn't risk my friends' lives just to save my own."

"Is that all?"

Darmik sighed. He might as well be honest. "No, that's not the only reason."

The man bent down so he was eye level with Darmik. His face remained concealed in the shadow of his hood. "Tell me your motives."

"She wouldn't want me to," Darmik admitted. "I also made a promise to a friend—no unnecessary killing." He let his head fall back against the wall. He'd failed. Not only was Rema going to die, but so were his companions.

"Excellent," the man said, pushing the hood from his head.

It was Trell.

"What are you doing here?" Darmik demanded, shocked to find Trell in Emperion. Was he working with Captain? Did he help bring Rema here? If Darmik weren't tied up, he would strangle the old man.

Trell held a finger to his lips. "Keep your voices low," he whispered. "Rema is here."

Darmik felt his heart pulsing in his chest. He'd

figured as much, but to have it confirmed was another matter. "Here in the compound?" he asked.

Trell shook his head. "I'm afraid not. The Execution Tower. She is scheduled for execution."

Darmik sat there, staring at the old man. "How are you even here?" he demanded. "Did you kidnap Rema?"

Trell shook his head. "It's a long story," he said. "I'll tell you another day. For now, all you need to know is that I'm here to help."

That was good enough for Darmik. He didn't have time to sit there listening to explanations. He had to save Rema. "Let me go."

"It's not that simple," Trell responded. He slid a dagger from the sleeve of his cloak. "Turn around. I'll cut your bindings."

Darmik did as he asked, and Trell sliced the rope around Darmik's wrists and ankles.

"Stand next to the door," Trell ordered. Darmik did as instructed, wondering what the old man had planned.

Trell knocked on the door. When it swung open, he said, "I need two guards in here to help with something."

Two soldiers entered, not noticing Darmik standing silently, against the wall. When the door slammed shut and locked into place, Trell took his sword and swung the hilt against the back of one of the soldier's head. He dropped to the floor.

Darmik used the same idea and hit the back of the other soldier's head with his elbow, then swiped at the guy's legs, sending him onto his stomach. Trell came over, whacking the back of the soldier's head, ensuring the man stayed down.

"You and Neco switch clothes with the guards," Trell ordered while slicing Neco's bindings.

Darmik quickly undressed one of the soldiers and exchanged his basic Emperion uniform for the soldier's elite one. Neco did the same with the other soldier.

"Put on the cape, too," Trell whispered. "Keep your head covered."

Darmik did as instructed, sheathing the soldier's sword on his belt, and shoving the dagger in his boot.

"Done," Neco said. "Now what?"

"Tie them up, just the way you were."

Darmik took his cut bindings and wound them around the unconscious soldier. He propped him up against the wall, next to Neco's soldier.

"If there's anything to cover their mouths with, use it," Trell said.

Darmik ripped off two pieces of his undershirt and shoved one into each unconscious soldier's mouth. Then Neco took the bottom of his undershirt and ripped two longer sections, tying them around the soldiers' mouths and heads.

Trell ordered Darmik and Neco to stand at attention with their backs facing the door.

Trell stepped into the hallway. "I need the rest of

you in there now." The remaining four soldiers entered the room.

Trell slipped his sword from its scabbard, flipped it around, and wacked one soldier on the back of his head, rendering him unconscious. At the same time, Neco went after another soldier, and Darmik knew he was responsible for the remaining two.

Savenek slid flat on the floor, ready to be of assistance. Darmik turned and tackled a soldier to the ground, next to Savenek, who lifted his bound legs and repeatedly kicked the guy until he no longer moved. Jumping to his feet, Darmik wrapped his arms around the remaining soldier and then rammed the guy's head into a wall, his body going limp.

"Quietly!" Trell insisted. "There are guards posted outside the window."

Glancing around, all the soldiers lay unconscious on the ground. Darmik started undressing the men, tossing their uniforms to his friends. Once everyone was freed from their bindings and dressed in the elite military uniforms, they tied the soldiers up, propping them against the wall.

"When we leave," Trell said, "I need two of you in front, two at my side, and two behind. You must walk in formation, in step, and not falter. Understood?"

Everyone agreed. Darmik noticed Vesha's hands shaking and Ellie remaining close to Neco, but both were moving quickly and appeared to be holding it together.

"Where to?" Darmik asked. He wanted to go

straight to the Execution Tower to rescue Rema.

"There's only one way for this to work," the old man said. "I'm expected at the palace. You will escort me to the entrance, where I will order you to the city for an additional patrol run. Then you can all head to the Execution Tower." Trell pointed to the limp bodies. "With any luck, these men will remain unconscious a while longer. If they wake and make enough noise, they'll alert the guards and we'll all be discovered."

Darmik examined the unconscious soldiers. One appeared ready to wake up at any moment, but he didn't want to hit him again and accidentally kill him. With their mouths gagged and bound, he hoped they wouldn't be loud.

"Let's not waste any more time," Neco said.

"Agreed." Since Darmik knew the way, he opened the door and led everyone from the room. He kept his shoulders back, head high, and walked with confidence, knowing he'd attract less attention that way. He made sure his hood was on, concealing his identity.

Walking under the hot afternoon sun, Darmik felt lightheaded. He realized they hadn't eaten or drank in over twenty-four hours.

As a group, they made their way to the outer wall of the palace without incident. For once, Audek managed to keep his mouth shut. When the soldiers opened the gate to admit Trell into the palace grounds, he turned to face Darmik. "I'll be traveling with the emperor to the city shortly for a public execution. Head that way and insure the route is safe. Dismissed."

Darmik spun around and took the lead. He wanted to tear the hood off his head because he was hot and sweaty, but he didn't. The risk of sunburn was great, and he didn't want to take the chance of someone recognizing him.

Traveling at a brisk pace, Audek finally broke the silence. "Do we have a plan?"

"I'm trying to figure one out right now," Darmik admitted.

"Do you know the layout?" Neco asked.

"Yes. It's a large courtyard surrounded on all four sides by tall buildings. There is only one entrance and exit for the public, who will number in the hundreds and be crammed in there to see the spectacle. Rema will be brought out onto a platform situated at the front."

"How many will be with her?" Neco asked.

"Usually just the person reading the charge and the executioner. Since Emperor Hamen is coming, I'm sure he'll want to be close to see the action. And where there's the emperor, there's also a large royal guard."

"I have one small dagger and a longsword," Savenek said.

Glancing at everyone, they each had a sword strapped to their waist. Would it be possible to enter the courtyard as soldiers on patrol, and kill the executioner before he murdered Rema? Possibly. However, the emperor's guard would probably take them all out, and then who would save Rema? Darmik balled his hands into fists, frustrated by his lack of options.

When they neared the city's edge, a man dressed in plain clothes ran out to greet them. "I have the items you requested," he said, waving them along.

"Thank you," Darmik replied, pretending to know what the man referred to. "Lead the way." He noticed Audek scrunch his face, looking confused. Neco wrapped his arm around Audek's shoulders, whispering something in his ear.

The man took them to a building two blocks away. "I've been watching all day for you," he said, opening the door and ushering them inside a dimly lit fabric store. Spools of wool, silk, and cotton hung on the walls.

"Here you go," the man said, handing a pile of clothing to Darmik. "You and your companions can change in the back room." He pointed to an archway.

"Thank you," Darmik responded. He went down a short, dark hallway and entered a small room with one window serving as the only light. His friends crowded in behind him. "Keep your voices low," Darmik whispered. "Quickly change and pretend like you know what's going on." He handed everyone a set of clothing typically worn by civilians. Darmik put on rough, brown trousers and a tunic. He felt something hard against his hip. Feeling inside the pants, Darmik found a dagger.

"Check for weapons," he told the others.

Ellie removed a small knife from her trousers.

"I have one, too," Vesha said. Neco, Savenek, and Audek all found similar weapons.

Darmik's heart raced. At this point, they had no other option but to trust Trell planned this. "Hide them," he ordered.

They exited the room and returned to the store.

"Hold on," the man said. He went behind a wooden counter and bent down, retrieving something. When he stood, he held fabric in his arms. "You must not forget the wraps for your face in case of a sandstorm." He smiled at them.

Darmik grabbed the top scarf and wrapped it around his head, mouth, and neck. Everyone else did the same.

"Let's go. There isn't much time." They exited the fabric store. Darmik waved them to the side of the street away from the few people walking down the road. "We're heading north-west to the tallest building in the center of the city. Does everyone see it?"

Once they all found it, Darmik continued, "We need to split up. Everyone head to that building. The execution site is at the base."

"What do we do once we get there?" Savenek asked.

"Wait," Darmik answered. "We'll see if Trell has anything planned. If nothing happens, then I'll kill the executioner before he harms Rema." Darmik balled his hands into fists, determination taking over.

"And then what?" Neco asked.

"I don't know," Darmik admitted. He had no idea how to get out of the courtyard with Rema alive.

"Once Darmik takes out the executioner, he'll be captured or killed," Neco said, folding his arms. "The only way to rescue Rema will be to create a scene of utter and complete chaos."

Darmik nodded. "Excellent idea. Audek and Vesha, you two will travel to the site together. Right when I kill the executioner, make a scene."

They agreed. "Where do we meet after?" Vesha asked.

"I don't expect us all to survive. If you do, head to the harbor and hide until I find you."

Vesha nodded. Audek grabbed her hand and the pair took off toward the tower.

"Savenek, I want you to take Ellie." Neco stiffened. "You two are responsible for grabbing Rema and escaping. If you manage to get her, go to the docks and hide."

"Where?" Ellie asked.

"Down by the water, under the pier. There are lots of dark places."

"Very well," Ellie answered, looking to Neco.

He wrapped her in his arms. "Be safe," he whispered.

"You too."

Darmik glanced away, giving them a moment alone.

Savenek came before him. "Thank you for your help and guidance," he said. "I will do my best to save her, or die trying."

"Me too," he said. They shook hands. "You better

get moving. You'll need to stand close to the front."

Savenek nodded, turning to face Ellie. Neco released her and she took a step back, still staring at him.

"I love you," Neco said, his voice gruff.

Ellie smiled. "I know. And I love you."

"Let's go," Savenek said, pulling his wrap tighter around his face.

Ellie did the same, and the two of them left, Neco staring after them. When they turned a corner and were no longer in sight, Neco asked, "What do you want of me?"

"I don't know," Darmik admitted. "But I only have one dagger. If I fail, it's up to you."

Neco nodded. "I promise."

"I'm sorry to ask this of you."

"You're not asking," Neco said. "I offered. We're in this together."

Darmik was at a loss for words. Neco had been like a brother to him.

"Stop," Neco said. "This isn't the end. Have a little faith." He smiled wryly at his friend.

During his time at Emperion, Darmik had witnessed several executions and beatings, not only at the military training facility, but here in the city as well. He knew from experience that there would be more military members in attendance than regular civilians, which led to the question—how would he kill the executioner and survive? He wouldn't. Darmik knew he was walking to his death. But as long as he saved Rema, it would be worth it.

They were one block from the Execution Tower. His hands trembled. Now was not the time to be afraid. He would need a steady hand to make the kill. There was honor in death, and saving Rema would be a noble act. She would bring peace and prosperity to Greenwood Island. In a land filled with evil and darkness, Rema was the bright, shining light.

"Is there usually this much activity going on?" Neco asked.

Darmik glanced at the people around him, hurrying to one place or another. "Yes," he answered. "Because of the large port, this city attracts a good number of people. When you add the army, well, there are thousands here."

They arrived at the entrance to the courtyard. People were already filtering in, so Darmik and Neco entered with everyone else, trying to blend in. Soldiers ushered people forward, trying to cram as many people in as possible. Darmik and Neco found themselves in the center of the courtyard.

Neco leaned in. "Do you have a clear shot?"

Darmik nodded; there was just enough room for him to throw the dagger.

He focused on the platform where prisoners were killed or punished. On the left side was a tall post with manacles attached to the top, stocks were situated on the right side, and in the center sat a large block of wood with chains hanging from each side.

Neco placed his hand atop Darmik's shoulder and squeezed. Their eyes met, and Neco nodded, giving him the support he needed to do this.

Behind the platform nestled into a building was a small area where the emperor sat while observing the spectacle below him.

Darmik looked to the tower, wondering where Rema was.

Commotion came from the front left, near the door of the tower. A young woman was dragged out and placed in the stocks. A soldier announced that she was being punished because one of her children had failed a class in military training. Another woman was brought out and chained to the post, her arms pulled tight above her head. She was being punished for being out past curfew.

No other prisoners came out. "Where's the executioner?" Darmik mumbled.

"No executions are scheduled for today," the man next to Darmik said. "There was an execution yesterday. Some girl, not from around here."

Darmik's vision swam, and he fell to his knees.

Nine

Rema

A knock sounded on the door. "It's time," someone called from the other side.

Rema pushed away from Nathenek. She must have cried herself to sleep in his lap. Her eyes were puffy and her head felt heavy. She sat, staring at the assassin. "How can you live with yourself?" she whispered.

Without answering, he stood. "I'm to escort you there." Nathenek reached down to help her up.

Ignoring his hand, Rema got to her feet on her own. "What is the official charge?" She adjusted her tunic and smoothed her hair down.

"Treason."

Rema laughed. This was her second time being accused of and sentenced to death for treason. It was comical that King Barjon and Emperor Hamen feared her. After all, she was just a simple girl.

Unfortunately, both men, both unworthy to rule, were on the verge of defeating her. She feared this execution would not end quite as well as her previous one. She couldn't possibly be so lucky as to escape death a second time.

Nathenek gently took her arm, leading her from the room and down the winding stairs. Her wrists weren't bound. She had to try—she wouldn't die without a fight. Pretending to trip on a step, she pulled her body down, hoping the assassin would let go. His grip only tightened. Rema twisted her arm, rolling to her stomach, and kicking with her right foot. He easily blocked her kick, yanking her to her feet. The entire ordeal was awkward since they were on the stairs and stone walls stood on both sides. "What are you doing?" he demanded.

"What do you think?" she spat.

Two guards appeared at the bottom of the stairs. "I've got this," Nathenek hollered to them. He half carried, half dragged her the rest of the way down.

At the bottom, she reached for the assassin's dagger in his pants, just like Darmik had taught her. Sure enough, strapped to his thigh, was a knife. She yanked it free. She needed to be quick, before he disarmed her. The blow had to be hard and well placed. Rema lifted her arm and plunged the dagger down, aiming for his side, by his stomach. Only she completely missed, and the knife got caught on his tunic. Strong hands grabbed her arm, pinning it behind her. In one swift, fluid motion, Rema found herself flat on her back, lying on the ground, Nathenek straddling her body, her arms held above her head.

His angry eyes bore into hers. "You just tried to kill me," he said.

Rema laughed. "You are taking me to my death." Her laugh transformed into sobs. She struggled to get free, but he was too strong. "Get off!" she screamed, thrashing her body. "I don't want to die!"

The assassin's grip tightened.

How could this be the end of her life? Her entire family and kingdom had been taken from her. For what? The emperor's quest for power? He'd destroyed her life, and now he was going to take it.

The fight drained from her body.

She wasn't strong enough.

Nathenek must've seen something change in her because his eyes softened. He released her, helping her to her feet. Strong hands clutched her shoulders, pushing her forward.

"Come on," he mumbled. "You can do this."

She wanted to punch him for his stupidity. A guard standing post next to a door pushed it open, and Nathenek ushered her inside, the door slamming closed behind them. Rema found herself in a small, windowless room lit only by two torches hanging on the walls. Another door stood on the wall opposite her. That had to be the exit to the courtyard—where she was to be executed.

"Would you prefer to be blindfolded?" Nathenek asked, startling her.

She stared at him, completely dumbfounded by

the question. "Does it matter?"

"I suppose not," he answered. "I just thought it might be easier."

The door behind her opened and Nathenek stiffened. He dropped to a knee, bowing his head.

"Rise," a familiar voice commanded. Rema turned and stood face to face with the emperor. "Ready?" he asked, raising his eyebrows, a smile tugging at the corner of his lips.

"To be slaughtered like a pig?" Rema spat.

The emperor laughed. "Such a befitting end for you."

She balled her hands into fists, wanting to punch the evil man.

Emperor Hamen went toward the other door.

Rema said, "Please let me go." Tears pooled in her eyes. "I don't want anything to do with this nasty place. I just want to go home." *And to Darmik,* she thought.

He paused, and then slowly turned around, studying her. "Your execution has nothing to do with what you do or do not want." He came closer to her, barely an arm's length away. "This entire empire is built on rules and structure. It may seem harsh at times, but it works. Your very existence threatens *my* empire. I have no choice but to have you executed."

Nathenek was right—the emperor's cold detachment was worse than King Barjon's mood swings. She quickly wiped her tears away.

"I don't know how your ancestor Nero could have

loved a commoner enough to not only marry her, but change the succession. Even though you have royal blood running through your veins, your blonde hair and blue eyes make you look like a commoner. No one would even know of your true lineage if it weren't for your tattoo."

He went to the door as if to leave when he paused and said, "I considered the possibility of you marrying my son. It would have officially sealed the line." He shrugged his shoulders. "But like I said, you look like a commoner, and I can't ask my only son to marry you. I've spent far too much on his upbringing to throw it all away now. There are far better choices for a wife, ones that will further my empire. Because you, my dear child, are insignificant, and no one will ever know who you really are."

Rema thought back to all the portraits she had seen at the palace when she first met Emperor Hamen. She recalled seeing a sickly girl of about fifteen years of age. There were no pictures of a son.

"I was unaware that you and the empress have a son," she mumbled.

His eyes bore into hers, sending chills through her body because they reminded her of Darmik. "We don't have a son together—only a daughter, Jana."

He threw open the door and stepped outside into the bright light of day.

Rema had a clear view of the raised platform covered with torture equipment.

She turned and ran. When she reached the back door, she yanked it, but it was locked and wouldn't budge.

Nathenek wrapped his arms around her, picking her up.

"No!" she screamed, kicking and punching.

He threw her over his shoulder and exited the other door, stepping onto the platform. Rema's tears were replaced with pure anger—at Nathenek for bringing her here, at the emperor for killing her family and ordering her death, and at life for being so cruel.

He had her legs pinned against his chest, so she used her fists to beat against his back. "Let me go!" she screamed. "I've done nothing wrong!"

Nathenek slid her from his shoulder, dropping her onto the ground on her bottom, knocking the wind from her. She glanced out at the crowd. Hundreds and hundreds of people stood silent and still, staring at her.

Rema decided to tell them who she was. She opened her mouth to address the crowd when someone came up behind her, shoving a piece of fabric into her mouth, gagging her. Then he took a long strip of material and wrapped it around her mouth and head, rendering her speechless.

Glancing to her right, she saw an area directly behind the platform where the emperor, Nathenek, Trell, and half a dozen guards stood.

Two soldiers roughly jerked her arms forward, dragging her to the wooden block at the center of the platform. She kicked her legs, trying to get free. They wrapped her arms around the block, locking her wrists into metal cuffs. She was on her knees, her chest atop the block, unable to move. Someone gathered her hair, pulling it above her head, exposing her neck.

Fear like she'd never felt before took hold of her. Out of the corner of her eye, she saw someone dressed in solid black approach, carrying an axe.

Another soldier stepped forward and spoke, "This woman is found guilty of treason. Her punishment is death by beheading." He nodded to the executioner, who raised the axe with both arms.

This was it.

The executioner lifted the axe above his shoulders, prepared to strike the back of her neck.

Rema squeezed her eyes

S

H

U

T.

Darmik

"Get up," Neco demanded.

Darmik couldn't imagine going on with his life now that he'd failed so miserably. He'd not only let his entire kingdom down, but the woman he loved. There was nothing left.

Neco reached down and pulled Darmik to his feet. "Look."

Darmik lifted his head, glancing at the platform. The previous two people were gone. Now, Rema was chained to the block, her neck exposed, the executioner standing over her with his axe raised in the air.

Without thinking, Darmik grabbed his dagger and threw it, embedding it in the executioner's chest. As the man fell and the axe threatened to harm Rema, Trell leapt forward and pushed him, sending the executioner tumbling from the platform, along with his weapon, into a wide-eyed and stunned crowd.

At the same time, while the crowd was focused on the executioner, the assassin stepped away from the other soldiers and, with lightning speed, unsheathed his dagger and slit Emperor Haman's throat. It took a moment before the guards on the platform realized what Captain had done, and charged at the assassin, who held up something in this hand, while yelling at them. The soldiers froze.

People in the courtyard started screaming, demanding to know what was going on. The emperor lay at Captain's feet, blood pooling around his boots. Trell stepped forward, and the courtyard fell utterly silent.

Darmik peered at Neco, who stood still as a tree, clutching a dagger in his right hand.

Darmik didn't know how the crowd would react to the sudden death of the emperor. At least they seemed willing to listen to Trell for an explanation.

"Release her," Trell ordered the soldiers. One bent down and unlocked Rema's manacles. She slowly stood, her legs appearing shaky. Her face was red and her eyes were swollen from crying. The guard untied the cloth from around her head, removing the gag from her mouth.

Trell took the item from Nathenek and came to stand next to Rema at the front of the platform. He held up his hand, and as Rema's key necklace dangled from his fingers, the crowd gasped. Rema glanced at Trell, her eyebrows drawn together in confusion.

"The false emperor wanted this woman dead because of who she is. Rema," Trell pointed to her, "is the true heir to the Emperion throne. She is the direct descendent of Nero, and is the bearer of the key." Trell placed the necklace around her neck. "I present to you, Empress Amer Rema, your true and rightful ruler."

Rema's eyes widened in shock as everyone dropped to their knees before her.

Rema

She saw Darmik standing there as everyone around him knelt on the ground. She wanted to scream with joy, run to him, and throw her arms around his neck. More than anything, she wanted to kiss him.

Rema smiled at Darmik, and he grinned back as he knelt on the ground. She was still trying to understand all that had happened. Apparently, she was now the empress of the largest empire known to man. And if she'd learned anything from her past experiences, it was to be confident, and to take control—immediately.

"You may rise," Rema told her subjects.

She turned to Trell, who stood smiling at her with an expression of awe and pride. "Do you have anything you want to say to the crowd?" she asked, raising her head high.

Facing the people, he said, "Tell everyone that Emperor Hamen is dead, and the true heir now reigns. Notices will be posted. Dismissed." The old man turned and knelt before her. "I am yours to command."

"As am I." Nathenek knelt next to Trell.

The crowd seemed unsure what to do, and many still lingered in the courtyard.

"Both of you have a lot of explaining to do. Rise."

"For now," Trell said, "we need to get you to a secure location."

"Am I not safe here, with you?" Rema inquired.

Trell's eyes darkened, and he didn't respond. Nathenek stepped in front of her, claiming her attention. "You are safe with me, I promise. However, until news of your ascension to the throne is well known, it is best to be cautious."

Rema stared into Nathenek's eyes, sensing something honest and sincere in them.

"Notices must go out to the commander and army immediately," Trell ordered.

Rema saw the soldiers on the platform staring at her with uncertainty. She made sure the key necklace was clearly visible, although she didn't understand its significance. Nathenek and Trell quickly ushered her back into the Execution Tower, where Trell started barking orders to the soldiers. The enormity of what had just taken place slowly sunk in. She was alive, Darmik was here, and she was the leader of Emperion.

"Where's Darmik?" she asked, eager to be reunited with him.

"He's here with a small group of people from your rebel army," Nathenek informed her.

"I want to see them. Now."

"Yes, Your Majesty," he said. "We'll take you to another location and have them brought there."

"Let's go," Trell urged them, gingerly taking Rema's arm and leading her to a locked door. A soldier opened it, revealing a long flight of stairs. Trell grabbed a torch and began descending into the cold darkness. Rema hurried after him, Nathenek right behind her. They started walking through a tunnel carved out of the earth.

Rema used the opportunity to examine the events from the last few weeks. She thought of Nathenek's behavior toward her on the voyage there, him training her, and his attitude since arriving at Emperion. When others were around, he had been hostile toward her, but when alone, he was kind. Had it been an act the entire time? He told her he swore an oath to the true line—he never said Emperor Hamen.

What was Trell's involvement in all of this? She wasn't sure how Trell and Nathenek were connected, but one thing was certain—she felt both men were trustworthy and had her best interests in mind.

After traveling through the dark tunnel for several minutes, they climbed a steep set of stairs, and entered a small, barren room. A soldier standing guard unlocked the door, and Rema stepped into a luxurious sitting room filled with plush velvet sofas and chairs.

"Where are we?" she asked.

"One of the emperor's safe houses. He has several throughout the city and empire that are used for secret meetings or when under attack.

"Who do we fear will harm me?"

"We're not sure," Trell admitted. "This is simply a precaution until we see where things stand."

"And Darmik and my friends?"

"Are being escorted here as we speak." He patted her shoulder.

Guards stood at the room's two visible doors. Someone knocked and a soldier was admitted, going directly to Trell, whispering in his ear. Rema didn't like the idea of allowing Trell to have control over the situation, but she didn't see any alternative right now. The army knew, trusted, and respected their former battle strategist. For now, he was the bridge between her and Emperion.

"How are you holding up?" Nathenek asked, standing at her side.

Honestly, she felt like she was dangling at the end of a very thin string and it was about to snap, but she couldn't let anyone know that. "I'm fine," she lied.

He was about to respond when commotion sounded from the other side of the door. Nathenek stood in front of her, shielding her with his own body. The door flew open, and Darmik burst inside.

Rema shoved Nathenek aside and ran, jumping into Darmik's arms. He held her tight. She breathed in his familiar scent, felt his strong hands on her back, and for the first time, felt truly safe and knew everything would turn out well.

Trell cleared his throat, and Darmik released her. The rest of her friends all stood behind Darmik, smiling. "Sorry to interrupt your reunion," Trell said, "but we need to move out. Word has reached us of civil unrest. People don't understand what's happening, and they're afraid."

Darmik grabbed her hand, brought it to his lips, and kissed it.

"It's good to see you alive and well." He smiled.

"You too," she said. Her cheeks hurt from smiling. She glanced at her dear friends, glad everyone was unharmed.

Darmik turned to face Trell. "I'm sorry, what were you saying?"

"Rema, you should go to one of the palaces outside the city. We will invite all the military leaders in and explain the situation. From there, they can tell those under their command. Announcements will be made to the civilians."

Rema tore her focus away from Darmik, and put it to the task at hand.

"Forgive me, Trell," she said, "but I need you to explain the *entire* situation to me, and I want you to start at the beginning. I'm not asking."

Trell removed his cloak and sat on one of the

sofas, rubbing his face.

"Sir," Nathenek said, "we really should get Rema to another location in case anyone followed Darmik here."

"No," Darmik said with authority. "I want a quick explanation, and then *Rema* will decide how to proceed." He squeezed her hand, giving her strength, and letting her know he was on her side.

Trell stared at Darmik, pride radiating from him. Rema suddenly remembered that Trell was Darmik's grandfather. She wanted to reveal their connection, but now was not the time.

"As you are aware," Trell said, "when crown Prince Nero left with Atta for Greenwood Island a hundred years ago, the line shifted. The true bloodline has always been Nero's first-born descendants. When Nero left Emperion, he wore the heir's necklace—a key with a ruby stone. The symbol can be seen everywhere around here. Just look at statues, paintings, or even buildings. Nero continued to pass the necklace down through the generations, as it had always been done in his family. He also carried on with the tradition of the secret royal tattoos. Our history and record books reveal both the key and the mark as the true line. Should anyone from the true line wish to ascend to the throne, they could, thus returning the line to where it truly belongs.

"When the line shifted, so did the colors, symbols, and marks in order to reflect that change and remind everyone that there had been a shift. When Hamen, a prince from a neighboring kingdom, married Empress

Eliza and ascended to the throne, he was furious to learn he married into a false line. He was painstakingly aware that even his descendants wouldn't carry the true line. He saw symbols every day that reminded him of this fact.

"After Empress Eliza's brother, Barjon, claimed he destroyed the line, Hamen thought he finally carried the bloodline. He sent out a royal decree stating Nero's descendants were dead, and he was now the true heir."

Silence hung in the air as Rema mulled over everything Trell revealed. "I want an explanation of your involvement," Rema said.

"I'm getting there." Trell leaned back on the sofa. "We Emperion people are all about rules. We adhere to them without question. Hamen told me to plan an invasion of a small, remote island and kill the ruling monarchy. So I did. It wasn't until after that I realized what I'd done, and who I killed. I swore I would protect the line in any way that I could. I demanded all artifacts and artwork, and searched through everything looking for the key necklace. When I couldn't find it, I knew someone had to be alive. Ever since I realized you are the heir, Rema, I have done everything in my power to keep you safe and bring you home, to Emperion."

"What he says is true," Nathenek added. "I've been aiding him for the past two seasons. Although, I wasn't aware of your identity until I saw the necklace."

All of this was overwhelming. Rema sat on the sofa, pulling Darmik down with her, trying to wrap her brain around all that was revealed. "What is the plan now that Hamen is dead?" she asked.

"We need to sort through those loyal to Hamen, and eliminate them. We must establish your identity as the sovereign ruler and meet with the neighboring kingdoms to declare peace."

"What about Hamen's wife and children?"

"His daughter has been bedridden for months. Empress Eliza lives with Princess Jana at the palace in Verek. They are rarely seen in public. We can either execute them, or have them sent to the dungeon for the remainder of their lives."

Neither option sounded appealing. "I want them exiled, not killed or imprisoned."

Darmik stiffened beside her. "I would recommend against that," he said.

Rema glanced at Trell, who was nodding. "Why?" She couldn't fathom killing two women because of the blood running through their veins. After all, that was what Barjon and Hamen did to her family. She would not stoop to their level.

"If they go to another kingdom," Darmik said, "they could be used as political leverage. It's simply too dangerous to allow them out of Emperion."

"In that case, let's exile them here, in Emperion. Find a suitable cottage in an unpopulated area. Have them guarded at all times."

"Very well," Trell said, nodding in approval.

"What about his son?" she asked. Perhaps he was here in the city, training to be a captain in the army.

"The emperor's wife only gave birth to a daughter," Trell revealed.

That didn't make any sense. "He told me he has a son."

"Excuse me," Nathenek said, stepping forward. "If you'll recall, he said he didn't have a son with the empress. Therefore, that implies he had a son with someone else."

"Where is the line entailed to go?" Rema asked.

Trell answered, "To Princess Jana. If she dies before she has children, then the line goes to the next living relative of the empress. That would be her younger brother, Barjon. Since he's the crown king, it would bypass him and go to his son, Lennek. However, since Lennek is in line to the Greenwood Island throne, it would go to Darmik." Rema felt Darmik stiffen. This was the first time any of them were hearing this news.

"Could anyone else lay claim to the Emperion throne?" Darmik asked.

"Not that I'm aware of," Trell said. "Nonetheless, right now, Rema's safety is our top priority. Until we learn where everyone's loyalties lie, I want every precaution taken."

"What about his son?" Rema asked. Could he claim the throne? Did he have any rights?

"That won't be an issue," Trell said.

"How do you know?" Darmik countered.

"Even if his son holds no rights to the throne, he could seek retribution for the death of his father," Nathenek added. "We must be cautious."

Trell shook his head. "There's nothing to worry about."

"Can we at least acknowledge the possibility?" Darmik asked. Trell reluctantly agreed. "There is one other issue I'd like to address," he continued. "What about Greenwood Island?"

No one said a word.

"Darmik is right," Rema said. "I have to help all my people."

"Your duty is here now," Trell said.

"Yes," Rema acknowledged. "But the people of Greenwood Island also fall under my jurisdiction."

Savenek cleared his throat. Rema had forgotten her friends were still in the room. "If I may," he said. "I'd like to offer a solution. What if, while you're waiting for the dust to settle here in Emperion, Rema returns to Greenwood Island?"

Trell shook his head.

"It's a great idea," Darmik agreed. "We need to get her to safety. What better way than on a ship to an island far away from here?"

"I understand, and that part makes sense," Trell said. "But she needs to be here."

"Why?" Darmik asked. "She also needs to return and eliminate Barjon and Lennek. They are her greatest threats right now. A portion of the Emperion Army can accompany her to ensure her safety."

"You want me to send her to war?" Trell asked incredulously, his face turning red.

"No," Darmik said, twisting his body to face Rema. "I'm asking you, Rema, as empress, what do you command?"

Rema stood with her hands on her hips, looking at every single person in the room. She knew her mind. "I am going to war."

TEN

Darmik

Darmik stood alongside Rema at the bow of the ship, watching Emperion fade away in the early morning sun. He grabbed her warm, sweaty hand, squeezing tight. They hadn't had a single moment alone since her almost execution yesterday.

After Rema declared she was going back to Greenwood Island, Trell immediately began preparations. They were now accompanied by a platoon of two hundred and fifty men, on a total of six warships.

Rema tried pulling her hand away, and Darmik reluctantly let it go. He glanced down at her. "Are you well?"

She nodded, not looking at him. It had only been a little over a fortnight since he'd last seen her, yet, she looked different. The lines of her face were a little sharper, her muscles toned.

Neco approached. "I'm sorry to disturb you two." He smiled at them. "But we need to go over a few things now that we're alone."

Darmik laughed—they weren't really *alone.*
Granted, the other ships had approximately fifty soldiers
each, and his boat only had a dozen, along with his
friends. He suspected Neco meant now that they were
away from the overprotective and watchful eyes of Trell
and Nathenek.

"Of course," Rema said. "Let's go below deck. It's
too hot out here for my liking."

Neco led them inside to the galley.

"I thought we were going to the meeting room,"
Rema stated.

"No," Neco replied, taking a seat. "We all need to
eat breakfast, so I figure we might as well talk here." He
shrugged his shoulders. "I've already told everyone to
meet us here."

There were several small, round tables, each able
to seat six people. Rema sat down across from Neco,
rubbing her face with her hands. Darmik sat next to
her. Soon the rest of their friends joined them. Savenek
grabbed an empty chair from another table and squeezed
it in between Audek and Vesha. Ellie found a large,
wicker basket filled with bread. She handed everyone a
loaf before taking a seat next to Neco.

Vesha leaned over and hugged Rema. No one
spoke, but Darmik suspected they were all thinking how
lucky they were to be alive. He reached under the table
and patted the top of Rema's thigh. She looked exhausted.
They only got a couple hours of sleep last night while

Trell had the ships loaded with goods and supplies for the voyage.

Since Darmik was starving, he tore into his bread.

Neco spoke with a soft voice, "I know Trell said the soldiers accompanying us are all trustworthy and loyal to Rema, but I think we should be extra vigilant."

"Agreed," Darmik said. "Since Rema appointed me as head of her royal guard, I'd like to officially recruit each and every one of you as members during our journey to Greenwood Island."

Rema quietly picked at her food. It was unlike her to be so silent and not offer an opinion.

Darmik continued, "I want her guarded at all times." Everyone nodded their heads in agreement, as they ate their bread.

Rema shoved away from the table. "I'm going to my room," she mumbled.

Darmik grabbed his food and stood, about to follow her.

"No," she said placing her hand on his shoulder and pushing him back onto his chair. "Ellie and Vesha will accompany me." Both girls glanced at him, so he nodded. They rose and followed her out of the galley.

Darmik wanted to have Audek accompany the girls; though he knew Rema would take offense that he insisted a male escort her. He forced himself to keep his mouth shut.

"What's wrong with Rema?" Savenek asked.

"She's probably just tired," Neco offered. "She's

been through a lot."

Darmik began to think it was more than that, that there was something bothering her. He'd have to speak to her in private regarding the matter.

"I asked you all here for a reason," Neco said, banging his fist upon the table.

"I know," Darmik mumbled, "but let's wait a bit. We'll start planning the takeover after we've all adjusted to being at sea."

Neco laughed. "No, that's not why I asked you here." He stood and went over to a cupboard where he pulled out four wooden cups and a bottle of ale. "We need to celebrate." He brought everything to the table.

"Here, here!" Audek cheered. "Lots to be thankful for! We got Rema back, and we're not dead!"

Savenek chuckled as Neco filled the cups to the rim and handed one to each of them.

"To Rema!" Darmik said. The four friends cheered and took a drink.

Darmik made his way to Rema's berth, concerned that he hadn't seen her all morning. Outside her door, Ellie and Vesha sat, quietly talking to one another.

"Rema's in there alone?" he asked.

Ellie nodded. "We've been out here the entire time."

"Do you know what's bothering her?" he quietly

asked.

"She hasn't said anything to us," Vesha said. "But she has been through a lot. Maybe she just wants some time to herself?"

"Or maybe she's sleeping?" Ellie suggested.

Darmik squared his shoulders, suddenly nervous. He knocked on the door and waited for Rema to answer. Nothing. Perhaps she was just tired and resting. Regardless, he wanted to stick his head in just to be sure. Turning the knob, he opened the door a couple of inches and peered inside. Rema lay on the bed, facing the wall, her back to him.

Darmik slipped inside, quietly closing the door behind him. She still had on an Emperion soldier uniform. He moved over to the bed, sitting down at the end, near her feet.

Rema's eyes were open. Her face was red and swollen, as if she'd been crying.

"Are you unwell?" Perhaps the motion of the ship bothered her, and she was seasick.

She didn't respond.

"Rema, what's wrong?" She closed her eyes, not answering. "You're starting to scare me," he gently said. "Do you need some water to drink? Should I get Ellie or Vesha?"

Rema shook her head. He scooted further up on the bed, near her back. Rubbing her shoulders, he said, "Please talk to me." Maybe something else had happened to her that he was unaware of. Nathenek hadn't mentioned anything before they left, but Darmik still didn't trust the guy—even if Rema did.

A thought suddenly occurred to him. "Did something happen between you and Nathenek?" he asked. Was she upset they were parted? Did she have feelings for the man?

Rema sat up, staring at him. They were only inches apart, and Darmik felt her warm breath on his face. He wanted to reach out and caress her cheek, but he kept his hands to himself.

"I'm sorry," she finally said, her voice weak. Her eyes darted down to her clasped hands.

"Please tell me what's the matter?" he begged.

The corners of her lips pulled up. "A lot has changed since we last saw one another." Her cheeks turned a rosy shade of red.

Darmik smiled, thinking of their last encounter at the rebel fortress when they were kissing. He'd been about to propose. "Yes," Darmik mused. "A lot has changed." He felt a wall between them. He very much wanted to tear down that wall with his bare hands. "I'm worried about you."

"I'm fine," she insisted. "It's just a lot to take in. Not only am I responsible for the people of Greenwood Island—where we're about to wage a war—but I'm now responsible for an entire empire. Do you have any idea just how large Emperion is? It's a thousand times bigger than Greenwood Island."

Darmik nodded. He was about to say something

when she continued, "I'm only seventeen. I have no idea what I'm doing. Most people in my position have spent their entire life preparing, and here I am, thrown into it. What if I fail?" She dropped her face to her hands, shaking her head.

He reached up, pulling her hands away from her face. "Rema," he said tenderly, "look at me." Her glassy, sapphire eyes peered up at him. "You will fail," he said.

Her eyes widened, and she jerked back. "What?" she incredulously asked. "If you know I'm going to fail, then what are you doing here?" Her voice had a hard edge to it.

"Shh," he said. "You misunderstand me." He put his hands on her shoulders, grounding her in place. "You will fail at some things. You can't possibly be successful in all you do."

She went to speak, but he held a finger to her lips, silencing her. "Each time you fail, you will learn from your mistakes. And it will make you stronger. You will be the strongest and most powerful woman in the world."

Rema sat perfectly still, as if she was processing all that he'd said. "I'm scared," she admitted. "To have that kind of power. To know how to use it."

"You have me and all of your friends. We are here to help you in any capacity you need."

She leaned forward and gingerly kissed him on the lips. "Thank you," she said, smiling.

ELEVEN

Rema

The events over the past twenty-four hours were so overwhelming, that she wasn't sure what to think or do. Her heart quickened and her breathing became labored just thinking about her almost execution. She thought she was going to die having failed her people and never seeing Uncle Kar, Aunt Maya, or Darmik again. Now, not only was she alive, but Darmik was there with her, and she was the empress of the largest known empire. Rema was now responsible for thousands and thousands of people, and she had an entire army at her disposal.

There was a tremendous amount of work to be done. While Trell and Nathenek stayed in Emperion to oversee the transition of power from Emperor Hamen to Rema, she was leading a platoon of soldiers to Greenwood Island to oust Barjon and Lennek. Once this war was over and won, she would return to Emperion and take her rightful place as empress. She planned to tour the entire kingdom to get to know and understand the people. Positive changes would be made to allow a more peaceful and fulfilling life. Without a doubt, the army had to be restructured. Children would no longer be required to enlist, and some of the cruelty Darmik spoke of would end.

Rema hoped Darmik would return to Emperion with her. She could use his knowledge and expertise to fix the army, but she wasn't sure what his intentions were. She couldn't ask him to abandon his soldiers on Greenwood Island just to accompany her. When they briefly spoke earlier, he said he'd be by her side. Rema foolishly hoped that meant for the rest of their lives.

After being below deck all morning, Rema wanted to feel the sun on her face and the wind against her body. When Darmik visited her earlier, he mentioned training everyone during the voyage to Greenwood Island in order to maintain their strength. It was time Rema pull herself together, and start acting the role granted upon her.

Exiting her room, she found Vesha and Ellie sitting on the floor. Both girls looked up at her with hopeful eyes.

"I'd like to go to the top deck," she said.

"It's about time," Vesha said, smiling. She was picking up some of Audek's candid humor.

"Yes, it is," Rema replied.

Following the girls through the dark hallways of the ship and up a steep ladder, Rema stepped into the bright sunlight, squinting.

"Her Royal Majesty," someone shouted. Everyone on the deck—crew, soldiers, and friends alike—bowed before her.

She had no idea what to do. Was the etiquette for an empress different from a queen? And why was everyone insisting on being so formal around her? She was just Rema, a seventeen-year-old girl, standing before everyone in a used Emperion military outfit. She certainly didn't feel like an empress.

"As you were," she said, hoping that was enough for people to go back to what they were doing. Rema walked over to Darmik, who stood at the center of the ship holding a sword, a half smile on his beautiful lips. "Are you training?" she asked.

"We are." He looked down at her through his dark eyelashes, making her heart skip a beat. She wanted to reach up and kiss him, but decided against it with so many eyes watching.

She glanced at Neco, Savenek, and Audek. They were sweaty and breathing hard. "All right," she said, turning to Ellie and Vesha. "Let's join them." Facing Darmik, she asked, "What are we working on?"

Audek dropped to his knees before her. "Rema...I mean...Your Highness...I mean, Your Majesty, right? Well, whatever your title is, I'm so glad you're here and safe." He hugged her legs. "And on *my* side!"

"Audek!" Darmik shouted. "Get off!"

"Oh, uh, sorry," Audek stuttered, releasing her. "Aren't you glad she's here?" He scratched his head, standing.

Darmik grabbed Audek's tunic, pulling him in close. "Of course I'm glad she's here. But people are watching you. You will treat Rema like the empress she is—especially when others are around. Are we clear?" Audek nodded, and Darmik released him. Rema wanted to intervene and tell Audek that it was all right, that nothing had to change between them. However, things were different now, and Darmik knew what he was doing. He had her best interests at heart, and she trusted him. If he said everyone needed to treat her like an empress at all times, then there was a legitimate reason, so she kept her mouth shut.

"We were just running through some basic drills," Savenek said, diffusing the tension.

"Excellent," she said, facing her friends. "Before we resume training, I have something to say." She looked at each and every one of them—at Vesha's warm smile, Ellie's bright and intelligent eyes, Neco's friendly disposition, Audek's wry smile, Savenek's intense gaze, and lastly, the love she felt radiating from Darmik. "I want to thank you for traveling all the way to Emperion to rescue me. I'm honored by your steadfast loyalty, and your courageous ability to put your lives on the line for what you believe in. Thank you."

"We are honored to serve you," Neco said.

Before she started crying, she turned and said, "Very well, let's get to work."

They spent the next hour running through

various hand-to-hand combat training exercises. It felt good to be focused on body movements instead of her new title and position. Still, Darmik was careful around her, and she was only ever paired with Vesha or Ellie. She suspected life would never be the same, and it was just something she'd have to get used to.

Rema sat on her bed while Ellie knelt behind her, combing her hair.

"So, you and Neco," Rema said, wanting to talk about something other than herself. Glancing back, she saw Ellie smiling. "How long have you two known each other? How did you meet?"

Ellie sighed, putting down the comb and sitting cross-legged before Rema. They never had a chance to talk about Ellie and Neco's relationship at the rebel fortress.

"We've been together for about a year now," Ellie revealed.

Rema wondered what that meant. Most people signed a marriage contract, courted, and then married shortly thereafter.

"Neco only came to King's City with Darmik, so I didn't get to see him very often. But whenever he was in town, we managed to spend some time together."

"Why didn't you ever say anything while I was at the king's castle?"

"It never came up, and in all honesty, Neco and I weren't serious until recently." Her face turned a crimson shade of red, and she glanced away.

"Serious?" Rema asked. "What does that mean? Are you two betrothed?"

Ellie chuckled, shaking her head. "While in the king's service, I was unable to marry."

"But you are no longer in the king's service," Rema mused.

Ellie buried her face in Rema's pillow, laughing. She glanced up. "I know," she said, smiling. There was a twinkle of excitement in her eyes. "And what about you?" She lightly smacked Rema with the pillow.

"What do you mean?"

"You and Darmik," she said, exasperated. "You two are...together?"

Rema nodded. She wasn't sure where their relationship was going, but she loved Darmik and wanted to be with him.

"Do you plan to marry him?"

Rema had undergone so many changes that she didn't have time to think about being married on top of everything else right now. "I need to worry about being empress over Emperion and Greenwood Island."

"Wouldn't you like to have someone by your side? Supporting you?"

Rema hadn't thought of it before. Darmik would make the perfect husband—not only did she love him, but he would be someone who would help share the burden of ruling.

"You're blushing!" Ellie teased her. Someone knocked on the door, and Ellie smiled. "I bet that's him!" She jumped off the bed and answered. Sure enough, Darmik stood in the doorway.

He'd changed clothing since the last time she saw him. He now wore a solid black tunic and pants, matching his hair and setting off his brown eyes.

"I'll leave you two alone." Ellie smiled as she left the room, closing the door on her way out.

Rema stood. Before they set sail, Trell gave her a footlocker filled with clothes. She suspected they belonged to the previous empress. Since it was nighttime, Rema had on a soft white gown that she assumed was a nightdress, although it was made of silk and finer than most dresses she'd seen.

Darmik's eyes bore into hers, and she felt her body temperature rise. She fidgeted with her hands, unsure of what to say or do.

"Hi," Darmik said, smiling. He took a step toward her. "I, uh, volunteered for the night shift."

Rema ducked her head, her blonde hair cascading down around her face. He planned to stay there all night? Why did things suddenly feel so awkward between them?

"So..." Darmik said, taking another step closer to her. "I assume you're tired?"

Rema nodded. It was rather late, and she hadn't slept much over the course of the past two days.

He took another step toward her. "Audek is

stationed outside."

"For the entire night?" Didn't Audek need to sleep? Did Darmik plan on sitting there all night watching her?

"No," he replied. "We're taking shifts." He ran his hands through his hair, nervous or unsure of what to do. "After my shift, Vesha will be in here with you."

Rema nodded her head. She had no idea what to say or do. The room felt stifling hot. During their time apart, she'd dreamed of being with him. Of having the chance to talk...of having the opportunity to kiss...of telling him how much he meant to her and that she loved him. Now that she was here, alone with him, she had no idea how to do any of those things. She felt like an incompetent child.

"Since you're tired, why don't you go to sleep?" Darmik suggested. His voice was husky and rough, sending desire through her.

"Good idea." She avoided eye contact, hoping it would be easier to breathe if she didn't look at him.

Since she was in the highest-ranking officer's berth, it was a little larger than the other ones. Still, it was rather stark. Besides her bed and footlocker, there was a small desk and a rickety, wooden chair. She wasn't sure where Darmik planned to sit during his shift.

"If you don't mind, and you're comfortable with it, I'll just lay on the ground."

She recalled her voyage to Emperion and being locked in Nathenek's room. Sleeping on the floor wasn't very pleasant. Pulling off the top blanket from her bed,

Rema handed it to him. "The floor is hard. Lay on this."

He took it, their hands briefly touching, sending a surge of warmth through her body.

"Rema," he whispered. She glanced up into his warm brown eyes. They were filled with desire. He tossed the blanket to the ground. "I love you." He took a step toward her, now only a hand's width apart. "When we were in Emperion, I thought you'd been executed." His eyes filled with tears. "I thought I'd lost you." He reached for her, and she melted into his arms. He held her tight. "I don't ever want to lose you."

Rema slightly pulled back, tilting her head and looking up at him. "I love you, too," she whispered. "But I'm afraid of the future. I have to go back to Emperion."

"I know." He gently kissed her lips. "And I plan to be by your side for the rest of my life."

Darmik knelt on the ground, clasping both of her hands. "Rema, I know this is unconventional, that Kar and Maya haven't given their permission, but I want to marry you. Please be my wife."

Tears slid down her cheeks. He wanted to marry her? To be her partner and love her for the rest of their lives?

She nodded. "Yes, I will marry you."

Darmik smiled the biggest smile she'd ever seen. He jumped up, grabbing her and spinning around.

He gently set her back down on her feet. They stood, staring at one another, then Darmik slowly lowered his head, and they kissed. Rema intertwined her fingers in his hair, pulling him closer. His hands roamed over her back, leaving a trail of heat. Rema wanted to feel all of him, but she knew now was not the time or the place. Darmik's kisses moved to her ear and then down her neck.

"We should stop," Rema mumbled.

"I know," Darmik admitted. "We should—but I don't want to."

"Neither do I," she said. Darmik gently took her face in his hands, gazing into her eyes, the love clear.

"We can announce our engagement after we win the war."

"Yes," Rema said. "But I'd like to marry soon."

Darmik smiled, melting her heart. "Me too."

Rema hated being below deck. The air smelled thick and musty, and there weren't any windows. Since they needed to plan their arrival and how they'd connect with the rebels, she called a meeting to order on the top deck. Even though they'd only been at sea for two days, the sun had already decreased in intensity.

Rema's friends and the dozen soldiers on board sat facing her. Darmik nodded encouragingly, giving her the strength she needed to take control. He told her the key to being an effective leader was to act with authority at all times in order to be taken seriously. Looking at everyone, Rema squared her shoulders and clasped her hands before her. She breathed in the cool, salty sea air and felt the wind against her body. She could do this.

"When we arrive at Greenwood Island, our presence will be noted immediately. Six warships and two hundred and fifty soldiers can't arrive at the island quietly. Therefore, we must plan accordingly. Let me introduce you to two key people in our mission."

Darmik and Savenek stood and came next to her. "This is Commander Darmik, from the King's Army. This is Savenek, a captain from the rebel army. I'm going to let each of them speak about the state of things, what we can expect when we arrive, and their ideas on how to organize everyone once on the island. When they're done, I'm open to suggestions from all of you." The soldier's eyes widened in shock. She doubted anyone encouraged or valued their opinion before. She smiled, knowing things were already changing for the better.

Savenek cleared his throat. "Thank you, Your Majesty." Facing the group, he began to address them. "Commander Mako has been organizing the rebels and getting everyone down the mountain. They should be located at various villages throughout the island by now, eagerly awaiting our arrival."

Darmik added, "The men from the King's Army who are loyal to me are amassing in Werden, a town a half-day's journey from King's City."

"Once word reaches Mako that we've arrived," Savenek said, "the rebels will travel to Werden to meet up with Darmik's men."

The boat lurched, and Rema widened her stance in order to maintain her balance. "What we need to figure out, and communicate with the other five ships, is how to get to Werden. Does anyone have any ideas?" she asked.

The soldiers stared at her as if she'd sprouted the head of a horse, so Rema kept calm and patiently waited.

Vesha raised her hand, and Rema nodded for her to speak. "Maybe we can arrive at night? Then we can try and get off the ship quietly. The crew can stay behind. Once we're on land, they can set sail and hide the ships off the coast, where no one will see them?"

"I like the idea of hiding the boats," Darmik murmured. "I'm not crazy about getting everyone off the ships in the dark, though. I fear we'll still be noticed because there are so many of us. Even at night, people work at the docks."

Neco raised his hand. "What if we split up? Each ship goes to a different port?"

"I like that suggestion," Savenek said. "We have a better chance of protecting the empress that way, too."

"Anyone else?" Rema asked. "I'd like a few more options to consider."

An Emperion soldier raised his hand. Rema nodded for him to speak. He stood. "If anyone is looking for us, they will have people watching the main ports. I think we should avoid the obvious and expected. Are there lesser known ports we can dock at?"

Another soldier stood. "All of us are trained to

swim. I do not see the need to dock."

Now they were getting somewhere. "What are the risk factors in swimming from the boat to the shore?" Rema asked.

"It depends on the water temperature, currents, and time of day," the soldier answered.

"I will not risk my soldiers' lives if there is another, safer way." Several soldiers smiled. "You need to know and understand, as your leader, I will always have your best interests as my priority, soldiers and citizens alike. Thank you for your suggestions. I want some time to think and consider the best course of action. Dismissed."

Rema stood, staring at the night sky. The crescent moon's reflection glimmered on the water. Thousands of stars twinkled above. Leaning her arms against the railing, she breathed in the crisp, cool air.

She heard her guards questioning someone, and hoped it was Darmik coming to join her. They'd been so busy strategizing their arrival at Greenwood Island that they'd barely had any time alone since his proposal. Glancing behind her, she saw Darmik dismissing her two guards. Her heartbeat sped up just seeing him.

"We should arrive tomorrow," he said by way of greeting. He stood beside her, handing her a heavy, wool blanket.

"I know." She wrapped it around her shoulders,

basking in its warmth. "I'm nervous."

"So am I," he admitted.

Peering over at him leaning against the railing next to her, she noticed his lips were pulled tight and his shoulders were tense. "I assumed you would be used to this sort of thing," she gently said.

"I am—to an extent."

"Then what are you nervous about?"

He turned toward her, clasping her hands in his big, strong ones. "I'm worried about protecting you." His thumbs rubbed small circles against her palms.

"Once we land and join forces with the rebel army and your loyal soldiers, overthrowing Barjon will be easy. There's nothing to be concerned about."

"I hope that's the case," he responded. "But if there's one thing I've learned, it's to never underestimate my father or Lennek."

She understood Darmik's concern; however, who could possibly stand in their way or oppose their mission? The people of Greenwood Island were repressed, starving, and would welcome the removal of Barjon and Lennek. The King's Army was loyal to Darmik, so there would be nothing to stop Rema from succeeding.

"There is one thing I'd like to ask you," he said.

She felt his hands stiffen. "What?" she whispered.

"Is there any chance of convincing you to hide somewhere until this is over?" He leaned back slightly, as if fearing her reaction.

Rema's eyes narrowed. He wanted her to hide?

While her people fought for her? Although it might seem like the safe route, she had no intention of being a leader who bid others to do her business. Her empire would not function that way.

Shaking her head, she answered, "No, there isn't."

She was about to explain her reasoning when Darmik smiled and said, "I didn't think so. Still, I thought I'd ask. If you hid, it would save me a lot of worry; although, the sort of person that would run and hide wouldn't be the one to have stolen my heart."

She reached up, tracing her finger along Darmik's cheek, down to his jaw, and then across his lips. His eyes darkened as he leaned down and kissed her. The blanket fell from her shoulders. She no longer felt the cold air as she leaned her body against his, craving his warmth.

TWELVE

Darmik

Since they were the lead ship, the other five vessels followed them to their current location, just off the coast of northern Adder. Darmik stood on the top deck, along with his friends and all the soldiers on board, searching for a small fishing village. Neco said it was hard to find and they needed to look carefully. These particular villagers lived a sheltered existence, trying to remain unnoticed, keeping the King's Army away.

"We've been searching for over an hour," Rema said, squinting from the bright sunlight.

"If Neco says there are fishermen here who can help, then we will find them," Darmik responded. "I promise."

"I don't want to be spotted. Isn't that the whole point of this?" She fidgeted with her key necklace, searching the shoreline.

"Don't worry," Darmik assured her. Although he told her not to worry, he was concerned. This was her first act as empress and events needed to unfold smoothly in order for her to gain the army's respect and utter devotion.

"Drop anchor!" Neco shouted. He raised a horn to his mouth and blew, alerting the other warships to do the same.

Darmik wished they could get closer to land; however, the helmsman had informed him that if they sailed any closer, they would run aground. Crew members shouted commands to one another as they brought in the sails and soldiers helped lower the anchor. Grabbing Rema's hand, he took her port side so they could have a better view of the shoreline.

Neco ran over. "I have my five companions chosen. All are strong swimmers."

"Excellent," Rema said. "You may proceed."

Neco smiled. "Will do!" He made his way over to where five soldiers were removing their boots, socks, and tunics. Ellie rushed over to Neco, jumping into his open arms. They kissed and Ellie's hair fluttered in the wind, wrapping around their heads, concealing the two of them. It felt good to see Neco so happy. Neco put Ellie down, gave a curt nod in Rema's direction, climbed up onto the railing, and then leapt into the turbulent ocean below, all five soldiers following suit. The water had to be freezing. The six men all surfaced and began swimming toward shore.

Ellie came over and stood next to Rema, biting her lip and fidgeting with a strand of hair.

"This will work," Rema assured her.

"Of course it will," Darmik added. He peered over the side, watching the group swim toward land. The shoreline was solid cliffs made from dark gray and black rocks, extending as far as the eye could see. Vibrant green trees lined the top. Following Neco's path, Darmik saw a channel so narrow that he had missed it when scanning the coast. The fishing village must be through there.

After a good twenty minutes, all six men entered the channel. Shadows from the towering cliffs made it impossible to see more than a dozen feet in.

"They made it," Rema said. She put her arm around Ellie, hugging her. "I didn't realize Neco was such a strong swimmer."

Ellie beamed. "I know. He has many hidden talents." She wiggled her eyebrows, and Rema laughed.

Darmik watched the shoreline for concealed threats. He didn't see a single person at the top of the cliffs; nevertheless, one could easily hide amongst the trees. All six ships had dropped anchor and were waiting. After about an hour, a small fishing vessel exited the channel.

"I hope there's more than one," Rema mumbled. "Otherwise, this is going to take forever."

Looking at the size of the boat, Darmik estimated that it could carry fifteen to twenty people. At that rate, the vessel would need to make thirteen round trips in order to get everyone to land. The small fishing boat went to one of the other warships first, just like they had planned. Darmik watched it come up alongside the ship, hooking several grapples to it, keeping the boats together, but preventing them from smashing into one another. A rope ladder was lowered over the railing and down to the small vessel. Once in place, soldiers began climbing down.

After twenty soldiers were on board, the grapples were withdrawn, and the boat moved away from the warship, heading toward the channel. Luckily, another fishing vessel, similar in size and appearance, exited the channel and headed toward the warship. Once all the soldiers were off that boat, Neco had instructions to send it with a minimal crew to the Great Bay. It was to dock at Plarek, the same port Nathenek used when he came to Greenwood Island.

Darmik suspected Barjon had men watching the ports. If so, the king would send what was left of the army there, far away from Rema's true location. The second reason for sending the warship there was to serve as a signal to Mako. Mako had rebels watching the port. Once they spotted the ship, they would alert Mako and word would go out to the rebels to amass in Werden. Darmik hoped that everyone would arrive at Werden within a fortnight. Then, as one, they would march to King's City and overthrow Barjon and Lennek.

Rema insisted on taking Darmik's father and brother alive, but if any threat were made toward her, they would be killed. Even though Barjon and Lennek were his family, he felt no love toward them, and either their deaths or capture was fine by him. All that truly mattered was ending their cruel and unjust reign, thus freeing the people of Greenwood Island.

The wrongs of Darmik's father and brother would finally be made right. Once that was done, he would be worthy of marrying Rema.

One of the fishing boats finally neared the warship Darmik was on. Men leaned out of the boat, attaching long, metal grapples to the side of the ship. Once in place, Savenek tied the rope ladder to the railing and let it unwind down the side of the ship. Neco stood below, giving the thumbs-up sign. Darmik wanted to go first, so he climbed onto the railing and over the side, his feet hitting the first rung. He smiled at the anxious look on Rema's face, and then climbed down. The wind blew hard, causing the rope to sway. Luckily, the rungs were close together, making the descent easy. When he reached the bottom, a wooden plank was extended from the boat out toward the ladder. After his feet were on the wood and he had his balance, he released the rope ladder. He turned around and made his way across the plank, jumping onto the deck of the fishing boat.

"About time!" Neco teased.

"How did getting everyone off the other ships go?"

"There were no issues. So far, everything is going according to plan."

Glancing behind him, Darmik saw Rema already

on her way down. "Is the village safe and secure?" Darmik whispered.

Neco nodded. "There is nothing to worry about."

Darmik noticed Neco had changed into fresh, dry clothing. Scanning the fishing boat, he wanted to know who was aiding them. Two older-looking men with white hair and gray beards stood near the helm of the vessel.

"They're good men," Neco said. "I've known them a long time."

Darmik suspected there was more to the story, but Rema had just planted her feet on the plank. With outstretched arms, she made her way across with ease. Ellie followed close behind.

"Move to the port side," Neco instructed them. "It's a tight fit." There were nets strewn all over the place on levers. Darmik assumed the nets were used to capture the fish.

Rema took his hand and led him closer to the railing. They were soon joined by their friends. Once everyone was on board, the grapples were removed and the boat lurched away from the warship.

"Come on," Neco instructed Darmik and Savenek. "Help me raise the main sail." Neco grabbed ahold of a thick rope, pulling it with all his might. Darmik took hold behind him, and Savenek clasped it further back. The three tugged until the rope went taut and the sail was raised. The boat continued to rock as it made its way toward the channel.

Darmik had never been on such a small vessel before. They bobbed up and down with the swell, and for the first time ever, his stomach felt as if it had dropped out of his body. Darmik feared he would vomit. Refusing to show any sign of weakness in front of Rema, he took a deep breath and headed toward the bow. He hoped the position out in front would ease his nausea.

As they neared the shoreline, the swell increased and the boat jounced up and down so violently that water sprayed him in the face.

"This is absolutely fantastic!" Rema laughed, coming to stand next to him. "Have you ever experienced something so exhilarating?" She wore an enormous smile that was contagious, and Darmik couldn't help but grin and bear the torture.

Even though the sun shined brightly in the sky, the air was chilly since the winter season had not yet ended. The boat lurched to the side as the main sail lowered and a smaller one rose in its place. The ship entered the narrow channel. Rocky cliffs towered on both sides of them, casting a shadow over the passageway. The boat slowed, and thankfully, the swell vanished. It was eerily quiet. After a hundred yards, the channel opened to a small harbor where one other boat sat docked.

"The smell is utterly atrocious," Rema whispered. "I guess it's from all the fish." She pointed to the landing where several piles sat discarded.

Although Darmik's stomach felt immensely better, he was still eager to be on solid ground. The ship pulled alongside the wooden pier and Neco jumped onto it with ease. He quickly tied the boat up and attached a board to the side of the ship.

When it was Darmik's turn to exit, he almost lost his balance because his legs were unstable. Luckily, Savenek was right behind him and he managed to steady Darmik so he didn't fall into the water. Darmik went to help Rema down the ramp, but she made it off with ease.

"Let's get everyone organized while we wait for the remaining soldiers to join us," Rema said. "So…how do we go about doing that?"

Darmik loved how she stood there with her hands on her hips, determined to accomplish her goals, but not really knowing what to do. "Would you like me to take charge?" he asked.

She nodded. There was only one problem with him taking charge—Rema's safety. He couldn't lead the platoon and watch out for her at the same time. He saw Neco out of the corner of his eye. Darmik waved, catching his friend's attention. He immediately came over. "We need to organize everyone," Darmik informed him.

"I agree," Neco replied.

Darmik glanced over at Savenek, who stood joking around with Audek and Vesha. It appeared money was exchanging hands. They were probably betting again. "Rema, if you want me to take control of this platoon while we travel to Werden, I will do it, but I'm going to place Neco in charge of your safety."

Rema nodded. "That's fine. Just find a job for

Savenek to do so he's occupied and not making mischief."

"Of course." Darmik chuckled. "Before I take command, I need to speak privately with Neco."

He watched Rema walk over and join Audek, Savenek, and Vesha. Turning to his friend, he said, "I want Ellie, and them," he nodded to Rema's group, "in her personal guard."

"I understand," Neco said. "But if you want me to watch over and protect her, I need someone to watch your back. I think you should consider Savenek."

"I can handle these men," Darmik replied.

"I know, but I'll only agree to head Rema's guard if you have Savenek with you."

"Why Savenek?"

"He's not from Emperion and he's more qualified than Audek."

They stood, staring at one another. The corners of Neco's mouth pulled up. He knew he'd backed him into a corner. "Fine," Darmik agreed, shaking his head.

He quickly got to work, organizing the platoon.

With two hundred and fifty men, he needed a scouting party in order to safely travel across the region of Adder to reach Werden unharmed. He surveyed his surroundings. There was only one wooden building at the end of the pier. There appeared to be a valley between the cliffs behind it. The area was rather exposed, and Darmik wanted to get further inland so they would be concealed among the dense vegetation.

The boat left to get another load of soldiers.

"Listen up!" Darmik shouted to the approximately seventy people standing around. "I need a scouting party. If you have this particular skill, let me know."

Several dozen raised their hands, and Darmik picked twenty men. "If you were chosen, come forward. The rest of you, wait patiently."

Darmik grabbed Neco's arm. "Assign twenty to serve as Rema's guard." Neco gave a curt nod, understanding the type of person Darmik expected to have guarding their empress.

Darmik met with his scouting party, telling them his expectations: he wanted a report every thirty minutes—no matter what, and they could organize themselves however they saw fit. Darmik scanned the ground until he found a small piece of driftwood. He wasn't sure of their precise location; but he had a general idea of where they were. Pulling out his dagger, he used it to carve a simple map of Adder and Shano. He marked the main towns to avoid, and the direction the scouting party needed to go in order to reach Werden. Once he was confident the men were ready, he sent them off to ensure the first leg of the journey was safe.

Darmik was concerned they didn't have the supplies necessary to travel so far. Luckily, the Emperion soldiers were not only trained to survive off the land, but they were used to it. Darmik appointed a squad of twenty to act as the hunting party. They were responsible for gathering enough food to feed everyone.

Darmik planned to travel during the day, and

to stop and sleep when the sun went down. He figured there would be approximately one hundred and ninety soldiers with him at any given time. The rest would be hunting or scouting, and twenty were assigned to guard Rema.

Almost all the soldiers had been transported from the warships to the harbor. Rema came up behind him, slipping her arms around his waist, hugging him.

"How are things going?" she asked.

He turned around so they were facing one another. "Excellent. We're almost ready to go."

She looked up at him with her sapphire eyes. "Before we do, I want to meet and thank those who helped us today."

Darmik wasn't keen on the idea of her interacting with the locals, but he understood her desire to do so. He looked behind her at Neco, who stood with her guard of twenty.

"Fine." Darmik kissed the top of her head. "But I'm going with you."

Neco came forward and took her arm, escorting her toward the wooden structure. Instead of going inside, they went around the shack toward the valley behind it. They climbed the small rise, all twenty of her guards in tow. At the top, it flattened out, revealing a small village, hidden from the harbor below. Two dozen wooden houses were situated in a horseshoe shape. A well was located at the end, along with a rickety-looking barn. About a dozen people of various ages milled about. Darmik came forward and stood at Rema's left side.

Neco raised his arm in greeting. "We'd like to meet with the elders. Are they available?" He held onto Rema's right arm while her guard spread out around them. The people of the village all stopped, staring. No one moved. "We mean you no harm," Neco added in a soft voice.

Darmik realized that the presence of so many strangers must be intimidating, not to mention the fact that most had blond hair and blue eyes, making it obvious they weren't from around here. "How about everyone wait just below the rise, out of sight?" he suggested. The soldiers went down the hill about twenty feet, still within earshot if called upon.

A middle-aged woman with tan skin and dark hair approached. "What do you want with us?" she asked.

"I want to thank you for your help," Rema answered in a clear, confident voice.

The woman looked Rema over. "Who are you?" she demanded.

"My father was King Revan, and my mother, Queen Kayln. I am the sole survivor." The woman took a step back, lowering her basket to the ground. "I mean you no harm," Rema continued. "I am here with an army to remove Barjon and Lennek from power. I will restore peace to the island."

The woman fell to her knees, bowing her head. Other people took notice, whispering amongst themselves. Two men came forward. One had long, white hair and a white beard. The other guy, who was much younger, had black hair and brown eyes. Both wore simple brown pants and tunics.

Neco bowed. "Thank you for your help today," he said. "It is greatly appreciated. I would like to introduce Her Majesty, Amer Rema."

Both men stared at her, not uttering a single word.

Rema stepped forward, toward them. "I am here to restore peace and prosperity to the island. I want to know how I can help you."

The younger man raised his eyebrows, skeptical of her claim. "How you can help us?" he asked. "We are the ones helping you. And you better not bring your war here."

"We will be leaving shortly, and no one will ever realize that we were here or that you helped us," Rema assured the man. "I want you to know that when I am in control of this island, you may come to me at any time for help, and I will give it."

Darmik suspected his father had no idea that this fishing village existed, and these people clearly wanted it to remain that way.

A small child ran up to Rema. "You look funny," the girl said.

Rema squatted down, coming eye level with the child. "I know," she said. "My hair and eye color are very different from yours." The little girl nodded. "But I'm from here, just like you." Rema held up her arm, revealing her tattoo of a curved stock of wheat with a sword down the center.

"You're from Jarko?" the child asked.

"I am."

The girl reached out and touched Rema's hair. "Why are you here?"

Rema smiled. "To thank these kind men for helping me and my friends."

The little girl nodded, as if she knew what was going on. "Maybe I'll see you again." She turned and skipped away.

Rema stood. "Thank you for your assistance." She nodded her head to the two men in a show of respect, turned around, and left.

Darmik hurried after her. He glanced back in time to see Neco shake hands with the older gentleman. As they went down the hill, Rema grabbed his hand, holding tightly. At first he thought it was to gain her balance; but he realized she was shaking.

"Are you well?" he whispered into her ear.

"Yes," she replied without hesitation. He squeezed her hand. "It's just that...well...I am responsible for *all* these people. It is a huge obligation."

"It is," Darmik agreed, "but one that you are perfectly capable of handling."

She squeezed his hand back.

THIRTEEN

Rema

Walking to Werden was a long, tedious journey. Rema wore the army uniform everyone else did—good, sturdy boots, long pants, and a tunic. Unfortunately, the outfit was made for sandstorms and protecting the body from heat. It did little to protect her from the cold, frigid temperatures of the island. However, it was better than traveling in a ridiculous dress.

She walked between Ellie and Vesha. Audek and Neco were in front of her, and the sixteen additional soldiers who'd been assigned as her personal guard were behind. They were asked to refrain from speaking in order to travel unnoticed. Rema understood the need for discretion; yet, there were two hundred and fifty of them on a narrow dirt road. If the king had soldiers nearby, they'd be easily spotted simply by the sheer number of the group.

Neco dropped back and squeezed between Rema and Ellie. "I just want to check in with you," he whispered.

"I'm fine," she answered. He could have just turned back and asked her. Perhaps something was bothering him? Or maybe he wanted to be near Ellie for a few moments?

He hesitated. "Audek is driving me nuts," he admitted. "The boy never shuts up." Ellie laughed, then quickly realized her error and closed her mouth. "I'm going to have him walk behind you, alone. I'll see if that keeps him quiet."

"I thought we weren't allowed to talk," Rema said. If she'd known she could speak quietly with Vesha and Ellie, she would have been doing it all along to help pass the time.

"We're not." Neco hurried forward, returning alongside Audek. He leaned his head in and spoke quietly to the man.

Audek looked around, like he was offended, and then he slowed, allowing Rema and the girls to pass by. He fell into step behind them, mumbling the entire time.

Before long, the sun began to set and the group stopped for the night. They left the dirt road and entered the forest.

"Are we sleeping on the ground?" Rema asked Neco.

"We are. Darmik is setting up a perimeter. People will be on patrol throughout the evening. There is nothing to fear."

Rema chuckled. "I'm not afraid. I've never slept under the stars before. With the exception of it being quite cold, this is turning out to be an exciting adventure."

Neco stood staring at her. He blinked several times, his face not revealing any emotion. "You and Darmik are perfect for one another." He turned and started barking out orders to her guard. Even though it was cold, Darmik refused to light any fires.

"He likes *you*," Vesha mumbled. "I thought he'd at least allow *you* to have a fire so you could be warm."

Rema laughed. "He does care for me and my safety, and that's exactly why he won't allow any fires."

"It's so cold that my feet hurt. How many days until we get there?"

"Neco thinks it will take us a little over a week at this pace," Ellie said.

The hunting group returned and started distributing food to everyone. A female soldier approached, giving Rema a handful of berries and nuts.

"Thank you." Rema took the food, sharing with Ellie and Vesha.

"I'll be back, Your Majesty, with a squirrel once it's cooked." The girl bowed and left.

"How are they cooking the squirrels if there's no fire?" Vesha asked. "Because if they're allowed to make a fire in order to cook, I'll go join them."

"Careful," Ellie teased, "you're starting to sound like Audek."

Vesha's face turned crimson, and she shoved several berries in her mouth.

Neco came over, sitting down before Rema. He

handed her a small, leather pouch. "There's not a lot, but it should be enough to tie you over until we find a water source."

Rema took a sip, and then handed the pouch to Ellie and Vesha.

After a skimpy meal of squirrel meat, Rema fell fast asleep.

The following days fell into the same routine. They were fortunate not to encounter anyone along the way. On the fifth day, Rema noticed a distinctive change in the atmosphere. The group condensed down to three wide, walking at a faster pace. Neco and Audek were on either side of her instead of Ellie and Vesha.

"What's going on?" she demanded.

"We're crossing the border from Adder to Shano, and the scouting party is late," Neco whispered.

They continued in silence; the only sound came from hundreds of boots walking on the dirt path among the forest trees.

Neco leaned down. "You do have a weapon, don't you?" he whispered in her ear.

She nodded, feeling the dagger strapped to her thigh.

Thick greenwood trees surrounded them. Birds chirped overhead, the sound echoing in the forest. The soldiers in front of her suddenly froze. Neco grabbed

Rema, pushing her back against the trunk of a nearby tree, while shielding the front of her body with his own.

Rema couldn't see around him, but she felt the presence of her guard nearby. No shouts rang out, indicating trouble. The birds still sang above. Neco moved away, and Darmik stood before her.

"What's wrong?" she asked.

"The scouting party has just returned and given their report." He took a step closer to her. "I can't be sure, but something isn't right."

"What did they say?" Rema asked.

Darmik ran his hands through his hair, a sure sign he was concerned. "There's a small city nearby, just south of us. I've passed through several times before. It's a busy town with lots of activity. It has an excellent market for leather goods. Saddles and such."

"What's the issue?" Rema asked. "Are we too close? Do we need to go off course in order to pass by unnoticed?"

He shook his head. "That's not the issue. The problem is the town of Ruven is completely deserted. The scouting party reported that not a single person was out in the streets. The windows are even boarded up."

"What does it mean?"

"I have no idea."

Savenek appeared behind Darmik. "Everything is ready."

Darmik nodded. "Savenek and I are going to investigate."

Fear shot through Rema. "Why?" she demanded. "You're in charge of everyone here. Shouldn't you send someone else?"

"Normally, that's what I'd do. Since everyone here is from Emperion, they have blond hair and blue eyes, making them stand out if seen. They are also unfamiliar with our customs."

She didn't want Darmik putting himself in danger. Discovering what happened to the town wasn't worth the risk or a priority right now. They needed to reach Werden.

She was about to use her title to overrule him when Neco stepped forward. "Excellent decision, Commander."

Rema looked from Savenek, to Neco, to Darmik. All three were well-trained soldiers. If they saw the need to investigate, she had to trust their judgment. "Very well," she said.

Darmik and Savenek turned and left. She wanted to scream, but she maintained her composure. "Who is in charge while they're gone?"

"Technically, you are always in charge. However, I am the acting commander now that Darmik and Savenek are away," Neco informed her.

She decided to focus on her people, instead of worrying about Darmik. "Are we going to remain here while they're gone?"

"I suggest we continue on course instead of sitting around. There could be undetected threats."

She agreed. Somehow standing there gave her the sensation of being watched. "Send the scouting party on up ahead, and let's get moving."

Neco gave the necessary orders, and the group continued.

Rema kept reminding herself that Darmik was a competent soldier, and she had nothing to worry about.

Her heart disagreed completely.

Fourteen

Darmik

At the edge of the forest, Darmik and Savenek hid behind a large bush, surveying the area. Darmik didn't like working this closely with Savenek. Although Savenek had proven he had the ability to take orders and listen to him, he did not fully trust the guy. They hadn't been in battle together, responsible for one another's lives. All they shared was a desire to protect Rema, and even that irritated him. He saw how Savenek still looked at her. He knew he was still in love with her. And there was nothing Darmik could do to change that.

The only reason he agreed to bring Savenek along was because Rema was safest with Neco. If something happened while Darmik was gone, he knew, without a doubt, his friend would protect her, no matter what. So Savenek would have to do.

"Smoke is coming from that chimney," Savenek observed. "The town can't be completely deserted." He stood.

"What are you doing?" Darmik demanded. "We can't just go walking in there. If someone's watching, we'll be spotted."

"I know," Savenek answered. "But we can't just sit here either. One of us needs to go and check things out. You're recognizable. That leaves me." He shrugged his shoulders and started walking toward the deserted streets.

This was not what Darmik had in mind. He planned to observe the area for a couple of hours before entering. Savenek, in his typical fashion, was acting before thinking things through. Darmik wanted to pummel him to the ground.

He watched him quickly make his way into Ruven, disappearing between the buildings. Scanning the area, Darmik didn't see any movement—nothing from the top of the structures or the forest edge. Where did all the people go? What happened here? There weren't any signs of a scuffle or attack.

After an hour with no change, Darmik saw Savenek walking along a street, exiting the other end of the town. He made his way into the forest—the furthest possible place from Darmik's position. Someone had to be watching Savenek. Darmik decided to climb one of the trees in order to get a better view of the area. He found a greenwood tree with a low branch. Grabbing on, he swung up into the tree and climbed the trunk until he saw most of the town. Still not a single person was about. He searched the forest for Savenek.

Several minutes later, he noticed him slinking between the trees, frequently glancing behind himself. Darmik climbed down, careful not to jostle the tree and shake the leaves. When Savenek neared, he nodded his head away from the town and kept moving. Darmik hurried after him. They continued in silence for a good mile.

"What's going on?" Darmik finally asked.

"No idea," Savenek answered, "but there's something scaring those people."

Darmik stopped walking. "What do you mean?"

Savenek turned around to face him. "Everyone is holed up in their homes with their windows boarded shut. I knocked on a few doors, but no one answered."

"How do you know people are inside?"

"I heard people walking around, plates hitting tables, sometimes people talking." Savenek shrugged his shoulders. "I can't help someone who doesn't want my help."

Darmik started walking again. *What could scare an entire town enough to make them to hide inside their homes?* He wasn't sure, but he had a feeling he was going to find out, whether he wanted to or not. For now, they needed to catch up with their group. Maybe he could check another town along the way to see if they were in hiding too.

The pair continued walking in silence through the woods. Darmik's stomach growled, and he wished he had a bow with him. Unsheathing his dagger, he kept his eyes alert for small animals. He spotted a rabbit munching on some grass. With a flick of his wrist, the dagger embedded into the animal.

"Next time, warn me," Savenek said, irritation clear in his voice. "I thought we were being followed."

Darmik chuckled.

"It's not funny," Savenek said.

After skinning the animal, Darmik made a small fire. They sat across from one another, keeping watch for threats. As soon as the meat finished cooking, Darmik kicked dirt on the fire, putting it out. He tore off a few pieces before passing the rabbit to Savenek.

"Can I ask you a question?" Savenek mumbled between bites.

Caught off guard, Darmik looked at him, trying to read his facial expressions and body language. Savenek's eyebrows were pulled tight, his body movements jerky.

"You can ask," he finally answered, wondering what had Savenek so irritated.

Savenek licked his fingers clean, and then dried them on his pants. "What are your intentions?" he demanded.

Darmik's eyes narrowed. "Regarding what?"

"Rema."

"That is none of your business."

"She's my sovereign," he harshly said.

Darmik couldn't help but laugh. "So now you admit she's your sovereign?" It wasn't very long ago when Savenek constantly questioned her authority.

Shaking his head, he responded, "I'd like to know if you plan to accompany her back to Emperion."

"Of course I am. I'm going to be by her side for the rest of my life."

The corner of Savenek's mouth pulled up in a half smile. "Better ask her about that."

Darmik wondered why Savenek was suddenly being so cocky. "How do you know I haven't?" he countered.

The color drained from his face. "Have you made her an offer of marriage?"

They didn't plan to announce their engagement until after Barjon and Lennek were dealt with, but Savenek needed to understand that he had no hope with Rema. "I have," Darmik admitted, "and she accepted."

Savenek blinked several times. "Oh," was all he said as his eyes became glossy.

"I'm sorry," Darmik said. "I assumed you knew we were heading in that direction."

He nodded. "I did. Hearing it is still hard. I hoped you would stay here on Greenwood Island, leading the army. I thought if you two were apart, that there'd be a chance for me." He picked up a short stick, twirling it between his fingers.

Darmik ate the last piece of meat, throwing the bone on the ground. "I assumed you would stay here on the island."

Savenek snapped the stick in half. "I'd like to be on Rema's personal guard, so I can protect her. Since she'll be returning to Emperion, I'd like to go, too."

Darmik didn't think that was a wise decision. "Hasn't Mako trained you to be a leader?" Savenek nodded. Darmik wanted to suggest that he remain here and command the army; however, that meant leaving Savenek in control of his men. He wasn't sure he liked that idea either.

"I don't inspire men the way you do," Savenek said, tossing the sticks behind him.

"Everyone at the rebel camp seemed to follow your authority."

"They did," he admitted. "But I've seen you with soldiers. Even the Emperion ones here with us, they'd follow you anywhere. I don't know how to gain that trust and respect."

"You can learn those things," Darmik said. "I can teach you." He couldn't believe he just offered to help Savenek.

"Rema inspires that same devotion, like you." He leaned forward, resting his arms on his legs.

There was one thing Darmik had to ask before considering Savenek's placement. "Knowing we plan to marry, how can you want to be around her every day? Feeling the way you do about her?"

Savenek stood, brushing the leaves and dirt off his pants. "I don't know. Sometimes she drives me crazy, and all I want to do is run far away from her. Yet, at the same time, I want to make sure no one hurts her."

Darmik understood those feelings since he

experienced them too. Looking around the area one last time, he scattered the firewood and bones, removing the footprints and any traces that someone had been there.

"Let's go," he said. "We don't have to decide anything right now. Let's just focus on usurping Barjon and Lennek. Then we can sit down with Mako and talk. Rema might already have an idea of who she wants where. And you know her, what she wants, she gets. We won't be able to talk her out of it."

Savenek chuckled. "You're right," he admitted. "She is stubborn."

A twig snapped, and Darmik froze. Someone was watching them.

Fifteen

Rema

It had been four days since Darmik and Savenek left to investigate the town, and they hadn't returned. Rema tried not thinking about it as she left the cover of the forest trees and trekked across the open field. She wanted to stay and wait for Darmik, but Neco insisted they keep moving. Traveling at a brisk pace, everyone vigilantly searched the surrounding area for potential threats. There wasn't much they could do to cover the trail two hundred and fifty soldiers left through the knee-high grass.

Neco fell in step beside her. "The scouting party just gave their update. We've entered Werden. Trell's place is just ahead."

Rema nodded, unable to utter a single word.

Ellie wrapped her arm around Rema's shoulder. "Don't worry. They'll return. I'm sure of it."

"What if something happened to them?"

"Don't," Ellie said. "Darmik's well skilled. He'll be

fine. Besides, you can't let everyone see you sulking."

All Rema wanted to do was cry. Yet, that wouldn't do her, or Darmik, any good. She would be strong for everyone else, and when she was alone, she'd allow herself to feel.

Up ahead, a large, gray, stone structure stood out among the vibrant green grass surrounding it. The massive house appeared abandoned and lifeless.

"That's Trell's home," Neco said. "Most of the scouting party has already been admitted."

"Is anyone there?" Rema asked.

"Mako, along with a large portion of the rebels."

It seemed as if the soldiers started walking a little faster, eager to be safely inside with a roof over their heads.

"I suggest a couple squads be on patrol at all times," Neco added.

Rema nodded. "I trust your judgment. Do what is necessary."

He took hold of her arm, pulling her to a stop. "Do you trust me?" Rema nodded. "Then trust me when I say Darmik will return, because he will."

She stared at Neco's intense gaze, wanting to believe him. But not a single word had been heard from Darmik. Even though he was a highly skilled soldier and an excellent plotter, if he ran into a portion of the army controlled by the king, he might be in trouble.

She voiced her biggest concern. "Do you think Barjon would hurt his own son?" Rema asked, knowing

Neco would tell her the truth.

His eyes darkened. "He would never hurt Lennek. However, Darmik is another matter entirely."

So what Neco revealed, without specifically saying, was that yes, Barjon wouldn't hesitate to hurt Darmik. Her chest tightened with concern.

Neco turned to face Trell's home, ignoring her piercing gaze. "Let's get you inside. Rain is coming."

The wind kicked up, making the tall grass around her sway, as if the field was an ocean. The clouds darkened, indicating a storm was on the horizon. By the time Rema reached the front door, a light rain started falling.

She eagerly stepped inside. A man she vaguely recognized from the rebel compound greeted her. "Welcome, Your Majesty." He bowed. "Everyone is being taken to a room and fed a hot meal."

"Thank you," she said. "What about my personal guard?"

"I will see they are taken care of and shifts are arranged," Neco informed her. "But for now," Neco held her elbow, leading her from the room, "someone wants to see you." He deviously smiled.

He took her through several dimly lit hallways before entering a sitting room decorated with tapestries depicting constellations. An enormous, stone fireplace warmed the room. Standing by the hearth, with his back to her, was a figure she recognized.

"Mako," she said. "It's good to see you."

Turning around, his warm, brown eyes met hers,

and he smiled. His gaze went to the sofa, and Rema followed his line of sight. Her aunt and uncle stood and rushed toward her. Rema threw open her arms, and the three of them embraced.

"We never thought we'd see you again!" Maya cried.

Kar took hold of Rema's face, staring at her. "My dear child, you're alive." Tears slid down his cheeks as he kissed her forehead.

Rema released her aunt and uncle. "We have much to discuss," she told them, not even knowing where to start.

"All in due time, dear," Kar said. "I suspect there are a few things you need to take care of first, since you just arrived. When you get a moment, come to our room. We can speak privately there."

Rema nodded and glanced over to the hearth where Mako and Neco spoke in hushed voices. Mako's smile dropped, and his shoulders slumped forward. Neco must have told him about Darmik and Savenek. Rema suspected Neco was worried too, but for some reason, he didn't want her to fret over the situation.

Mako noticed her watching them. "Neco has given me a brief overview of what has taken place since your kidnapping. Apparently, events have not unfolded quite as we anticipated."

"What's wrong?" Kar asked, placing his hand on Rema's shoulder as if to protect her.

"Nothing," Mako responded. "Just that our dear

Rema will not be with us much longer."

"Why not?" Kar demanded. "You said she would be restored to the throne!"

"She has been," Mako said, "to the Emperion throne. Rema is now the Empress of Emperion *and* Greenwood Island." He shook his head in disbelief, smiling. "Never in my wildest dreams did I think this would happen."

Rema was still getting used to the idea of being an empress. It sounded so strange and foreign to her.

Aunt Maya clasped Rema's hands, her face filled with concern. "Are you going to Emperion?"

Rema nodded. "I have to. They need me. I have a lot of work to do to bring peace and change for the better."

"Are you ready for this responsibility?" she asked.

Kar patted Rema on the back. "It doesn't matter if she's ready or not. Rema is the true reign heir."

Neco cleared his throat, speaking for the first time, "I'm sorry to interrupt, but I must get Her Majesty situated and taken care of."

Maya hugged Rema again. "I can't believe it."

"Me neither," Rema mumbled. After saying goodnight to her aunt and uncle, Neco showed Rema to a large bedchamber where Vesha and Ellie sat waiting for her. A fire roared in the hearth, and food was brought immediately.

After eating, Rema washed up and climbed into bed. She wasn't sure how she would manage to sleep when Darmik was out there. *Why was something always coming between them?* At least Darmik wasn't alone—he had Savenek. She fell asleep praying he would return safely to her.

The following morning, Rema woke to pouring rain outside. If Darmik was still out there, then he was stuck traveling through these treacherous conditions. Unease filled her. Something was wrong; she just knew it.

Sitting up in the canopy bed, she saw Ellie and Vesha sleeping near the hearth. Not wanting to wake them, Rema slipped out of bed and put on her clothes from yesterday. If any news of Darmik came while she was sleeping, then Mako would know. Rema slowly opened her door, careful not to disturb the girls. Standing outside her room were two soldiers from her personal guard.

"Good morning, Your Majesty," they said in unison.

"I'd like to speak with Mako."

"Of course. Follow us."

The men led her down two flights of stairs, stopping before the door to the sitting room. "We'll wait here, Your Majesty."

Taking a deep breath, Rema squared her shoulders and entered the room. Mako sat at the desk, writing. She quickly surveyed the room, but no one else was there.

Mako glanced up. "Good morning. I trust you slept well."

Rema closed the door behind her. "I did," she answered as she moved before the hearth, basking in the fire's warmth. "Now I'd like your report. How are things? Do we have a plan? Is everyone from the rebel camp here?"

"Yes, I can tell you definitely had a good night's sleep." Mako chuckled. "I will try and answer all of your questions. Everything is running smoothly. All rebels from the compound, except a few dozen, are here or on their way. I expect the remaining people to arrive in the next day or two. Everyone is eager to see you, although I have not yet explained that you are the empress now."

He stood and came next to her. "I'd like to ask you a question." Rema nodded. "How are you holding up?"

Steady rain pattered against the windows. Dark gray clouds loomed outside. Darmik was out there somewhere. Tears threatened, but she didn't want to show weakness. She squared her shoulders. "I'm fine, thank you." Darmik would advise her to be the empress she was born to be. "I'd like to address my people."

"Excellent idea. Not everyone has eaten breakfast yet, so I suggest waiting an hour. I'll let everyone know you'll speak in the hall downstairs."

"There's a level below the main floor?" Wouldn't that be underground? She had never heard of such a thing before.

"Yes," Mako replied. "There's a room filled with

your family's artifacts—priceless heirlooms. Alongside is an empty gathering hall. It should be large enough for everyone to fit comfortably."

"My family's things are there?" She wanted to see the items, to see pieces of her history. Would they make her feel connected to her family on a deeper level? She didn't know, but she was eager to find out.

"Yes, and I will show everything to you later. For now, Kar is in the stables waiting for you."

Why didn't Mako say anything sooner? Rema hurried from the room, wanting to spend some time with her uncle.

Her two guards greeted her. "Are you going to escort me everywhere today?" she asked.

"No," one of them responded. "We're your guards for the first shift. We rotate throughout the day, so who's guarding you changes, but there will always be two people while you're inside, and twenty when you step foot outside."

Rema sighed. She was never going to have a moment's peace. The men led her to a door at the east end of the house. When she stepped through the archway, she spotted Kar near a stall in the small barn, brushing a white horse.

She ran, her guards chasing after her.

Kar glanced up. "I have an old friend here who misses you." He smiled and stepped aside.

Snow snickered, greeting her with his wet nose. Rema buried her face in her horse's mane. Snow was here.

An immense sense of relief filled her.

After spending time with Kar and Snow in the stable, just like old times, Rema felt rejuvenated. She found Ellie and Vesha playing cards and asked them to accompany her back to her room.

"I need both of you to help me," Rema said, leaning against the bed.

"Of course," Ellie responded. "What do you want?"

"I'd like to address the people here." She glanced down at her army uniform. "Can you help me look like an empress?"

Ellie smiled. "I would love to."

Vesha went through Trell's closet and pulled out several tunics. Then she tore them at the seams. "I can make you something with this fabric."

Rema laughed. "I'd like to address everyone today."

"I can do it!" Vesha said. "Give me an hour and I'll have something magnificent for you."

"And while she's working on that," Ellie said, taking Rema by the shoulders and moving her in front of the mirror, "I'll do your hair." She went to a wooden box and opened it up. "Look what Trell left for you," she said, lifting a gold crown from the box. "This was your mother's." She handed it to her. "I'll arrange your hair around it."

Rema stood there, holding her mother's crown in

her hands. It was solid gold with twelve keys etched into it. Beautiful red rubies were set in each one. She'd never seen anything so striking and unique—it was perfect. Placing it atop her head, Ellie carefully braided Rema's hair, securing the crown to her.

When Ellie was done, Vesha came forward holding a simple, yet stunning dress. Rema slipped it on and looked in the mirror. The heavy, black fabric clung to her body, making her appear thin and tall. The sleeves were green, matching the color of Emperion. A red sash was tied around her waist, complimenting the rubies in her crown.

Mako told everyone she wished to speak to them. They all gathered in the large room downstairs, awaiting her. She entered, and the room fell silent. Her stomach was queasy with the idea of speaking before so many people, especially without Darmik's silent, steady support beside her. Taking a deep breath, she smiled and tried to appear confident.

Her guards helped her stand upon a table, overlooking everyone.

"Thank you all for coming here," Rema said in a loud, clear voice. "I am grateful to have you by my side." She looked into her people's eyes, wanting them to know she was sincere. "As you know, I was kidnapped and taken to Emperion. What I want to share with everyone is that while I was there, it was discovered that I am the true heir to the Emperion throne. I am Empress of Emperion and Greenwood Island." Many of the rebels whispered to one another, surprised by the news. "I want you to know that I plan to bring peace to both great kingdoms."

Cheering arose. "However," Rema said, holding up her hands, "before I can begin to help you, we must remove Barjon and Lennek. With you by my side, we can rid the island of these fiends. Justice will be served. Who's with me?"

Everyone stood, clapping and cheering. Rema smiled.

Mako accompanied Rema to a small library. "I thought you said we were going to the archives room?" There was nothing but books here.

He smiled. "Watch." Moving to one of the shelves, his hand felt along a book, jiggling it. A loud groan erupted and the bookshelf swung open, like a door.

Rema's eyes widened. "A secret passageway?" she asked, curious to see what lay beyond.

"It's not secret anymore. Trell left a letter detailing the location of the room, and who is permitted access to it."

"I'm not sure what right Trell has to the items," Rema mumbled.

"He agrees. In his letter he states that everything is yours to do with as you please."

Her heartbeat quickened. Her family's history was in there, only a few steps away.

"Follow me." They walked into a short hallway and down a flight of stone stairs, stopping at a heavy oak door. When Mako gave it a push, the door they had entered through swung shut with a bang.

"There are several torches. Wait here while I light them."

The room gradually lightened, and Rema looked around, astonished at the sight before her. The large space was divided into sections. One contained statues and artifacts, another area was filled with books, while to her right were shelves filled with boxes of various sizes. The last area was completely covered with white sheets, concealing the identity of what lay underneath them.

"The room you spoke in is on the other side of that wall," Mako said, pointing to the left.

Rema walked through the area, unsure of where to start. "Have you been in here before?" she asked.

Mako nodded. "After I read Trell's letter, I located the room. Although, I haven't investigated anything in here yet."

She went over to the boxes and pulled one down. Sliding an envelope out, she found a picture of a young man with a crown atop his head. She glanced through a few more and found similar pictures. Pushing the box back in place, Rema went to the area covered with sheets. She gently tugged on the white fabric, and it slipped off a desk covered with papers. Rema sat on the chair, observing all of the documents and maps, afraid to touch or move any of them.

"What have you found?" Mako asked.

"I'm not sure." The maps appeared to be of the various regions of the island. Some of the paperwork had names written on it, others had dates with events.

Mako pulled one sheet of paper out from under the others, and set it on top. It appeared to have the layout of a large castle. He tapped the edge, lost in thought. "I'd like to study this one in greater detail."

"Here," she said, offering him the chair. He sank down on the seat, staring at the paper.

Rema went over to the statues, observing their intricate detail. One was of a young girl wearing a crown. Engraved on the girl's outstretched hands was a key. Rema took off her necklace and held it next to a statue—the keys were identical.

The room suddenly became overwhelming. So much of her past was hidden in here. She headed toward the door, needing some fresh air. Pushing on the knob, it refused to budge.

"I didn't know there was another door," Mako announced, coming up behind her. "Step aside and let me try. It's probably just stuck from lack of use." He turned the latch and banged on it. It flew open, revealing a solid black room. Mako grabbed one of the lit torches and went inside. He whistled in awe.

Rema stepped into the room. All the walls were covered with weapons. Swords, different sizes of knives, daggers, longbows, crossbows, arrows, and spears. There were hundreds and hundreds of weapons—enough to equip a small army. *How long had Trell been planning this?*

Sixteen

Darmik

Darmik had no idea if the sound of a twig snapping was from an animal or a person, but they couldn't afford to stand there waiting to find out. He grabbed Savenek's arm and pointed up. Savenek nodded. Darmik clasped his hands together and crouched down so Savenek could use it to hoist himself up to the lowest branch. Once he took hold, he climbed higher until he disappeared among the leaves.

A nearby tree had several broken limbs protruding from the trunk. Darmik grabbed one and pulled himself up. Then he clasped onto another, lifting himself higher on the trunk. He was about to take hold of another branch when he heard the sound of leaves crunching below. He froze, trying to peer down without moving.

Two soldiers wearing the King's Army uniform crept past. "Are you sure you heard something?" one asked.

"I thought I heard talking coming from this direction, but I must have been mistaken," the other replied.

"Let's return to the rest of the squad."

Darmik didn't hear any more of their conversation. Just to be certain the soldiers were gone, he remained in the tree, unmoving, for several minutes. When his arms and legs could no longer hold the position, he lowered himself to the ground. Savenek joined him a moment later. Darmik nodded in the direction of the soldiers, and the two of them silently went the same way through the forest. Darmik searched the ground, easily tracking the two men.

He followed the trail as it circled dangerously close to the area where Darmik and Savenek had been hidden in the trees, and then it veered back toward the town. Darmik lost all traces of the men when he reached a dirt path. The road had several different footprints, and he guessed at least twenty had recently passed through there.

The two men were probably part of a squad of soldiers who were either scouting ahead, or sent to reconnoiter when with they heard Darmik and Savenek talking. He looked to Savenek, who nodded in agreement—they needed to follow the soldiers to investigate. Perhaps they would shed some light on what was going on in the deserted town.

Darmik followed the dirt road in the direction of the footprints—heading away from the village.

After a short distance, he heard the sound of boots crunching on dirt. He moved to signal Savenek to leave the path so they could get ahead of the soldiers, but Savenek didn't know the signals of the King's Army. They would have to stay together then, instead of splitting up. This endeavor would have been much easier with Neco.

Darmik silently left the path and headed deeper into the forest, Savenek following close behind. When he was a good fifty feet from the path, he preceded parallel to it, sprinting as fast as he could between the trees. Once he estimated he was far enough ahead of the soldiers, he slowed his pace and cautiously made his way back toward the road. Thankfully, Savenek had enough skill to remain quiet as well. When the path was in view, Darmik pointed up, and Savenek nodded in understanding. Darmik found a tree with a low enough branch to grab onto. He hoisted himself up the trunk, climbing until he found a solid branch to watch from. Savenek found a nearby tree and did the same.

After a few moments, the squad of soldiers neared. They walked two wide and passed without speaking. Darmik recognized several of the faces. This was a squad from the Third Company. He wondered where they were heading because this particular company did not normally patrol this area. Once the squad was far enough away, Darmik climbed down, and Savenek joined him.

"I want to follow them," Darmik said.

"Where does this road lead to?"

"I'm not sure. I don't know of any towns north of here."

He recalled docking at the fishing village he had

been unaware of until only a few days ago. Feasibly, there could be others like that one.

"Then let's get moving," Savenek said, "because they're obviously going somewhere."

They headed away from the road about twenty feet and then walked parallel to the trail, remaining silent so the soldiers wouldn't overhear them. Darmik thought back to when the squad passed by. They hadn't been carrying any supplies, so they must be arriving at their destination soon.

After traveling about eight miles, the sun began to set. Darmik expected them to stop for the night, but the soldiers gave no indication of doing so. Instead, several of the soldiers gathered large sticks, wrapping green ferns around the tops and lighting them on fire. Once the torches were lit, the soldiers continued walking on the road. Darmik couldn't light a torch or he'd be seen, and it was too dangerous to follow the squad in the dark. As much as he hated the idea of stopping, he and Savenek had to for their own safety.

He ran his hands through his hair, trying to figure out what was going on.

"Wise decision," Savenek whispered.

Darmik looked at him. "Something's wrong. I can feel it."

"I'm sure you're right, but we need to focus on getting back to Rema. When we reach Werden, we can talk with Mako. Perhaps he knows what's been going on since we left."

"I agree—it's a better idea than us traipsing around out here in the pitch black forest. Let's find a place to rest for the night. I'll take the first watch."

They veered further off course than Darmik realized. It took them an entire day just to backtrack enough to head in the right direction toward Werden. He estimated they were now two days behind Rema. He was eager to reach Trell's home to ensure she made it safely. Thankfully, with Neco watching over her, there was little to worry about.

Soaking wet from the torrential downpour, Darmik and Savenek climbed the last rise and descended into the valley where Trell's house was located. Darmik's body shook from being so cold. He could barely feel his hands. The Emperion uniform he wore was ill suited to Greenwood Island's winter conditions. About a mile from the house, a group of Emperion soldiers stopped them. Once the soldiers realized it was their commander, they let him and Savenek pass. Darmik was glad the Emperions were there—that meant Rema was safely inside. He was also thankful a patrol had been set up.

When he neared the front door, it flew open and Rema stormed out, Vesha and Ellie close behind her.

"Where have you been?" she demanded, standing in the pouring rain. "I have been worried sick about you." She pointed at him. The rain drenched her hair and clothes, but she gave no indication it bothered her.

He opened his arms, and Rema rushed into them, kissing his cheek.

"I thought something happened to you," she said, holding on tight. He could feel the warmth of her body against his. "You're not hurt, are you?"

Before Darmik could respond, Savenek said, "No, we're fine. Thanks for your concern." He pushed by them and went inside.

Rema ignored him. "I want a full report." He loved it when she fell into her role as empress and took control. "Why are you looking at me that way?" she asked.

There were too many people around, watching, so he just shook his head, giving her a devilish grin. Her cheeks turned a rosy shade of red.

"Let's go inside," he said. "I'm freezing."

After changing into dry clothes, Darmik made his way to the sitting room. He found Savenek and Mako talking in front of the fireplace while Rema sat on the sofa next to Neco. Darmik stepped into the room, and Neco rushed over.

"It's good to see you." Neco patted him on the shoulder. "I'm not used to you being on a mission without me."

"It was a different experience," he admitted. "I want to thank you for bringing Rema here safely."

Mako cleared his throat. "I'd like to thank you for doing the impossible and saving Rema from an Emperion assassin." He came over and shook hands with Darmik. "I never thought I'd say this, but I'm glad to see you."

Darmik chuckled, "Likewise."

Rema stood. "I'd like to know what you and Savenek discovered."

Darmik quickly told them what happened in the town. He also explained how they ran into the squad of soldiers and followed them. Mako suggested a group be sent to investigate. Savenek offered to organize two dozen soldiers and show them where to go. Darmik agreed, but insisted Savenek remain at the house; there was a lot of planning to do, and Savenek was a captain of the rebels. He was needed here to help organize. After Savenek left the room to get to work, Rema took hold of Darmik's hand, pulling him to the sofa.

Mako and Neco sat on the sofa opposite them.

"I'm surprised everyone fits inside Trell's home," Darmik commented. The house was quite large; however, there was no way it could hold more than five hundred people. Where was everyone?

Mako sighed, leaning back on the sofa. "Not all my men are here. There are two-hundred fifty on patrol at any given time, and another ten groups of twenty from here to King's City are spread out, watching. I don't want to be taken by surprise. That leaves approximately six hundred people here, in the house. I also have a few hundred scattered throughout the kingdom. I didn't want to consolidate all my resources and have something happen that I'm unaware of."

"And my men?" Darmik asked. He'd sent his trusted soldier, Traco, here to Werden to organize the soldiers loyal to him from the King's Army.

Mako shook his head. "There were only a couple of squads when we arrived."

That didn't make any sense. His army consisted of over ten thousand men. He knew that some would have a hard time deciding whether to remain loyal to King Barjon, or side with Darmik, but he assumed most would pledge allegiance to him, and not his father. He dropped his head into his hands. How could they defeat Barjon and Lennek with less than a thousand men?

"Where's Traco?" Darmik asked.

"He's here," Neco said. "I've spoken to him. Only a couple of hundred men from the Fifth Company arrived. That's all."

"If Darmik's men aren't here, where are they?" Rema asked.

Mako shook his head.

"What about the deserted town?" Darmik asked. "Have you heard of any other cities or villages with people hiding indoors?"

"I haven't," Mako responded. "But I didn't receive any reports during the last week either."

"What are you indicating?" Was there nothing to report? Or had something happened to Mako's men that prevented them from returning?

"That something is amiss," Mako admitted.

Hopefully, the two dozen men being sent to investigate those soldiers would uncover something.

In order to build morale, Darmik suggested they have a celebration in the large, underground room Mako referred to as the gathering hall. Even though only a couple of hundred men had arrived from the King's Army, Darmik still wanted to unify them with the rebels and the Emperions.

Looking in the mirror, he adjusted his tunic. This was an important event, and he wanted to look like a respectable soldier who knew what he was doing. Although he didn't recognize any members from the Emperion Army, he was sure most had heard of him as the *soft prince* who came to train in Emperion, and on the mainland, his reputation was one of little authority.

It was strange to no longer be a prince or commander of his own army. He was supposed to be in charge of Rema's royal guard, but for the time being, he was serving as commander alongside Mako. Most valued his opinion and he had an esteemed position there; yet, Darmik found it difficult to give up the army he had worked so hard to put together and build.

He ran his hands through his hair, pushing it away from his face. He was finally ready for the celebration.

Since there wasn't enough room for everyone in Trell's home, Mako assigned four to five people per bedchamber. Darmik shared a space with Neco, Savenek, and Audek, who all stood at the door waiting for him.

"I'm ready," Darmik mumbled.

Neco smiled and opened the door.

"Are you sure you're ready?" Audek said. "Because we can all wait here for you to run your hands through your hair and adjust your tunic a few more times. It's not like we have anything better to do than to stand here watching you."

Darmik grabbed him by the back of the neck as they headed down the hallway. "I am not one to joke with," he said, his tone harsh. They came to the railing overlooking the floor below. Darmik released Audek's neck and swiftly grabbed his legs, hanging him over the side, head down.

Audek screamed. "I was only joking! You can take as long as you like to get ready! Please don't drop me!"

Darmik lowered him a bit. "You need to learn to keep your mouth shut."

"I'll try, I swear. I won't talk so much. Really, I promise. I think I can do that."

Neco laughed. Darmik worked to keep his face blank as he brought Audek back onto solid ground. Audek's face was red from hanging upside down.

"I'm truly sorry, sir—I..." He stopped, at a loss for words.

Darmik leaned in. "You're not the only one who

knows how to make a joke." He started laughing, slapping
Audek on the back.

"What?" Audek asked, dumbfounded.

Darmik wrapped his arm around his shoulders.
"How does it feel to be on the receiving end for a change?"

"You really had me there," Audek replied, relief
washing over his face. The four friends laughed. It was
wonderful to be joking with one another instead of
worrying about the upcoming battle.

A group of Emperion soldiers exited the room
near them.

"Are you heading down to the celebration?" Darmik
asked. They nodded, but didn't speak. All five stood with
stiff, awkward postures, appearing uncomfortable. "Walk
with us," Darmik said. "We're heading the same way."
The Emperions exchanged looks with one another, and
then joined Darmik's group.

As they descended the stairs, one Emperion said,
"It is rather cold here. It's a welcome change."

After some more idle talk, they reached the
gathering hall. Darmik couldn't believe the transformation
that had taken place in a few short hours. Tables had
been brought in and were lined with food and drinks. A
group of rebels stood in the corner of the room, singing a
fast-beat tune while dozens of couples danced.

Ellie ran over and grabbed Neco's hand. "If you
don't mind," she said to Darmik, "I need some time with
my man." The two of them melted into the crowd of
dancers.

He searched for Rema, but she was nowhere to be seen. Vesha headed in their direction. She asked Savenek if he wanted to dance, but he gracefully declined.

"Do you know where Rema is?" Darmik asked her.

"She's with Mako. Two Emperion soldiers are guarding her tonight." She turned to face Audek. "Would you like to dance with me?"

He rubbed his hands together. "I would love to." The two of them joined the others dancing.

"Care for a drink?" Savenek asked. Darmik nodded. He could use a cup of ale to calm his nerves. Savenek returned a few minutes later, carrying two pewter mugs. He handed one to Darmik. They clanked them together. "To Rema," Savenek said.

"To Rema!" Darmik took a drink.

"The way I see it," Savenek said, "if we could make it to Emperion, rescue Rema, and safely return… overthrowing Barjon and Lennek should be easy." He took a sip.

Darmik couldn't believe he stood there conversing with Savenek over drinks. He glanced sideways at him, "Nothing with my father is ever easy."

"I'm surprised you don't have any qualms about killing your own flesh and blood."

It was Savenek's lack of tact that bothered him. Like right now, he wanted to smack him. Instead, Darmik finished his drink. "King Barjon has never treated me well. Phellek was more of a father figure than Barjon. As for Lennek, well, we've never been close." He recalled all the times Lennek had gotten him in trouble, lied, or even whipped him. No, their relationship was not a normal one, and he had no idea why. Until Rema, he didn't feel loved by anyone. The music stopped, and all heads turned toward the entrance. Mako stood there, holding Rema's arm. She wore a simple dress, but atop her head was the Greenwood Island crown. She looked absolutely stunning.

"Her Majesty, Amer Rema of Greenwood Island and Emperion," Mako said. Everyone bowed their heads, and Rema entered the room with a graceful smile, walking straight to Darmik.

"That's quite the title," he said.

She laughed. "I know. I can't make someone say all that every time I enter a room."

The group of singers started a fast-beat tune that Darmik didn't recognize. People all around them began dancing. Savenek said he needed to speak with Mako, and he left the two of them alone.

"Will you do me the honor?" Darmik asked, offering Rema his arm.

She took it, and they moved closer to the singers. "I can't believe we're all here."

"I know," he responded, squeezing her hand. Darmik swung her around so she faced him. He glanced to the couple next to them, who appeared to be doing a basic four-step dance. He smiled. The last time they danced together, she was engaged to Lennek; now, here they were, and she was all his. "Ready?"

She nodded.

He lifted his hands, palms out, facing Rema. She placed her hands against his. Together, they raised their arms up and out. They stepped to the side and slowly turned around. Facing one another again, Darmik stomped his feet to the beat of the music, Rema mirroring him step for step. The music sped up, and Darmik moved his feet faster and faster, keeping to the rhythm.

Rema lifted her skirt up a bit, allowing her feet to dance uninhibited. She tossed her head back, laughing. The song ended, and everyone clapped and cheered. The group started singing another fast-beat tune.

Darmik slipped his arm around Rema's waist, picking her up and spinning her around. When her feet touched the ground, everyone clapped four times, and then stomped their feet four times. Sweat covered his brow, but he dare not slow down.

Finally, the musicians decided to take a break and a woman replaced them, singing a slow tune. Darmik pulled Rema tight against his chest. He held her firmly, tucking her head under his chin. Her crown poked his skin, but he didn't care. It felt too good to have her so close. Her arms wrapped around his waist, hugging him. He wished they could stay like this forever.

Glancing over, he saw Neco and Ellie in each other's arms, slowly moving to the music. Vesha and Audek also danced together, although they held one another at arm's length. It appeared Audek was doing most of the talking. Maya and Kar stood off to the side, intently, but proudly, watching Rema.

Darmik had been so wrapped up in enjoying his time with Rema that he'd failed to see the obvious until now. While most people were dancing and having a good time, they were separated into three groups: the rebels, the Emperion soldiers, and the members from the King's Army. Observing each group, it was easy to tell them apart. The Emperion people all had blond hair and fair skin, while everyone else had dark hair, eyes, and skin. Darmik's soldiers seemed hesitant of the rebels, and the rebels distrustful of them. These three groups would never be able to fight in battle together if they couldn't even mingle with one another.

"What are you thinking?" Rema asked.

"I'm wondering what I can do to unify everyone."

She stared into his eyes. "I think that's a job for the both of us."

"Do you have an idea?"

"Yes," she said, "I do. I look Emperion, but am from Greenwood Island. I think I should start to bridge the gap between the two. But you, my dear Darmik, can help merge your soldiers with everyone else. They need to know they can trust the rebels and foreigners."

He kissed her nose. "I have one suggestion for you."

She glanced up at him. "Yes?"

"Emperions enjoy strong ale. We always celebrated with a drink."

"So you're saying to offer them wine?"

Darmik smiled. "No, I'm not. You're the empress. You *suggest* they have a drink. Then make a toast. It's simply customary."

"Oh, right. Got it." She squared her shoulders and headed toward the Emperions, her guards close behind.

Darmik went over to his soldiers from the King's Army. Since he forbade women from entering, and there were only men, none of them were dancing. Instead, they sat around talking and laughing with one another near the food tables.

When Darmik approached, they all lifted their cups in salute. He sat down among them.

One nudged his shoulder. "So, you and the new empress, eh?" Several laughed.

He waved them off, not wanting to talk about her with other people. "Why aren't more of you here?" He took a sip of the cider and waited for someone to respond.

"We're wondering if word didn't reach the other companies," a soldier replied.

Darmik had wondered the same thing. When he spoke to Traco earlier, his man told him he sent messages to all ten companies. He decided not to push the matter right now. His objective was to unify everyone, not question the loyalty of his army. "Why are you all over here? The Emperions won't bite."

"They look and talk funny," someone answered.

"Did you forget that I was born in Emperion and was trained there?"

"But you don't look or talk like them."

"No, only the lower class has blond hair. The royalty have dark hair and eyes, like mine."

"Then why is the empress blonde?"

Darmik sighed. "Prince Nero fell in love with a commoner. When the emperor forbade the marriage, Nero came here with the girl—who had blonde hair and blue eyes. Rema is their descendent. And let's not forget, Nero brought other Emperions here. A lot were upper-class citizens with brown hair. So, a lot of you are likely descended from them. We are tied to the empire."

Neco came over and joined them. "I've been to Emperion," he said. "Let me tell you, we're a lot alike. They, too, suffer from a cruel leader who rules with an iron fist. Her Majesty is going to change all that. But in order for her to do so, we need to help her by removing Barjon and Lennek." He finished off his drink.

Darmik stood. "We have to be able to work together and trust one another." He glanced over at Rema, who spoke with the Emperion people. "Let's go toast our new empress." He walked toward her across the room, not looking back to see if his men followed him.

"Thank you so much for your suggestions," Rema said. "I appreciate it." The Emperions she talked to smiled kindly at her. "When we return to the mainland, I will be forming a committee of soldiers to help restructure the army. You are all welcome to join."

"Hello," Darmik said, interrupting her. He didn't want her making too many promises, especially ones regarding the army. Soldiers were used to following orders and needed the hierarchy of command. "I'd like to make a toast." He went over to the singers and asked them to wait before starting another song. Grabbing a chair, he stood on it and whistled, getting everyone's attention.

"Thank you all for coming tonight to celebrate with our beloved Empress Amer Rema!" Cheering rang throughout the room. Darmik raised his cup. "I'd like to make a toast. May our conquest be swift, the punishment just, and victory sweet!"

"Here, here!" people yelled.

Darmik took a sip of his drink, everyone else doing the same.

The door to the gathering hall burst open, and a servant rushed in. "Commander Mako!" she shouted. "Someone is here to see you. It's urgent." Mako hurried forward and left with her.

Darmik jumped off the chair and took Rema's hand. "Something's wrong," he said. "Let's go."

They dashed from the room, Neco and Savenek right behind them.

"Wait," Rema said, coming to a halt. "Someone needs to stay behind and make sure people remain calm. I don't want anyone to panic unnecessarily."

Of course, she was correct, but Darmik really wanted to stay with her and discover what was going on.

"I'll stay," Neco offered.

"As will I," Savenek said.

"Excellent," Rema replied. "Please make sure

people continue to sing and dance. Darmik will inform you of the situation as soon as possible." She spun around and hurried down the corridor.

When they reached the main floor, Darmik heard voices coming from near the entrance. He rushed forward and saw a man standing by the door, dripping wet. Mako gave the servant orders for blankets and food.

"He has hundreds of them," the man said. "Hundreds."

"What's going on?" Rema demanded.

"Everyone to the sitting room," Mako said, ushering them down the corridor. "Quickly now."

Once inside the room, Mako shut the door. "This is Parek, one of my scouts."

Parek removed his wet cape and went before the hearth. "I've been traveling for almost two days straight to reach you," he said, rubbing his hands together and holding them near the fire.

"What news do you have?" Mako asked.

There was a knock on the door, and a servant entered carrying a tray of food. She set it down, and then excused herself.

"I infiltrated the King's Army and discovered what's going on," Parek said, his face grim. "Lennek has control of the army."

"Impossible," Darmik said. "There's no way my men would willingly follow him." Even though he renounced his position as prince and commander, he expected his men to follow him. He didn't think they supported a corrupt crown.

"They're not doing so willingly," Parek revealed, shaking his head.

"I don't understand what's going on," Rema said.

"Barjon and Lennek have kidnapped hundreds of the soldiers' children."

"What?" Rema yelled, jumping off the sofa and pacing the room. "He kidnapped children? He's using them to control the army!" She balled her hands into fists.

Darmik had always known his father and brother were ruthless, but this was excessive, even for them.

"Yes," Parek answered. "Lennek claims that once Rema and Darmik are dead, the children will be released." He rubbed his face. "There's more," he said. "For each person who defects and joins Darmik, a child is killed."

That accounted for the lack of men here from the King's Army. The few that had managed to come join him must have done so before Lennek implemented his demented plan.

"Where are the kids being held?" Darmik asked. They had to be in a secure location, but he couldn't imagine the army guarding them since the children belonged to their fellow soldiers.

"No one knows. They haven't been seen."

"We'll just have to defeat Barjon and Lennek with the men we have," Rema said, seething with rage.

"I'm not sure we're fully equipped to go up against ten thousand soldiers," Darmik admitted. "I intended to have my men on our side. Now I'll have to fight them."

He didn't think he could kill people he'd trained.

"We have weapons here," Rema said. "We will succeed." She stared into Darmik's eyes, a fierce determination taking over. "We will." He wanted to believe her, but he'd been in battle before, and he knew what was ahead of them.

"Is there anything else, Parek?" Mako asked.

"Yes. Barjon has the army out searching for the rebels."

Darmik rubbed his face. This location was no longer secure.

"I suggest we organize and leave as soon as possible—before Barjon discovers we're here," Mako suggested.

"I agree," Darmik said.

Rema nodded her head. "Very well. Prepare for battle."

Seventeen

Rema

After receiving the news from the scout, Rema climbed into bed, exhausted. How was she supposed to be responsible for all the people here? For the entire island? For Emperion? She couldn't do this. People's lives were at stake, and it was up to her to save them.

How could Barjon and Lennek steal the army's children? Those poor kids—taken away from their parents and locked up, not knowing when and if they'd be released. The only option Rema had was to quietly lead her army to King's City, and defeat Barjon and Lennek before the King's Army was raised to fight against them. Then the soldiers could have their children back.

She tossed and turned, unable to relax. Ellie and Vesha each breathed heavily, indicating they were asleep. Throwing her blankets off, Rema slid out of bed and padded across the room to the window. The stars shone brightly overhead. Grabbing her robe, she left the room, quietly shutting the door behind her. Two Emperion guards stood in the corridor.

"Is something the matter?" one asked in his thick accent.

"I can't sleep," she answered, "I want to go outside to see the stars."

"We have orders to keep you inside the premises," he said, "for your own safety."

"I understand. What about the roof? Am I allowed to go up there?" She felt silly asking if she could or could not do something, since she was the empress and technically in charge of everyone. However, she knew Darmik and Neco set parameters with her guards for her own safety, and she would respect them.

The guards looked at each another. One shrugged his shoulders and replied, "We don't see why not."

Rema had no idea if she could even get to the roof, but it was worth a try. She went up the stairs to the top floor, and then searched the hallways. She finally saw what she was looking for—an iron door. She shoved it open and sure enough, there was a ladder. Climbing up, Rema found herself on the top of the castle. She pulled her robe tight and went to the edge, looking out upon the land before her. Breathing in the fresh air, she stared at the stars and thought about the task ahead of her.

This was *her* island. These were *her* people. It was *her* duty to make things right and help everyone live peacefully.

Someone cleared his throat and she spun around,

coming face to face with Savenek. "What are you doing here?" she asked. She waved to her guards, indicating she would speak with him. They melted into the background, out of sight.

"I couldn't sleep," he said, his voice soft. "I was pacing in the corridor when I caught a glimpse of you going upstairs. It didn't take long to figure out where you went." He shrugged his shoulders.

Rema turned around and leaned against the half-wall, gazing back at the stars. Savenek came to stand next to her.

"Have you considered staying behind?" he asked.

She'd wondered when someone would make a suggestion such as this.

"You won't consider it, will you?"

Rema shook her head.

Savenek sighed. They stood side by side in silence. "After we get rid of Barjon and Lennek, are you going to Emperion?" he asked.

"Yes," she replied. "They need me."

"We need you here, too."

"I know," she said. It wasn't that she necessarily wanted to go to Emperion, but she had to. If she didn't return, someone else would steal the throne and they could be even worse than Hamen. It was her responsibility to bring peace and stability to Emperion. She hoped to leave Mako on Greenwood Island to see a smooth transition and to act on her behalf.

"I need you here," Savenek whispered.

Rema peered over at him. He stared into the night sky, not looking at her. She wondered why he revealed such a thing. "I've agreed to marry Darmik."

He nodded, like he already knew. "I'd like to accompany you, to be a member of your royal guard, if you'll have me."

She wasn't sure that was the best of ideas, especially if he still had feelings for her. In addition, Savenek was reckless and unpredictable; yet, she trusted him. "I would be honored," she answered, not wanting to turn him down again. "But you have to know, my heart belongs to Darmik. It always will."

"I know."

She reached over and placed her hand on Savenek's cheek. "Thank you for your friendship and loyalty." His eyes softened. Rema hurried and walked away.

Rema woke to a flurry of activity. People had already started assembling outside. She quickly dressed while Ellie braided her hair. When the three girls were ready, they headed downstairs together. People ran around, some carrying armfuls of weapons, others bags of food.

Maya and Kar rushed over to her. "You're not going with them, are you?" Maya demanded.

Rema sighed. "Of course I am," she said. "It's my army, after all. I can't send them to do my bidding without me."

"Yes, you certainly can," Maya said, crossing her arms.

"Your aunt is correct," Kar added. "Now that you're in charge, you can send your army and servants to do jobs for you."

"I know I can," Rema replied. "But just because I can, doesn't mean I should."

"I'm not sure if I should be proud of you," Kar said, "or slap you across the head to knock some sense into you."

Rema laughed. "I'll take the first option."

Mako came over. "I want everyone who's coming, outside," he said.

"Very well," Maya mumbled. "If you're going along, so are we."

Rema stood, staring at her aunt and uncle. They were too old to partake in such a journey. However, she always despised when someone told her what to do. Therefore, she would to allow them to make their own choices.

"Are you reconsidering?" Maya asked, a smug look across her face.

"Absolutely not," Rema replied. "We should all head outside, since we're all going."

Kar chuckled. "That's my girl."

Squinting in the bright sunlight, Rema saw that Darmik had everyone organized into smaller groups. He walked around, giving instructions to what she assumed were the squad leaders. Someone came over and ushered

Maya and Kar to one of the groups.

"I've been meaning to talk to you about the command situation," Mako said, recapturing her attention.

"What do you mean?"

"Well, exactly who is the commander of the army? Me? Darmik? You need to make it clear."

Rema intended to have Darmik head her royal guard, but seeing him in charge right now, made her realize that he had to be commander of the army. Wanting him to be on her royal guard was a selfish request on her part, and she should never have asked it of him.

"Darmik is the commander of my entire army, both here and in Emperion."

Mako nodded. "Very well. And who is in charge of your personal safety?"

"I will speak with Darmik on the matter." Her inclination was to choose Neco as the permanent head of her royal guard; however, Darmik might need him more.

As if sensing her, Darmik glanced up and she waved him over. "I am officially appointing you as commander of my entire army."

His eyes widened. "As you wish."

"As commander, who would you suggest head my royal guard?"

"Neco," he answered without hesitation.

"I think you may need Neco by your side," she countered.

He rubbed his chin, lost in thought. "I agree. If

I'm to head the entire army, then I want someone I trust."

"So that leaves Mako, Audek, and Savenek," Rema mused.

Mako cleared his throat. "I would be honored to hold the position. However, I would like to stay here on Greenwood Island when this is over."

"I understand," Rema answered. "And I would like you here, protecting my interests."

"I want Savenek in charge," Darmik said, surprising her. She didn't think he cared for Savenek. "He will have your safety as his priority," he explained.

"I will ask if he'll take the position." Mako nodded and left.

Rema and Darmik stood alone. "I didn't think you'd choose him, giving his feelings toward me."

"That is precisely why I selected him." He kissed her on the forehead.

"I'd like to address the people before we go," Rema said.

"Of course."

Within five minutes, Darmik had everyone's attention. Rema stood on the steps by the front door of Trell's house, Darmik at her side. She felt silly wearing the standard army uniform—pants and a tunic—since she also donned her crown. The weight of it atop her head reminded her of the responsibility she bore to these people.

"Thank you all for being here," she said in a loud, clear voice. "Today, we begin our trek to King's

City. Leading my army is Commander Darmik. He will be appointing temporary positions of captains and lieutenants for our mission. We have but one goal—to quickly and efficiently storm into the castle and either capture or kill Barjon and Lennek, thus ending their tyranny." Cheering and applause rang through the air. "Let's move out!" Darmik descended the stairs and began shouting out orders to his men.

Savenek came up to her. "Thank you for the honor of allowing me to protect you. I swear, on my life, to serve you until the day I die." He knelt before her.

Rema touched his shoulder. "Thank you for your loyalty."

Mako approached. "Your horse is ready."

"You want me to ride Snow?" she asked. Mako nodded. "Is anyone else on horseback?"

"No," he replied. "There aren't enough for everyone."

"Then I'll walk with my people."

Savenek rolled his eyes. "I forgot how difficult you could be."

They traveled all morning before stopping for a quick meal, and then continuing. Word came from one of the scouting units that the small village town of Vara was deserted.

"Darmik has decided to pass through in case anyone needs our help," Savenek informed her. "But he doesn't want you sitting outside the town watching. He thinks you'd be too vulnerable. So we're going to be somewhere in the middle of the army as we enter the town."

Word came down the line for everyone to prepare for battle. Savenek unsheathed his sword. The men assigned as her guard carried either a sword or a bow. Rema removed her crown and hid it in one of the soldier's sacks, so she wouldn't stand out among them.

The town came into view. It appeared perfectly normal—no buildings destroyed and no signs of a battle or struggle. There also weren't any people about, no smoke rose from chimneys, and no dogs or animals roamed around. Rema removed her dagger, ready in case danger presented itself.

"If a skirmish should arise," Savenek whispered in her ear, "stay at my side—no matter what." Rema nodded. "No," he said, "I want you to promise me."

"Fine," Rema said, "I'll stay with you. I give you my word."

The first section of the army reached the edge of the town. Rema tried to find Darmik among them.

"Let him do his job," Savenek said. "If you're worrying about him, and he's worrying about you, someone's going to get hurt. Understand?"

"I do," Rema said. "But if you keep me better informed, then there will be no need to worry." One of her guards snickered, and Savenek glared at him.

The first group of soldiers entered the town. The

rest of the army waited for the signal to attack or retreat. No one uttered a single word. Rema held her breath, her heart pounding.

A soldier ran back, stopping before Rema. "Commander Darmik requests your presence."

"What's going on?" Savenek demanded.

"I'm not at liberty to say."

The rest of the army quickly left formation and started to circle the town. Savenek and her guard surrounded her as she made her way toward the small city. At the village edge, she paused, listening. No signs of distress or indications of a scuffle.

"Let's go," she whispered. They entered the town of Vara. Small, two-story structures stood on either side of the dirt road. "Where did all the people go?" she mumbled.

"They could be hiding inside," Savenek said. "Possibly watching us." He looked at the windows of the buildings.

An eerie sensation came over Rema. She started walking faster, wanting to find Darmik. She spotted him up ahead standing with a squad of soldiers, who surrounded something. As she got closer, she realized they had a dozen men dressed in the King's Army uniform on their knees, hands on their heads.

Savenek's eyes darted to the nearby buildings. "Stay close."

Darmik turned to face her. "Your Majesty," he bowed. "We encountered these men who claim to be stationed here. We apprehended them with ease, and with your permission, I'd like to interrogate them."

She stared into Darmik's intense gaze. He nodded ever so slightly. "Find out why they're here and where all the people have gone. Use whatever means necessary."

"Of course, Your Majesty."

"I'd like to stay," Rema added.

Darmik froze. "You want to witness the interrogation?" he asked.

"Yes," she responded. He scrunched his forehead, which was an unusual gesture for him since he normally maintained a neutral expression. He had to be weighing his desire to shield her from harm and anything unpleasant with her outranking him.

He nodded curtly and turned to face his men. Neco stood above one of the prisoners, pointing a sword toward the man's chest. Rema expected to see him near Darmik; however, she did not expect to see Mako and Kar there. Both of them stood near the prisoners, also with their swords drawn.

"Bring him here," Darmik said, indicating the captive on the end.

Neco grabbed the man's collar and yanked him forward. He threw the man to the ground, stepping on his neck, forcing him to stay down.

"Are you the only soldiers here?" Darmik demanded.

"Yes," the prisoner croaked.

Rema wondered if he was telling the truth. There

were a dozen captives here. A squad usually consisted of twenty individuals.

Darmik knelt down, close to the man's head. "Pratok, we've known each other for quite some time."

Shock rolled through Rema. Darmik knew this man? Of course he did, he was from his army. It must be rather difficult to interrogate someone he knew. She squeezed her hands together, trying to remain calm and in control.

"We have," Pratok said, pursing his lips.

"So you know I can tell when you're lying, and you know what I do to people who don't provide worthy information during an interrogation." Darmik's face was hard and hands balled into fists, giving him a menacing look.

Tears formed in the man's eyes. "I'm sorry," Pratok said. "I have no choice." His arms started shaking.

"Tell me why you're here," Darmik demanded. "If you lie to me, I'll chop off your hand."

Rema didn't think Darmik would actually do that, but she couldn't be sure.

"We were told to wait here." Neco removed his foot from Pratok, giving him some more room to speak.

"Who ordered you?" Darmik inquired.

"Prince Lennek."

"What are you waiting here for?"

Pratok let out a small yelp. "You," he cried, "but that's all I know."

Darmik cursed. He stood and came over to Rema.

"He's telling the truth. I'm not sure he knows anything else. I'll ask the others a few questions, but I don't think we'll get any more information."

"What makes you so sure?" Savenek asked.

"I know Pratok, and I know when people are lying." Darmik crossed his arms. "What I find more concerning is that Lennek specifically sent them here. Almost as if he knew we were coming."

Savenek chuckled. "Lennek is a moron. There's no way he's aware we're here yet. He probably just sent soldiers all over the kingdom."

"No," Darmik responded. "He's smarter than you realize. And I fear we've walked into a trap."

Cold fear shot through Rema. She felt people watching them, and she wanted to leave the town. She glanced at the nearby buildings.

"If so," Savenek snidely said, "then why are we the ones standing here while they," he pointed to the prisoners, "are tied up?"

"I don't know," Darmik admitted. "I'm afraid we just willingly walked into a trap. Although, I have no idea what it is."

Savenek laughed. "Who would have set it? Lennek?"

Rema knew that while Lennek might appear to be rash, careless, and a fool, he definitely wasn't. He was more intelligent than anyone realized.

"Never underestimate my brother," Darmik said. "Or my father. Both are cunning and shrewd."

Rema wondered if the people hiding had anything to do with the missing children.

"Tie everyone up," Darmik ordered. "The prisoners are coming with us."

Rema didn't think dragging a dozen men along with them was a wise decision; although, leaving them free to report to the king and prince wasn't any better.

"He should just kill them," Savenek mumbled.

She hated the idea of Darmik harming another person, and was glad he didn't willingly partake in it. Instead, he chose to try and rescue these men.

"I promised Trell no unnecessary killing," Darmik said. "I intend to keep that promise." Reaching up, he took hold of Rema's key necklace. He traced the edges of it before slipping it under her tunic. "Let's get moving. I'd hoped to be in King's City by now."

EiGHTEEN

Darmik

Darmik hated the fact that Savenek was continuously with Rema.

"Stop staring," Neco said. "We're almost at King's City. Will you please focus?"

"Sorry," Darmik mumbled. He knew Rema was safest being guarded by Savenek, but the guy still irked him.

Greenwood Forest loomed to the right side of the dirt path they traveled on, open land lay to the left. There was only one more hill before King's City was in sight. Darmik estimated they'd reach the wall in about two hours, the same time as sunset. Attacking the king and prince would be more effective in the early morning hours.

Darmik raised his hand, signaling for everyone behind him to come to a halt. He told his runners to inform all captains and lieutenants to make camp for the night—they would attack at daybreak.

Everyone started to leave the dirt path to get situated. A horn blared in the distance and then the ground rumbled, as if hundreds of horses were coming toward them. Darmik turned to Neco, whose eyes widened in shock.

"Weapons ready!" Darmik shouted. "Incoming!"

Unsheathing his sword, he faced the open land before him. At the crest of the hill, he saw a single horse rider point his sword directly at him. "Attack!" echoed through the air. A sea of horses, ridden by armor-clad soldiers, thundered down the hill toward them. Darmik had never gone into battle against men he knew. He shook his head; he needed to get into fighting mode.

Neco stood beside him. "Rema and Ellie are in the middle, surrounded by four squads of soldiers."

"Hopefully, there's only one company of the King's Army," Darmik mumbled. Any more than that, and they wouldn't stand a chance.

The horses stopped a hundred yards away. The riders pulled out longbows and aimed at the forest. Darmik moved behind a tree, using it as a shield. Arrows sailed through the air. A couple dozen of his men fell to the ground. Peering around the trunk, he saw the soldiers nock arrows and aim high into the air, which meant the arrows would be raining straight down this time.

"Stay close to the trees!" Darmik shouted.

Arrows whistled through the air and sailed at them once again. A few dozen more men dropped to the forest floor.

"Should we attack?" Neco asked.

"No," Darmik answered. "We can't fight them on horseback. We'll be slaughtered. Our best chance is to lure them into the forest."

"Here they come!" Neco shouted.

The horses moved aside, and another company of soldiers marched over the rise toward them. Panic shot through Darmik. Two thousand men from the King's Army were here. They were outnumbered two to one. There was no way to win this fight. Good men on both sides were about to die. He widened his stance, raised his sword, and mentally prepared for battle. He would not die today. The armed soldiers drew near.

"Ready?" Neco asked.

"I always am," Darmik replied, thankful his friend was at his side.

"After you." Neco nodded his chin toward their attackers.

Darmik smiled and charged at the enemy, the Emperions and rebels following him. The clash of steel rang through the air. Darmik knew he had to strike hard and fast. With Neco at his back, he raised his sword and sliced toward the first soldier he encountered. The man went down. Darmik automatically swung again, parrying a blow from another man. He countered with a wide swing, slicing his attacker across his stomach.

He fell into a routine—swing, parry, thrust. It felt like he fought for hours and yet, the enemy soldiers kept coming. Men littered the ground all around him.

"Commander!" Neco shouted. "They broke through our line. I believe we need to assess the situation and locate our empress." There was a hint of panic to his voice that Darmik had never heard before.

Darmik kicked the man in front of him, sending him to his knees. "Let's go!" He and Neco retreated, running into the forest area where the enemy soldiers had infiltrated. Darmik desperately searched for Rema, but she was nowhere to be seen. He ran deeper into the forest, looking for her. Everywhere he turned, he saw men from the King's Army. They were desperately outnumbered.

"Neco, tell the Emperion soldiers to fight forward for ten, and then back flank two back."

"What the heck does that mean?" he asked as he kept pace, running behind Darmik.

"Just repeat the order, they'll understand. Then find Mako and tell the rebels to fight for another ten minutes. Then I want them to fall back the way we came from, approximately two miles. We'll regroup there. Go quickly and relay the messages. I'm going after Rema." Neco took off.

Chaos surrounded Darmik. He continued running, scanning faces for her. Up ahead, he saw a group of men standing shoulder to shoulder. Intuition told him it was her guard. Sprinting toward the fray, Darmik unsheathed a dagger, both hands now armed, ready to join in the fight. Two members of the royal guard went down, allowing the enemy to break through their line.

Rushing forward, Darmik threw a knife into the back of one soldier. He reached for his last dagger and hurled it into the neck of another. Several men turned to face him. Darmik caught a glimpse of Savenek and Audek fighting, Rema still nowhere in sight.

The enemy came at him. Darmik swung his sword, blocking a blow and responding with a strike of his own. The sword he wielded was heavier than the one he typically used, and his arms grew tired. He had to force himself to be quick with his movements. He swung again, the soldier blocked, and Darmik kicked his leg, hooking it around the man's ankle, bringing him flat on his back.

Darmik ran toward Savenek and Audek. When he got closer, he saw Rema fighting with a soldier behind them. She stood with her feet shoulder-width apart, both hands on the sword, parrying each blow dealt. Darmik almost stumbled when he saw her. He'd never been more proud, or more frightened, in his entire life.

A sound rustled behind him. He spun and ducked as a sword flew over his head, narrowly missing him. Jabbing his sword forward, he sliced his opponent's leg. When the man went down, Darmik turned and saw a soldier's sword arc toward Audek's chest, cutting him open. Audek stumbled and fell to the ground. Savenek faltered. Darmik knew Savenek would be next. Without stopping, Darmik threw his heavy sword toward Savenek's opponent, hitting his back. It didn't knock him down, but the distraction was enough for Savenek to refocus and stab the man.

Darmik picked up his sword from the ground and ran toward Rema. She'd been disarmed. As she stood there, defenseless, the man she'd been fighting raised his sword to strike.

"No!" Darmik yelled.

Savenek threw his knife, embedding it into the man's thigh. While distracted, Rema pulled out a dagger, stepped forward, and thrust it into the man's stomach. His eyes widened as he lurched backwards, dropping to the ground. Rema stood frozen in shock.

Darmik grabbed her shoulders. "Are you hurt?" he demanded.

She looked at him with wide eyes, shaking her head.

"We need to get you out of here." He started to pull her further into the forest.

"No," she said. "We aren't leaving without Audek."

He glanced back and saw Audek on the ground, Vesha and Savenek kneeling at his side. "Where's Ellie?" he asked Rema.

"I don't know. I haven't seen her since the fighting broke out."

"Is he alive?" Darmik called to Savenek.

"Barely," he responded.

Darmik ran back to them. "We must hurry." Enemy soldiers fought all around them. At the moment, everyone was currently engaged. "I'll grab one arm, Savenek, you grab the other. Vesha and Rema, start running deeper into the forest." The girls did as instructed while he and Savenek lifted Audek between them. Audek moaned, blood soaking his tunic.

They supported him while heading after the girls. The trees thickened, and darkness descended. He heard the sound of crunching leaves. "We're being followed," Darmik whispered.

"Duck," Rema said. They did as instructed, and Rema threw a dagger at something behind them. She smiled. Darmik glanced back and saw an enemy soldier lying on the ground, a knife protruding from his chest.

"Where'd you learn to do that?" he asked, shocked by her accurate throw.

"Nathenek taught me."

"That was impressive."

"I know." She spun around, grabbed Vesha's arm, and they continued.

Once Darmik was positive no one else followed, they headed north—the direction they came from earlier in the day. After they'd gone a solid two miles, Darmik directed them eastward toward the dirt path. It was difficult to see now that it was night and the moon was concealed behind clouds. Audek passed out. If they didn't tend to his wounds soon, he'd die.

"I hear something," Rema whispered.

"I told everyone to meet in this general area. Vesha, come take my place. I'll go and investigate. You all wait here." He removed his arm from around Audek and Vesha slid under his arm, holding him up.

Darmik crouched low, staying close to the tree trunks as he moved through the forest. He heard a twig snap and spun around to find Neco.

"Am I glad to see you," Darmik said, relieved.

"Is Ellie with you?" His eyes were pulled tight with concern.

Darmik shook his head. "Let everyone know I'm bringing in an injured man who needs medical attention immediately."

Neco hurried away, while Darmik returned to his friends. He switched places with Vesha, and he and Savenek dragged Audek to where everyone else was. When they arrived, two Emperion men rushed forward to help. Darmik handed Audek over to them.

"We have a fire going over there," one Emperion said. "That's where we're assessing the injured."

The two men lowered Audek to the ground next to the fire. One ripped open Audek's tunic, revealing a nasty gash across his chest. Vesha gasped and fell to her knees next to him.

"Audek, listen to me," Vesha said, taking hold of his hand. "You're going to be all right." Audek remained unconscious.

"He's not going to make it, is he?" Rema asked, coming to stand by Darmik, tears dripping down her cheeks.

"I don't know," he answered.

Neco appeared at his side. "Ellie isn't here. I'm going out looking for her."

"It would be wise to wait until daybreak," Darmik said.

"I know, but if she's lying somewhere, bleeding, I have to find her."

He realized Neco's hands shook from fear. If the roles were reversed, and something happened to Rema, Darmik would do the same thing. "I'll go with you."

"No," Neco responded. "I want you to stay here. I'll take Savenek with me."

Darmik nodded. "Very well. Please be careful." Neco patted Darmik's back and left.

Rema went and sat near Vesha, rubbing her friend's back.

"He needs stitches," one of the Emperion men stated. "But I am not very good at closing wounds."

"And medicine to fight infection," Vesha mumbled, her healer training kicking in.

Darmik watched the Emperion soldiers mix some herbs together and spread it over Audek's wound.

"I can do the stitches," Vesha said, wiping the tears from her eyes. "I'm good at it." She took the needle and thread, very carefully pulling Audek's skin together. The two men helped hold the skin in place while she sewed it shut.

"Rema," Darmik said, "can I speak with you?" She stood and came over to him. "We must find Mako and get the people organized. There's much to be done."

"Of course," she said. Rema glanced back at Audek and Vesha. "There's nothing I can do to help him anyway.

I might as well do my duty to my people."

They searched for Mako. Most people lay sleeping or tending to wounds. If Darmik had to guess, he'd say there were a little less than half their people present. Did that mean the rest were dead? Or missing? He finally spotted Mako sitting on the ground, his head between his legs.

"How are you holding up?" Darmik gently asked.

Mako sighed. "Better now that I know Rema is safe." He stood and joined them. "We…we lost so many." He rubbed his face with his hands. "It's like they knew we were coming. It was an ambush."

That was what Darmik had been thinking, but hadn't wanted to say. "I saw Lennek there," he admitted. "He was wearing my commander's helmet."

"Lennek was there? Leading the King's Army?" Rema asked, her eyes darkening. "I'm going to kill him."

"Your Majesty," a young soldier said, coming to kneel before her. "I'm so glad you're safe."

"Thank you," Rema replied, placing her hand upon the man's head. He smiled and left. "I suppose I should speak to my people."

"That would be most wise," Mako said.

"I don't want to address everyone as a group. I will go and speak to each person individually. I think that will help build morale. Plus, I need to thank each and every one of them for their service and sacrifice here today."

Now that Savenek was gone with Neco, Darmik wanted to stay by Rema's side to ensure her safety until

he returned. She went up to the first couple she saw
sitting about ten feet away. She knelt down, speaking
in low tones so Darmik couldn't hear. He simply stood
a few feet away and observed. The two men she spoke
to nodded, their faces haggard. Rema said a few more
words and then both men smiled, their moods improving.

She stood and moved to the next group, doing
the same thing. Each person she spoke to smiled, their
face softening as if they truly appreciated her taking the
time to talk to them and offer encouraging words.

After visiting a dozen groups, Rema came over to
Darmik, kissing his cheek. "Have you seen my aunt and
uncle?"

"No, I haven't. I'm sure they're around here
somewhere." He'd been looking for them for the past
twenty minutes, but hadn't spotted them anywhere yet.

Rema nodded and went to the next group. While
she spoke, Darmik continued to scan the area for Maya
and Kar.

Rema stood, looking in every direction, her face
pulled tight in concern. Then she went to the next pair
of soldiers and talked with them. When she finished, she
bit her lip. Darmik noticed her wiping her eyes. He went
over and gave her a hug, rubbing her back. "You can do
this," he said encouragingly.

"I want to know where they are." She kissed his
cheek and moved to the next group of people. Kneeling
down, she kindly smiled and began speaking to them.

Darmik couldn't help but marvel at her beauty,

strength, and passion—he both admired and loved her.

Someone nudged Darmik's shoulder, and he turned to see one of his soldiers standing there. "Commander, I'm glad you're back."

"Thank you," Darmik said. "I'm thankful you were there today. Even though we didn't win, I'm honored to fight by your side."

"I didn't realize you and the empress were courting." He smiled cheekily at Darmik.

Darmik laughed. "Yes, we plan to marry."

"She's a mighty fine woman. You're lucky to have someone so compassionate." He patted Darmik on the back and left.

Darmik was definitely the lucky one to have Rema in his life. As Rema spoke to the next group of people, she kept glancing back at Darmik—panic in her eyes. He needed to find Kar and Maya for her.

Movement off to the side caught his attention. He saw Neco and Savenek walking toward him, Ellie lying limp in Neco's arms. Darmik rushed over, Rema immediately at his side.

"Is she alive?" Rema demanded.

"Yes," Neco responded. "She's just exhausted and fell asleep in my arms." He gently nudged Ellie, and her eyes opened.

Rema's shoulders relaxed, and she smiled. "Wait, why is there blood on you if you're well?"

Ellie and Neco exchanged a brief look. Savenek stepped back as Neco carefully set Ellie on her feet. He also took a few steps away, giving Rema and Ellie privacy. Whatever Ellie was about to say, it must not be good. Darmik knew he should also give them space, but he wanted to be by Rema's side in case she needed him.

"I do have blood, but it's not mine." Ellie reached forward, hugging Rema.

"Whose blood is it?" Rema asked in a high-pitched voice.

"Shh," Ellie said, rubbing her back.

"Whose?" Rema demanded, crying.

Ellie looked into Rema's eyes.

"I'm so sorry," Ellie tenderly said, "but Kar and Maya are dead."

Nineteen

Rema

Rema's world swayed, everything went black, and she collapsed to the ground. Strong hands held her tight. It must be Darmik embracing her. Things were blurry, gradually coming back into focus, and she could see again.

Darmik hovered above her. "Someone get her water," he demanded.

She remembered what Ellie had said—Kar and Maya were dead. She wrapped her arms around Darmik's neck and squeezed, the tears coming. How could they be dead?

"Here," Ellie said, handing her a waterskin.

Rema shook her head. She just wanted to be left alone.

Darmik stood, pulling her up with him. "I'm going to find her a place to rest for the night. We'll regroup in the morning," he said.

She caught a glimpse of Mako's stricken face, and

she felt her heart squeeze in pain. "Ellie," she whispered. "Will you please come with me? I'd like to know what happened."

"Of course."

Darmik led them about twenty feet away from the small crowd that had gathered. Rema sat with her back against a tree trunk, Ellie on one side of her and Darmik on the other.

"Please tell me what happened," Rema whispered.

"I'm so sorry," Ellie said.

Rema leaned against Darmik's shoulder, taking comfort in his steadfast strength.

Ellie took a deep breath. "When the battle broke out, Savenek ordered us to form a protective circle around you. I was to your left. I saw Kar and Maya nearby, the panic clear on their faces. They were heading in your direction. They...they were so focused on you that they weren't watching behind them."

Tears formed in Ellie's eyes. "The enemy came. I was fighting off a man. Out of the corner of my eye, I saw a soldier running toward Kar and Maya." Ellie wiped her cheeks. "Savenek sent me to help them. As I ran over, I saw a man shove Maya out of the way. She fell down, smashing her head on a rock." The words started coming quickly, and Ellie's eyes glazed over. "Kar turned around and saw her. He screamed and engaged the soldier in a sword fight. More enemy soldiers came and Savenek started condensing the line down, closer to you."

Ellie brought her legs up, hugging them, resting

her head on her knees. "While Kar fought the soldier, I saw another approach him from behind. I screamed, but it was too late. The soldier plunged a sword into his back. He tumbled forward, flat on his face. An Emperion came to my aid. We attacked the two men who killed Kar and Maya. After we took them down, I turned to see if you were all right, but you and Savenek were gone. Bodies were all over the place. I saw Maya's body jerk and ran to her. She tried talking, but I told her to be quiet. I grabbed her arms and pulled her out of the mess. I heard more soldiers coming. There was a large tree with huge roots that formed a small, cave-like place to hide. I slid inside, pulling Maya down with me. I held her in my lap, while listening to people run by."

Rema reached out, taking hold of Ellie's hand, squeezing it.

"Maya started mumbling. She begged me to watch out for you. She asked me to promise her. I did. Then her body went limp—she was gone." Ellie buried her head between her knees.

Rema scooted closer to her, hugging her. "Thank you for what you did."

"I'm sorry I couldn't save them." Ellie's face was red and her eyes swollen.

"There was nothing else you could have done," Rema said.

"I need to be with Neco right now." Ellie stood and left.

Rema couldn't believe her aunt and uncle were

gone. The people who raised her, cared for her, and loved her. She buried her face in her hands, crying. She was a terrible leader. She couldn't even save her own family—how was she supposed to save a kingdom? An empire?

Darmik wrapped his arms around her.

"I just want to be left alone," she cried. "I can't do this."

"Shh," he said, consoling her.

"Go away." None of this would be happening if she'd never met Darmik in the forest that one day. She'd be married to Bren, and Kar and Maya would be alive. Sure, she'd still be confined to her home in Jarko, but everyone she loved would be alive. She wouldn't be responsible for all these people. She wouldn't bear the weight of the crown.

"I'm not leaving you," he said. "I know how you feel."

"How could you possibly know?" she demanded. "You've haven't lost almost everyone you love."

Darmik shook his head. "You're wrong." He sat across from her, not touching her.

She couldn't see his features very well in the darkness.

"You know Barjon isn't kind and loving toward me. He doesn't act like a father. But there are others I love—and have lost. Phellek was as close to a father figure that I've ever had. Captain killed him right in front of me. Almost my *entire* personal squad died saving me from Lennek. Those were the men I spent every day with, fought with, and trusted with my life. *They* were my brothers. And you forget—my mother died delivering me into this world. How do you think that makes me feel? To know, and be reminded by Barjon, that I am the reason my mother is dead?"

He scooted forward, taking her hands in his. "I know you're hurting right now. I know because I have felt your pain—I understand it. You are not alone because I'm here for you."

She stared into his eyes, at this beautiful man before her. "I love you," she whispered. "I don't want to lose you, too."

He leaned forward, kissing her forehead. "I don't want to lose you either. When I heard the front line was broken, I was scared to death that the soldiers got to you. I don't know what I'd do if I lost you, too."

"Does it get easier? Does the pain go away?" It hurt just to breathe. It felt like her heart had been ripped from her chest.

"With time, it becomes manageable."

She wiped the tears from her face. Mako walked over and sat down beside her. "I'm so sorry," he said. "Kar was like a brother to me. Losing someone is never easy."

"No, it's not," Darmik added, patting her hands. "Just remember, they spent their lives protecting you. You can honor them by finishing what they fought for. You can end Barjon and Lennek's tyrannical reign."

"We will end this," Mako promised.

"Thank you both," Rema said, glad to have these

wonderful people in her life.

Darmik pulled out a dagger from the sheath strapped to his thigh. "Phellek gave this to me." He handed it to Rema. She recognized it as his prized possession. "I want you to have it. I want you to use it to end this."

Mako stiffened beside her. "Let me see it," he asked, his voice trembling.

Rema carefully handed the knife to him. He took it, his hands shaking. For several minutes, Mako just sat there, staring at it. The weapon was beautiful. There was a silver sun on the hilt, and the tip looked sharp and deadly.

He handed it back to Rema, his face white. "Are you well?" she asked him.

Mako shook his head. "That is the knife used to kill my daughter, Tabitha. I removed it from her chest, tossing it to the ground."

Rema stared at the weapon lying on her palms. "I want you to have it," she said. "Use it to kill the man responsible for all this."

With quivering fingers, Mako delicately picked up the dagger, his eyes glassy. "I will kill Barjon and avenge my wife and daughter's deaths." His hands curled around the weapon, squeezing it tightly.

When Rema woke the next morning, she immediately went to check on Audek. Vesha was sitting by his side.

"How's he doing?" Rema asked. He lay on the ground, covered with tunics that people had freely given to him.

Vesha glanced up at her. "Ask him yourself," she said.

Rema knelt down. His eyes were closed, and she didn't want to wake him. Leaning in closer, she examined his face. His cheeks had some color to them. That was a good sign.

"Hey," he said, his eyes flying open. "The all-mighty empress is here to see me!" She jerked back, and he laughed. "Ah, forgot I can't laugh. It hurts too badly. Did you see they stitched me up?" He started to lower the tunics covering him.

"Stop," Vesha said. "She does *not* need to see that."

Rema couldn't believe he was awake and coherent. She'd expected him to die, too.

"He's been like this all morning. He thinks it's funny," Vesha said, the corners of her lips pulling up like she was trying not to smile.

Rema noticed Vesha holding Audek's hand.

"Is he going to make a full recovery?" Rema asked.

"I am," he answered. "You don't need to look so shocked. I might not be the beauty I once was," he said, pointing to his torso, "but I will most definitely live." He looked at Vesha. "Thanks to you."

Vesha's face turned red, and she glanced down at their joined hands.

"I need to speak with Darmik," Rema said, standing. "I'm glad you're well, Audek."

She spotted Darmik talking to Neco, Savenek, and Mako, and walked over to join them. They were all on their knees, studying a map lying on the ground.

"What's going on?" Rema asked. Peering at the map, it seemed familiar. Everyone looked at her, but no one spoke. "Someone needs to tell me." She pointedly looked at Darmik.

"We have an idea," he said, focusing on the map.

"Which is?" Rema prompted.

"The King's Army is following Lennek because he and Barjon have taken their children." Darmik glanced back up at her. "If we rescue the kids, then my men can fight for me."

"Are you certain?" Rema asked.

"I'm positive."

"Regardless," Neco added, "we need to save the children. It's the right thing to do."

"So what's this?" she asked, pointing to the map between them.

Mako cleared his throat. "It's your parents' home," he said. "This is the castle Barjon stormed and slaughtered everyone in."

"This is different from King's Castle?" she asked, kneeling on the ground and studying the map in greater detail.

"Yes," Mako said. "After the massacre, the place was abandoned. Since Barjon easily overtook the fortress, he didn't want to live there. He chose a location further inland, surrounded by flat land. That's where he built the new castle."

Rema still didn't know why they were all staring at the floor plan of her parents' home. What did this have to do with anything?

"Mako found it on Trell's desk," Darmik said. Rema remembered finding it there, and Mako asking permission to study it. Darmik cleared his throat. "Mako has a theory." His intense eyes met hers. "That the king is hiding the children there, and I agree with him."

Rema focused on the map of her parents' home. She observed the stables, courtyards, great hall, towers, kitchen, throne room, bedchambers, and the royal nursery—*her* nursery.

Savenek pointed to the map. "It would be an excellent place to hide the children since no one knows of its existence."

"I'm not so sure," Neco mumbled. "I'd like to sneak into the enemy's camp and see if I can discover the location from a captain or Lennek himself."

"I doubt even a captain knows," Mako said. "The only way Barjon taking the children hostage works is if no one knows where they are."

"I agree," Rema said. "And it's too risky to have you sneak into enemy territory. I don't want anything to happen to you."

"He's more than qualified," Darmik said. She glared at him. "Well, he is."

Mako pulled out the dagger he received from Darmik. He sat there staring at it, lost in thought.

"This is what I propose," Rema said. "We go to this castle and see if the children are there. If they are, we rescue them. Hopefully by doing so, we will get the men from the King's Army to join our side, so we can overthrow Barjon and Lennek. If the children aren't there, then we've lost nothing by simply checking." She looked at Neco. "Then we return to Emperion and bring a larger army here. That way, we'll attack Barjon and Lennek with significantly less loss on our side."

She grabbed her key necklace, waiting for their responses. Everyone started nodding in approval.

"I think it's a wise move," Darmik said, crossing his arms. "I'd rather get the King's Army on our side than fight against them."

"Very well." Rema released her necklace. "Tell everyone we're moving out. I want to be on our way as soon as possible." In the battle yesterday, more than half of her army had been killed. She didn't want to sit there and make it any easier for Lennek to finish them off.

"What about those who are injured?" Neco asked.

"There is a rebel cave a few miles from here," Mako offered.

"Excellent," Rema said. "Assign one person to assist each injured individual to the cave. Tell them to stay there until they hear from us. Vesha should accompany them as well since she is skilled in healing."

"Yes, Your Majesty," they all said in unison.

⌒⌒⌒

They traveled to the northern section of Shano toward the Great Ocean, Rema's guard surrounding her at all times. She feared Lennek would be out searching for them, so she ordered Darmik to keep them far from any roads or trails.

When night came, everyone slept on the hard ground. Rema tossed and turned, imagining an army riding in and slaughtering them all while they slept. She knew Darmik had men guarding the perimeter; yet, it wasn't enough to keep the nightmares away.

Mako stood and watched the queen. She kissed the princess, and then tenderly laid her down on Mako's bed. Queen Kayln removed the baby's blanket and slipped a red velvet pouch out of the bodice of her gown, tucking it under the collar of the princess's dress.

"I love you, my darling child. Keep this close to your heart. I'll always be watching over you."

With trembling hands, Mako picked up his dead baby and removed the knife, tossing it to the ground as if it were on fire. The queen handed Mako the princess's royal blanket. He wrapped Tabitha in it, and kissed her forehead like she were still alive.

"Princess Amer is all that is left," the queen said, wiping her tears. "Even if she never fulfills her duty as ruler of our land, I want her to live."

She bent down and pressed her lips to her

daughter's cheek one last time.

Rema's eyes flew open. Everything around her was calm. She felt her key necklace against her chest and rolled over, closing her eyes and trying to fall back asleep.

Soft whispers drifted toward her and she strained her ears, listening.

"Please, I beg you, don't fight. You can stay back where it's safe." It sounded like Neco, but she wasn't sure.

"I understand your concern," Ellie answered. "But I promised Maya I would watch out for Rema."

"Neither one of you should be there when we go in."

She sighed. "I know you're worried, but I'm perfectly capable of taking care of myself. You know that."

"I do," he responded. "It's just that, I've never been in battle knowing the woman I loved was in it, too." There was a shuffling sound. "And I've never had anything to live for, until now. If I died, it was always for a good cause. Now I don't want to die. I want to live—with you by my side."

This was a conversation Rema should not be hearing. She rolled over, making as much noise as possible.

After traveling hard and fast for a week, early one morning Rema and her soldiers arrived at a twenty-foot high stone wall. They walked alongside it until they came to a section that was crumbled, allowing them to easily climb over the rubble. Once inside the wall, Rema froze, stunned at the sight before her. In the middle of the lush, green valley, among tall greenwood trees, stood an enormous castle, one side collapsed in, another section black as if it had been burned, while another side stood untouched by time. A stream wound its way around the place. Even though she didn't remember being here before, she felt a connection to the castle, as if it called to her.

Mako came over. "There's a secret entrance. That's how I escaped with you. I suggest we use it, so no one knows we're here."

She placed her hand on his forearm. "How are you doing?" she asked, worried about the memories this place stirred for him.

"I'm not going to lie. This will be one of the hardest things I've ever had to do." He stared into the distance, lost in thought.

Darmik approached. "We need to get to the bottom of the hill and hide among the trees before someone spots us."

Savenek took her arm, leading her down the rise to the forest below. Once they were out of sight, Rema asked, "Any suggestions on how to proceed?"

"It appears lifeless," Savenek said. "I don't see anything that indicates someone is inside." He kicked the toe of his boot into the moist soil.

Rema thought so too. Although, if Barjon had the children hidden there, he would make sure they were well concealed.

"A small group should be sent in to investigate," Mako said. "While that's happening, the rest of our army can surround the castle."

Darmik agreed. "I'll send Neco in with five men to locate the children."

"I'll show them the entrance," Mako said, "and explain the layout, but I don't want to accompany them."

Rema turned to Darmik. "Are you going, too?"

"I want to, but I'm not leaving. I need to be here directing everyone."

Relief washed through Rema. She feared what lay behind the castle walls.

Mako left to show Neco and his men to the secret tunnel, while Darmik started organizing his soldiers into position. Rema leaned against a tree trunk, waiting, Ellie by her side. The sun rose high in the sky.

"What could possibly be taking so long?" Ellie asked, fidgeting with her hands.

"There's a lot to investigate," Rema answered. The castle was huge. She had no idea where Neco would even start.

"What's that noise?"

It sounded like horse hooves. Savenek ran over to Rema, grabbing her. "Someone's coming!" he took her and Ellie deeper into the cover of the trees, where they stood in silence.

After several minutes, Mako joined them. "A dozen soldiers were spotted riding their horses to the castle. Among them are Barjon and Lennek."

"Are you sure?" Rema asked, stunned.

"Yes," Mako said. "Which can only mean one thing—the children are here."

Rema never imagined finding the king and prince here too. Everyone looked at her for guidance. "We need to do something about Lennek and Barjon. Now may be our only chance."

Mako stood staring at her. "What do you suggest?"

"We're going in," she said. "Take us to the entrance."

"I won't escort a large group of people inside," Mako said. "Otherwise Barjon will know we're here."

"Very well," Rema conceded. "Then take Savenek, Ellie, and me."

Mako led them through the trees to an area dotted with large boulders. Climbing over the mossy rocks, she recognized a boulder shaped like a bird—it was almost identical to the one near her home back in Jarko. She froze.

"Do you know this symbol?" Mako asked. She nodded and headed left, stopping before a cluster of rocks. Mako looked at her with his eyebrows raised.

"There," she said, pointing to an area where the stones were piled high.

Mako smiled. "Kar taught you well." He went to the side of the mound and moved some vines aside, revealing a narrow entrance to a cave.

She was just about to take a step forward when Darmik ran up behind her.

"Everyone is in position," he said, "spread around the castle. Neco has located the children in the dungeon. He's going to start bringing them out."

"Barjon and Lennek are here," Rema told him.

Darmik's eyes widened, clearly not expecting to run into his father and brother today. "Are you sure? We haven't encountered many soldiers. There's just a few inside with the kids."

"The army is probably nearby," Savenek said. "I bet Barjon and Lennek came here with only a couple of guards in order to keep this place a secret."

"That's plausible," Darmik mumbled. "Very well. Rema, wait out here with Savenek and Ellie. Mako and I will deal with them."

"No," she said, standing tall. "I'm going in." She pointed to the cave. "And the four of you will accompany me. We end this today." She pushed past Darmik and entered the tunnel. Blackness engulfed her. A dripping sound came from somewhere inside. Her heart pounded. Grabbing her key necklace, she whispered, "Mother, Father, Davan, and Jetan, please watch over me and give me strength. With your help and guidance, I will destroy the men responsible for ruining the kingdom and countless lives."

A hand slid around her arm. "This way," Mako whispered, pulling her forward. "Everyone keep a hand out to the side so you don't run into a wall. Keep walking."

They continued in darkness for a good thirty minutes before Mako stopped.

"There are three ways in and out of the castle," he said. "I'm trying to figure out the best approach."

Rema still couldn't see a single thing and was surprised when Darmik spoke right behind her. "Neco is bringing the children out through the west entrance, near the dungeon. I suggest we avoid that route."

"Very well," Mako said. "Then we should enter on the east side of the castle."

They traveled in silence for a few more minutes. Mako came to a stop, the hand holding her arm shook. "I always hoped to bring you back here one day," he said. "I didn't think it would be under these circumstances, though." He released her. She heard what sounded like wood sliding, and then pale light illuminated the tunnel.

Rema stepped past Mako and entered a small room. A bed was positioned against one wall, while a bassinet stood in a corner. A worn rug covered the stone floor. Looking closer, she noticed fabric on the ground. It appeared to be a dress—along with bones. She glanced to the bassinet, now noticing the rusty brown on the frayed, ivory bedding. Rema covered her mouth with her hands, tears pooling in her eyes. She stood in Mako's bedchamber where his wife and baby daughter, Tabitha, had been murdered. Darmik, Savenek, and Ellie all exited the room and entered the castle's corridor. Mako came next to her.

"I'm so sorry," she said.

"So am I," he whispered before turning and leaving through the arched doorway.

Rema hurried after him. The stone flooring of the hallway was covered with dried, bloody footprints. Part of the ceiling down the hallway had collapsed in, allowing sunlight to filter through and vines to climb down into the castle.

"This way," Mako whispered. He led them along the corridor. At an intersection, he peered around the corner and waved them forward. Rema walked up steps covered with worn, red carpeting, clutching onto the wooden banister, feeling the presence of so many lost.

She climbed four flights of stairs and then Mako led them down an empty corridor. A tapestry hung on the wall, faded from time. Looking closer, she saw it depicted a castle shrouded in clouds on a mountaintop— just like the rebel fortress. She reached out and traced the lines of the castle with her fingertip.

"Move it aside," Mako whispered. She did as instructed and found a secret passageway. "I'll go first."

Rema followed him into the darkness. A musty smell engulfed her. Whispering, Mako counted to thirty and turned left. He counted to fifty and stopped.

"The royal wing is through this wooden door. My guess is that's where Barjon and Lennek are. Ready yourselves. Ellie, I want you guarding this door so no one sneaks up behind us. No matter what happens, do not leave your position. The rest of you are inside with me. I'll count to three, and then open the door."

Rema unsheathed her daggers, clasping one in each hand. She was ready to face the man responsible for murdering her family.

"One, two, three." Mako threw open the door and rushed inside. Rema squinted against the bright light and hurried after him. Darmik, Savenek, and Mako quickly spread throughout the room.

No one was there. Rema glanced around at the three sofas and two chairs. A large, empty fireplace stood against one wall. Several portraits hung on the walls. It appeared someone had taken a knife and slashed them to pieces. Rema stepped forward while everyone else held their positions. This was the sitting room her parents had used. An overwhelming sense of grief engulfed her.

She crept to the nearest doorway, peering inside the nursery. *Her nursery.* Tears filled her eyes, and she moved to the next archway. The door was closed. She leaned against it, listening for voices, not hearing anything. Mako shook his head and waved his hand, wanting her to come away from the door. She slowly turned and crept toward Darmik, who suddenly threw his hand up. Rema held still as the sound of voices floated out of the corridor to her right. She looked up and saw a few people walking directly toward her. All she could focus on was Lennek. Their eyes locked, and a cruel, vicious smile spread across his face.

"It's about time you showed up," Lennek sneered as he stepped into the sitting room.

TWENTY

Darmik

Darmik watched his brother saunter into the room with his royal-blue cape billowing behind him and his circlet encased with sapphires upon his head. Barjon came in next, followed by the steward Arnek, and the captain of the Third Company. Darmik wondered if any other soldiers were nearby.

Lennek chuckled smugly. "I told you, Father, they would try and save the children. Kindhearted fools that they are." He folded his arms, standing before Rema. "I knew they would walk right into my trap."

"It's a good thing the Third Company is nearby," the king said, his eyes focused on Rema, hatred radiating from them.

"Yes," Rema said, squaring her shoulders and standing tall. "It is. I'm sure they're very interested in learning the whereabouts of their children."

Darmik smiled at Rema's ability to see things clearly. "Yes," he added, "my men are escorting the children to their parents as we speak."

Lennek's cheek twitched, indicating he was nervous.

Rema said, "So while you thought you'd lure us here to murder us, just like you did to my parents and brothers, we'd thought we'd expose you for the fraud you are. You're under arrest."

Barjon laughed. "I'm under arrest? I beg to differ. You are the one under arrest, you churl." His face turned an angry shade of red.

Mako stepped forward. "I don't think you've been introduced to Her Majesty, Empress Amer Rema of Greenwood Island *and* Emperion."

The color drained from Barjon's face, and his black, beady eyes narrowed.

"That's right," Darmik added, "you probably haven't heard yet. Our dear Rema is the true heir to not only *your* throne, but to Emperion's as well. She was named empress a month ago. Hamen is dead."

"Brother." Lennek turned his attention to Darmik. "You always have to take what's mine." He unsheathed his sword, the sound of steel ringing through the room.

"I can't take something from you when you never had it in the first place," Darmik calmly said. He held the hilt of his sword, ready in case Lennek attacked.

"I hate you," Lennek said, seething with rage. "You think you'll gain power by supporting this harlot? Well, you won't." He unclasped his cape and when it dropped to the ground, he kicked it away. "I'm going to kill you and then Rema."

"Your own brother?" Darmik asked. "You despise me so much, you'd kill me?"

"With pleasure." Lennek lifted his sword, holding it before him.

"And you, Father," Darmik said, turning to face Barjon, while still keeping an eye on his brother. "Why do you hate me? I've always done what you've asked."

"I hardly think supporting the girl who's trying to overthrow me is doing as I've asked." Barjon removed his sword from its scabbard.

Although he'd always known it would come to this, it still hurt to see his family prepared to fight against him. Darmik hoped to arrest his father and brother, instead of killing them. He had hoped they'd learn from their errors while imprisoned for the rest of their lives. It seemed a just punishment for all they'd done.

"Is it because Mother died in childbirth?" Darmik asked, finally voicing the question he had always wanted to, but was afraid to ask. "Is that why you can't stand me?"

Barjon's face reddened, and he leaned forward. "You're not even my own flesh and blood," he spat. "When you were born and Hamen showed up, I knew that you were his. Your mother didn't die in childbirth—I killed her for being the whore that she was."

Darmik felt as if he'd been thrown from a cliff and was falling through the air.

Lennek laughed, lunging forward while Darmik was momentarily distracted by what his father revealed.

Darmik automatically swung his arm up and his sword clashed with Lennek's. Barjon thrust his sword toward him, but Mako parried the blow. The captain of the Third Company rushed forward, and Savenek stopped him. Darmik went on the attack, and Lennek met him strike for strike.

Arnek slunk against the wall, attempting to leave the room. He couldn't be allowed to go and get help. Darmik saw Rema step in front of Arnek, blocking the steward's path.

Darmik sped up his moves, maintaining his offensive position. Lennek still met every strike—he'd drastically improved. But Darmik had never lost to his brother, and he did not intend to lose now. He swiped his leg out, tripping Lennek, who went down on the ground. Darmik glanced over to Rema. She swung her daggers at Arnek, causing him to turn and run. She pulled her arm back, flicked her wrist, and released a knife. It embedded into Arnek's back, the mousy man tumbling to the floor and onto his face.

Lennek stood and slashed his sword toward Darmik's chest. Darmik stepped closer to avoid the strike, lifted his elbow, and slammed it into his ribs. Lennek wrapped his arm around Darmik's neck.

Mako and Barjon moved around the room, their swords clanging against one another, sparks flying.

Darmik bent forward, tossing Lennek over his head and throwing him onto his back.

Savenek lunged toward the captain, swung the

blade down, and delivered a killing blow.

Darmik turned to see Mako's sword tumble to the ground, his eyes widening in shock as Barjon smiled while lifting his sword and pointing it at Mako's chest. Barjon pulled his arms back to gain momentum, about to plunge the sword into Mako. Mako whipped out the dagger with a silver sun on the hilt, flinging it into Barjon's stomach. He stumbled as he tried to thrust his sword toward Mako, who moved aside. Barjon wavered before collapsing onto the ground, blood pooling around his body like water.

Darmik turned to face his brother. Lennek twisted around, grabbed Rema, and pulled her against his chest, a small dagger to her throat.

"Drop your swords," Lennek demanded, "all of you."

Darmik didn't trust his brother and knew Lennek planned to kill her. Seeing no other option at this point, he lowered his sword to the ground, near his feet. Savenek followed suit. Mako was already without a weapon, and Ellie remained hidden in the corridor.

Lennek laughed. "You're all idiots, the entire lot of you." His arm tightened around Rema's shoulders and he dug the tip of the dagger into her skin, drawing blood. "I'm going to walk out of here, and no one is going to lay a finger on me. Is that clear?" He started moving toward the door, still facing everyone, dragging Rema along with him. Rema slid one arm down her leg, slipping her hand into the slit of her pants, and ever so slowly pulling out her last knife. Darmik nodded at her—she couldn't wait too long; otherwise, Lennek would see her weapon. She needed to do it now.

In a flash, Rema leaned to the side and plunged the dagger into Lennek's thigh. When he faltered, Rema bit his hand and ripped the knife from him. He screamed. Rema twisted out of his embrace and thrust the weapon into his side, near his stomach. He hunched over and Rema ran to Darmik as Lennek sunk to the ground.

Darmik wrapped his arms around her, holding on tight. "It's over," he whispered in her ear. "You did it." He'd never been so proud, or relived, in his life.

Lennek screamed, pulling out the dagger from his side. With his hands covered in blood, he aimed the weapon at Rema's back and threw it. Darmik shoved her, hoping to move her from the knife's path, but it was too late. The dagger was aimed right at her.

Savenek leapt in front of Rema, and the knife embedded into his chest. He crashed to the ground. "No!" Mako screamed.

Rema rushed over to Savenek, kneeling next to his body and pulling his head onto her lap. With shaking hands, she removed the dagger. Blood trickled from the corner of his mouth.

Darmik grabbed the dagger and stalked toward Lennek, who retreated to the hallway.

"We're still half-brothers," Lennek wheezed.

"No, we're not." Darmik ran at him. He wrapped his arm around Lennek, holding him in place. "Now you'll never hurt anyone ever again." Darmik drew the knife across Lennek's throat, slicing it open, and killing him. He shoved Lennek away from him and he tumbled to the ground, lifeless.

Darmik quickly removed his tunic and ran over to Savenek, pushing the material against his wound, trying to stop the profuse bleeding.

"You're going to be all right," Rema said to Savenek, her eyes filling his tears.

"I...I'm dying," he choked out, a gurgling sound coming from his mouth.

Mako leaned down, kissing Savenek's forehead. "I'm honored to have filled the role of your father. You turned out to be a man who I'm proud of in every way." His shoulders shook as he hunched over, crying. "Thank you for being my family."

Rema turned and hugged Mako, holding him tight.

Savenek reached up, taking hold of Darmik's wrists. "Take...care...of... her."

Darmik nodded. "Thank you for saving Rema. I'll protect her with my life, just like you did."

Savenek's eyes rolled back and he stopped breathing, his hands falling from Darmik.

This man, who Darmik started out hating, turned out to be more of a brother than Lennek ever was. And Savenek died with the greatest honor of all—saving someone he loved.

Twenty-one

Rema

Rema couldn't believe that Savenek lay lifeless before her—that he'd died saving her. She swore to live a life worthy of his sacrifice. Wiping the tears from her eyes, she stood and looked at the disarray before her. Without uttering a single word to anyone, she exited the room. Her hand traced along the wooden railing as she walked down the hallway and descended four flights of stairs. She went through the crumbled great hall, littered with weeds, hanging vines, and bones. The crooked front doors of the castle stood hanging open. She walked out into the bright sunlight.

Neco stood on the steps, surrounded by dozens of haggard-looking children. Behind them were hundreds of soldiers dressed in the King's Army uniform. The wind tossed Rema's hair as she stared at everyone before her. The soldiers removed their tunics, tossing them to the ground. Then, silently, they all dropped to one knee, bowing their heads.

Darmik came up next to her, slipping his hand into hers and squeezing it. Then he, Mako, and Ellie joined Neco, kneeling on the ground before her.

∾∾∾

The next day, a ceremony was performed honoring Savenek and everyone who died at the castle seventeen years ago. Rema never had the opportunity to say good-bye to her mother, father, or brothers. Mako never got to honor his wife and daughter. Rema also needed to thank Kar and Maya. This was for all of them.

Just outside the castle, among the tall greenwood trees, Savenek's body was placed on a large pile of wood. Mako positioned the dagger with a silver sun on the hilt between Savenek's hands.

Darmik, Neco, and Ellie all stood alongside the pile of wood. Rema and Mako approached the body, and Mako handed her a lit torch. She reached down toward the hay under the wood, lighting it on fire. The flames quickly grew, enveloping the wood, and then Savenek's body. She stood back, holding Mako's hand.

"This is for all the ones we've lost. May they find eternal peace." Rema closed her eyes. She was grateful for Kar and Maya's love, Savenek's steadfast devotion, her parents and brothers, and her living friends here today. With her free hand, she reached up and took hold of her key necklace. She vowed to never forget those who died. Rema was the true heir, and she would reign with compassion and love for her people. She would be the greatest empress that ever lived.

She imagined her family there, smiling down on her, proud of the woman she'd become.

The following weeks passed in a blur. Notices were sent to the seven governors and all willingly chose to claim loyalty to Rema. Darmik took control of the army, ensuring a peaceful transition.

Rema decided to stay there at the castle, in her parents' rooms. Darmik sent word to Trell, letting him know Barjon and Lennek were dead, and asking if it was safe for Rema to return to Emperion. Most of the time, Rema was in meetings with governors and members of the army. She appointed several leaders, as well as decided who was staying on Greenwood Island, and who would accompany her to Emperion.

Early one morning, while Rema was getting ready for the day, someone knocked softly. "Your Majesty, Mako is here to see you."

Rema glanced out the window; it was still gray outside. "Show him to the sitting room. I'll be there in a moment."

Ellie cinched up Rema's dress in the back. "I'll go and fetch your breakfast," she said with a smile. "That way, I can run into Neco before he heads out for his morning drills." She turned and left through the servant's passageway.

Rema looked at herself in the mirror, imagining her mother doing this very thing seventeen years ago. She heard a shuffling noise in the other room, so she went to speak to Mako.

Entering the sitting room, she saw him leaning against the hearth, his back to her. "Good morning."

He turned and faced her, smiling. "Sorry to disturb you so early."

"You may seek me out any time, day or night. What can I do for you?" she asked, sitting on the sofa.

"I've considered your offer to join you in Emperion. After much thought on the matter, I have decided to stay here on Greenwood Island." He came and sat next to her.

Rema figured he would want to stay. However, she felt obligated to at least offer him a position at her side. "Since you plan to remain here, I want to bestow the title of lord upon you, and have you serve as the leader of Greenwood Island."

"I would be honored." He angled his body toward hers, looking into her eyes. "I don't want to sound grim, but we need to talk." Rema nodded, waiting for him to continue. "Your parents were able to save you and thus preserve the royal line because they had the foresight to plan for an invasion. When you go to Emperion, I want you to take their advice."

Rema wasn't sure what he meant. "You mean to have a plan in case we're invaded?"

"It's more than that," he said. "Their ancestors built

the rebel fortress decades ago, knowing they needed a secret location in the event that anything ever happened. Only a handful of loyal subjects even knew it existed."

She grabbed her key necklace, fidgeting with it. "So I'm responsible for carrying on the line."

Mako smiled. "Exactly. You must make contingency plans to ensure the survival of your family."

Rema released the key. "I have a question for you," she said. "How did this necklace get engraved?"

He shook his head. "I'm not sure. The last time I saw your mother, she gave it to you. I assume Kar and Maya had the message engraved inside in case something happened to you before they had a chance to explain your lineage."

They sat in silence for several moments. "I'm sorry about Savenek," she whispered. "He was a good man."

Mako nodded. "Yes, he was." He patted her hand. "There has been too much death and destruction. I'm ready for your reign of peace."

Someone cleared their throat. "Your Majesty," the servant said. "Neco is here to see you."

"Please show him in."

Mako stood. "I need to go. Just remember what we talked about."

"I will," Rema said. "Plans will be made to protect the line."

Neco was escorted into the royal sitting room just as Mako exited. "Is there something I can do for you?" she asked.

He stood tall. "I wish to speak freely with you."

"Of course." Rema motioned to the sofas. "Please have a seat."

Neco sat and looked into her eyes. "I wish to marry Ellie." Rema had expected as much. "And I would like your consent."

Rema didn't feel it was necessary to seek her approval. One of the laws she reinstated was that people could marry the person of their choice—there was no longer any contracts or governor approval.

"You do not need my blessing," Rema kindly responded.

Neco leaned forward, resting his arms on his knees. "I believe I do," he mumbled. "Ellie is your lady in waiting and I am Darmik's second in command. If you think our relationship would compromise your safety, or my duty, then you have a right to refuse us."

Rema stood and came before him. "Neco, I am indebted to you. I want nothing more than to see you and Ellie happy." She took hold of his hands. "You're one of the most honorable men I have ever known. I trust, and believe, you will do your job." She wondered if Darmik felt the same way. She would need to speak with him on the matter to ensure his support as well.

Neco smiled. "Thank you." He stood and hugged her.

Someone cleared their throat. "Your Majesty," a servant announced. "Darmik is here to see you."

Neco released her. "I'll leave you two alone." He

turned and left just as Darmik entered the sitting room.

"You wanted to see me?" he asked.

Rema laughed. "Yes." She felt silly for summoning him. However, she had been trying to speak privately with him for the past four weeks. It seemed that every time they finally had a moment alone, someone interrupted with an urgent matter. She decided the best way to see him would be to summon him in the early morning hours before their work for the day began.

He kissed her cheek. She wanted to throw her arms around him, holding him tight, but she refrained from doing so. She needed to tell him about Trell while she had the chance. "There is something you should know," Rema said.

Darmik's eyes quickly scanned her body. "Are you all right?" he asked, concern etched on his face.

"I'm fine." He wrapped her in his arms, pulling her against his chest. "I learned something in Emperion about you."

He leaned back, searching her face for clues. "About me?"

"Yes. When I spoke with Hamen, he said that Trell is your grandfather." She waited for his reaction.

His eyebrows pulled in and he appeared confused. "Trell?" He released her and paced about the room. "The emperor…I mean, Hamen, told you Trell is my mother's father?"

She quickly explained the conversation she'd heard between Nathenek and Hamen.

Darmik ran his hands through his hair, letting out a sigh. "Barjon would never talk about my mother, or her family. Now I realize it's because he murdered her. No wonder Trell hates him so much. But why didn't he ever tell me?"

"You'll have to ask him. Maybe it was the only way he could be around you?" Rema suggested.

Darmik scratched his head. "It actually explains a lot, not only about my childhood, but about my father's relationship with Trell." He stopped pacing and came before Rema. "Did he say anything else?" he softly asked.

She remembered Hamen's sickly daughter who she'd exiled along with her mother. "You have a half-sister."

Darmik leaned his forehead against hers. "I think I've had enough half-siblings to last a lifetime. Are you sure you still want to marry me? I mean, I don't come from the best lineage."

"It doesn't matter who your parents are," she said. "What matters is who you are. And I love you."

He leaned down, and they kissed.

Someone cleared their throat. "Your Majesty," the servant said. "There are two people here who seek an audience with you. Mako said they should be admitted directly."

Rema wondered who it could be. Holding Darmik's hand, she instructed the servant to escort the two visitors in. She heard his voice before she saw him.

"See, I told you," he said, "now that she's the all-mighty empress, we're horse hay."

"Will you please stop talking," Vesha responded.

"May I present, Audek and Vesha," the servant said.

Rema ran over and hugged her friends. She hadn't expected to see either of them. "Look at you!" she said to Audek. He was able to stand and walk on his own, although he was hunched over a little bit.

"As soon as he was well enough, we began the journey here," Vesha declared.

"I assume you've heard the news," Darmik sighed, shaking hands with Audek.

"We have," Audek muttered, blinking several times. "Savenek was a good man."

Vesha's eyes filled with tears, and she looked away.

Ellie burst into the room, breathing heavy. "You won't believe who's here," she huffed, smiling. "Trell and Nathenek just arrived. Apparently, it's time for your coronation and wedding."

Rema held onto Mako's arm as he walked her down the long aisle, leading to the dais containing the chairs her parents had sat on while presiding over court. Even though the castle was still being renovated, it seemed only fitting that her coronation and marriage to Darmik take place here, where her family had lived.

Nearing the throne, Rema saw Ellie and Neco

holding hands, Vesha and Audek standing right next to them. Behind her friends, were all the governors, hundreds of commoners, and dozens of soldiers. Nathenek, Trell, and hundreds of Emperions stood on the other side of the aisle. Darmik waited on the dais for her. His eyes shone with love and admiration as she walked toward him. When she reached the throne, she turned and faced everyone, Mako standing at her side.

"Citizens of Emperion and Greenwood Island, welcome." He turned and stood before Rema, holding her ruby ring. "I, Mako, Commander of King Revan's Army, do hereby grant and name Queen Amer as Empress Amer Rema of Greenwood Island and Emperion, sole surviving heir of the royal family, to hereby lead, rule, and govern our great empire." He slid the ring on her finger.

Trell stepped forward, carrying the items of regalia. He knelt before Rema, handing them to her. Taking the ceremonial mace and family sword, she held them for all to see. Trell stood and returned to his bench.

Clutching the items, Rema turned to face Mako, who held a red velvet pillow with her mother's crown sitting atop it, along with her key necklace. He lifted the crown and placed it on her head. Then he took the necklace and clasped it around her neck. Kneeling before her, he laid his sword on the ground by her feet. "I, Commander Mako, do hereby pledge my life to you." He stood and sheathed his sword.

"I give you Her Majesty, Empress Amer Rema!"

She stood tall as everyone inside the throne room

dropped to one knee, bowing their heads.

"Rise," Rema commanded her subjects.

Mako took the items of regalia from her and laid them aside as Darmik stepped forward and knelt before Mako.

Mako unsheathed his sword, placing the tip on Darmik's right shoulder. "I tap thee once, in the name of the empress, our protector. You have willingly and bravely come to this place today, hereby declaring that you are worthy to take Empress Amer Rema's hand in the marriage binding. Is this so?"

"Yes, My Lord."

"You may rise." Mako faced the crowd of people. "Citizens! We are gathered here today to witness this man and this woman in a binding of life."

Rema and Darmik joined hands, facing one another.

"Commander Darmik, will you have this woman to be thy wedded wife? To love her, comfort her, honor and cherish her, in sickness and in heath? Forsaking all others, keeping thee only unto her, so long as you both shall live?"

"I will."

"Empress Amer Rema, will you have this man to be thy wedded husband? Will you obey, serve, love, honor, and cherish him, forsaking all others, so long as you both shall live?"

"I will."

Mako handed each of them a solid gold ring.

Darmik slid his onto Rema's finger, and she slid hers onto his.

Mako continued, "These rings symbolize your never-ending love for one another. May you be faithful to one another, live and grow old together, and may you be blessed with many children."

Darmik leaned forward and gently kissed Rema's lips. Warmth seeped through her body as she hungrily kissed him back.

"Tonight," he whispered, sending shivers down her spine.

Everyone cheered as they turned and faced the crowd.

Outside the throne room, in a hidden alcove, Rema and Darmik embraced. "Thank you," she murmured against his chest.

Darmik chuckled. "You're thanking me? For marrying you?"

"And saving me. Multiple times. We're going to make a great team."

"Yes, we are." He leaned down and kissed her lips. "We need to make an appearance at the celebration before someone wonders where we are."

Rema took his hand and together they walked down the corridor and to the Great Hall where the gala took place. Food was served to everyone in attendance. For those unable to come, Rema insisted food be distributed to as many people as possible throughout Greenwood Island.

Thousands came to honor her—now that travel was no longer forbidden and people could move freely about the island.

After a week of celebrations, Rema and Darmik boarded the Emperion warship, ready for the journey ahead of them. They were accompanied by Trell, Nathenek, Neco, Ellie, Audek, Vesha, and hundreds of loyal soldiers.

The sails went up, and the ship slowly moved away from the dock. In the distance, the sun was just rising over the horizon, casting a warm light over them.

Although she was sad to leave Greenwood Island behind, she was eager to return to Emperion and face the challenges ahead—because where one story ends, another one is only beginning.

The End

EPILOGUE

The nurse handed the baby boy to Rema.

"I don't understand," Rema said, taking the child in her arms. "I had twins?"

Darmik sat on the edge of the bed beside her, holding their daughter. "Can you believe it?" he asked in awe. "A girl and a boy. We're truly blessed."

"You say that now, but can you imagine all the mischief they'll get in when they're older?" Rema glanced at the precious boy in her arms. "What should we name them?"

"How about we name the girl after my mother, Allyssa," Darmik suggested.

"And the boy?"

"I'm sorry to interrupt," the nurse said, "but I must inform Trell of the situation. He wants to make an announcement to the city."

Rema glanced into Darmik's beautiful brown eyes. "Tell him that the Crown Empress Allyssa is doing well, and her brother, Prince Savenek, is equally healthy."

The nurse bowed and left.

"Savenek?" Darmik questioned her. Rema nodded. He looked at the boy wrapped snug in her arms. "Savenek it is."

ACKNOWLEDGEMENTS

There are so many people who helped make this book possible. First of all, I need to thank my husband for putting up with me. Writing, editing, and publishing a book in a few short months is no small undertaking. Thank you for watching the kids, running them to their activities, and basically being Mr. Mom around here. I love you and cherish the support you give me.

My mom and my sister were a huge help with this book. There is no way War would have been complete in time if it weren't for them. Thank you, Mom, for the countless hours you spent helping me. And Jessica, I don't know where I'd be without you. You're a remarkable sister and I am lucky to have someone so strong, fun, and loyal in my life.

Some very special people gave valuable feedback that helped shape War into what it is today. Thank you Elizabeth Nelson, Angelle LeBlanc, Stacie Buckingham,

Rebecca van Kaam, Jan Farnworth, Hope, and Jen Lord. You girls are amazing, and I'm honored to have your help and support.

There are two talented people who read through the manuscript numerous times: Debi Barnes and Allyssa Adkins. I couldn't have written this book without the two of you. Not only did you offer insightful input, but you kept me going when I was exhausted and didn't think I'd ever finish. You put a smile on my face and remind me why I write. Your enthusiasm means the world to me.

Everyone on the Davis Divas Street Team—thank you for spreading the word about my books!!! You girls are wonderful and I'm honored to have your help.

Amber Douglas McCallister, thank you for writing a beautiful poem about Rema. Even though it didn't make it into the book, I'm privileged you took the time to do so. You're a talented writer and I'm grateful to know you.

I'd also like to thank Ashley Uribe at East West MMA for answering all of my silly questions and offering far more realistic fight maneuvers and techniques than what I come up with. If there are any fighting scenes in War that don't work, it's entirely my fault.

To everyone at Clean Teen Publishing—thank you for believing in this series and bringing it to life. I would especially like to thank Dyan Brown, Rebecca Gober, Marya Heiman, and Courtney Nuckels. I am proud to be a part of your team. You truly are publishing ninjas! Also, a special thanks to Cynthia Shepp for doing a fantastic job with editing.

Last, but not least, thank you for taking the time to read this series. Thank you for entering the worlds I create and falling in love with my characters. Your support and encouragement exceed my wildest dreams.

About the Author

Jennifer graduated from the University of San Diego with a degree in English and a teaching credential. Afterwards, she finally married her best friend and high school sweetheart. Jennifer is currently a full-time writer and mother of three young children. Her days are spent living in imaginary worlds and fueling her own kids' creativity.

Visit Jennifer online at
www.JenniferAnneDavis.com

CPSIA information can be obtained at www.ICGtesting.com
Printed in the USA
LVOW11s0750290116

471861LV00002B/12/P